EXIT TO ETERNITY?

I turned the bike toward it. There was no sensation of it summoning me, but on the other hand I didn't feel any resistance. As I got closer the streaks of light began to look like sharp-edged bands of metal. I would be sliced going through them, like rye bread. But you know what Conan's girlfriend says in the movie: "Do you wanna live forever?"

Actually, yes . . .

BICYCLING THROUGH SPACE AND TIME

MIKE SIROTA

ACE BOOKS, NEW YORK

For Jackie Sweet—the singular most wonderful thing ever grown in the state of Iowa.

And to the forces of the Universe, for guiding her to my field of dreams.

CHAPTER 1

The Old Guy

There was this room, this really strange white room. It was where I first saw the Old Guy.

I mean, who ever heard of *everything* being white? The floor and walls, a sectional sofa, an end table, a floor lamp, the whole thing! There was even a solid white framed picture hanging on one wall. (I only knew that because I bumped into it. Untitled; might have been Casper eating a powdered donut or the KKK doing the downhill at Aspen.)

What was even stranger was how I got into this white room. Because I don't have a *clue*.

The last thing I remember was walking along Broadway in downtown San Diego, near Horton Plaza. Interesting area. Here's this beautiful multilevel shopping mall with brightly colored architecture and lots of neat trendy shops—fronted by a little park filled with dozens of down-and-outers.

Anyway, it was midmorning and I'd just biked here from my place in Del Mar, about twenty-five miles up the coast. Don't know why, on a Wednesday, I had this urge to see preoccupied men and women in proper business attire scurry in and out of office buildings, or to cross streets crammed with cars, trucks, taxis, and buses. It usually happens about as often as Qaddafi goes to a bar mitzvah.

So, after locking my bike in front of the plaza, there I was, waiting to cross Fourth Avenue, surrounded by lots of the aforementioned wage slaves, three down-and-outers, and a young male Chicano with the world's biggest and loudest dual-speaker Sony radio superglued to the side of his head.

That's it.

Now I was here, in this white room, with the Old Guy—who was coming toward me.

"You want to know what's happening?" he said.

Surprise, the Old Guy was dressed in white, something like pajamas with enormous sleeves and no visible fasteners. His complexion was mostly white, but flecked with tiny dark spots, like his face had been carved from a block of Oreo Cookies & Cream. He didn't seem to be crotchety-old, like Scrooge before the ghosts, or lovable-old, like Marcus Welby or Gramps on *Lassie,* but crotchety-lovable-old, like Uncle Charlie on *My Three Sons* or any character played by Wilford Brimley. Though stooped, he moved around quickly with short steps.

"Well, do you?" He was in my face now.

"Do I what?" Unlike his voice, mine sounded hollow in the room.

"Want to know what's happening?"

"For openers, that would be good."

He fluttered his fingers, like dismissing an irritating kid. "Don't worry, everything's cool."

"Everything's . . . *cool?*"

The Old Guy stuck a finger in his ear and twirled it around. "Didn't I say it right?"

This was starting to annoy me. "Look, if you don't tell—!"

"Yes, okay." He pulled the finger out. "I didn't think you'd be so excitable." He looked me over carefully, like he wasn't sure about something. "No, there can't be a mistake. You *are* Jack Miller."

I started to slip off my backpack, shouting, "You lifted my wallet, didn't you?"

"Oh, I did not!" he said peevishly. "I know everything about you. We've made a complete study of Jack Miller, ever since . . ."

"Ever since what?" I asked, checking for the wallet anyway.

"Since you acquired the bicycle."

"Bicycle," I said numbly.

The Old Guy put a finger back in his ear, this time twirling it longer than before, like he was rotating an internal Rolodex. "'Nishiki Pinnacle mountain bike. Light but powerful, twenty-one speeds, chromoly frame and fork, linear response mountain brakes, front and rear derailleur indexing, great in the boonies and on the street—'"

"That's mine," I interrupted, "bought it last week. What are you, CIA or something? I know, there's a blueprint hidden in the frame. Some nuclear doomsday thing that can fry eighty percent of the world in under an hour! Or a microdot with a list of all satanic cult headquarters in southern California!"

"Nothing like that," he said.

I took a few steps, nearly tripping over a white throw rug that I hadn't noticed, and sat down on the white sofa. "Then let's cut the mystery and tell me what this is about—from the beginning!"

"You wouldn't understand half of it," the Old Guy said.

"Then tell me the half that I would!"

The Old Guy smiled, or twisted his mouth, or something. "Okay. First, you want to know where you are. Actually, you're right where you were. You never left."

I don't know if he did anything, but the white room was suddenly gone. The corner of Broadway and Fourth was there: people, traffic, a Carl's Jr., the whole thing. Only problem was, *nothing moved*. Just me and . . . the Old Guy. He was there— sort of—but all wrong, like a negative. And he was floating—I think—right next to the kid with the blaster.

We were back in the white room again. The Old Guy's white tennis shoes were solidly on the floor. I looked at him.

"You're not from around here, are you?" I asked.

He twisted his mouth. "At least you understand *that*."

"So, where's home?" I was trying to be cool, failing.

"That's part of the half you wouldn't understand. Let's just say it's . . . far off. It's the best I can do, Jack."

"Okay, assuming I accept this, and you're not Doug Henning in disguise putting on one hell of an illusion that Phil Melkowitz or my other friends paid through the nose for . . . then what do you want with me?"

"We came to offer you something."

"What?"

"A challenge, Jack. Adventure on a grand scale! A chance to travel to . . . places, yes, places, to do things that no one on your rather pragmatic world can *begin* to imagine! Does that appeal to you?"

I was dubious. "Great. How did I get singled out for this?"

"It was . . ." He cocked his head and stuck a finger in much farther than before. "We have no word for it. You, on the other hand, have many. It was destiny, fate, providence, karma . . . that's enough." Out came the finger. "Over here we had Jack Miller, planet Earth, North America, Dilber California—"

"Del Mar."

"Yes, isn't that what I said? And over there we had the Anlun Bicycle Factory, on the *same* planet, East Asia, Taipei, Taiwan."

"An amazing coincidence," I nodded.

"Your profile suited our requirements well," he continued. The finger again. "Jack Benjamin Miller, age thirty-four, five feet eleven and three-quarter inches—"

"Six feet."

The Old Guy nodded, or moved his head with the finger. "Yes. Continuing: 170 pounds, married six years, now divorced. No offspring. Heterosexual . . . An interesting idea. Where I come from . . . never mind. Works as a writer, lecturer, but mostly supports self from . . ." The finger was in as deep as it would go, but he looked puzzled. "We had trouble with this. Can you explain Lotto?"

"Sure. It's a game of chance. You pick random numbers, get lucky, win money. That's what happened to me last year. It wasn't one of those mother lodes of jackpots, forty or fifty million, but it wasn't bad. Every year I get a check for about the same after taxes as what I was taking home when I was a worker bee, sitting in freeway rush-hour traffic twice a day, doing stuff that bored me to death—wearing a *tie*. So when the chance came, I took it and got out of that life. I have to be careful but I manage okay, and the freedom's great."

"So you write your stories."

"Uh-huh."

"But without much success."

"I've had a few books published!"

"But . . ."

I shrugged. "Without much success, you're right."

"I absorbed all of your stories."

"You *read* them?"

"It was required as part of the briefing. My people absorb rather quickly. One of them, *Tree Men of Quazzak*; interesting, but inaccurate."

"What do you mean, *inaccurate*? It's a fantasy. I made the whole thing up!"

"No, Quazzak *does* exist. A planet in a rather insignificant solar system, the second, I think—no, perhaps the third—quadrant of the Helios 84 galaxy. Wretched pile of sand and rock, Quazzak, not a forest world like you described, and its nomadic primitives would have no more concept of a feudal society than—"

"Wait a minute!" I exclaimed. "I've been going along with this till now, but—!"

He held up both hands. "You're right, you're right, I digressed. Back to the point. So you write your stories of adventure, and it's satisfying, but because of all the time you have to yourself, it's not enough. You wish that you could *live* those adventures, don't you, Jack? Be a part of Earth's barbaric past or uncertain future, explore some distant world. Don't you?"

"I suppose . . . Yeah, of course, who wouldn't? But it's not—"

"But it *is*!" You *can*!" The Old Guy was really getting charged. "That's what this is all about, Jack. The bicycle. *Your* bicycle can take you anywhere because of the Vurdabrok Gear, which we put in while it was being assembled!"

"The *what*?"

"Vurdabrok Gear. It's, ah, part of the half you wouldn't understand. Named after its creator, one of the wisest men in our history. Quite a *cyclist* in his own right. Once your bicycle left the factory we followed it across the ocean and ultimately to the San Dieguito Cycle Emporium, where you would buy it. We . . . looked ahead to make sure it would be you. But we didn't have to interfere."

This was either getting good or I was beginning to freak out. "I've run through the gears from top to bottom," I told him, "all *twenty-one*, and there was nothing weird about any of them."

"You couldn't have tried this one, Jack. It's your *twenty-second* gear. I'll tell you how to use it."

"That would be a wonderful thing," I said wryly. "So okay, to summarize all this, you're a visitor from another world and you came looking for me because I fit the profile and you want to send me to great and glorious adventures on worlds all over the universe, or the past and future of my own world."

He tried that smile again. "See how easy?"

I felt like my brain was going to short-circuit. But you know, I *wanted* this to be true and looked at him hopefully.

"No shit?"

The Old Guy's smile was getting better. "No shit, Jack. I think that was the proper response." He withdrew the finger. "We are in earnest about wanting you to undertake this journey."

"But what's in it for you?"

"An appropriate Earther question. You think *you* have time on your hands, Jack? My race has more time than you could comprehend. So our diversions must be of considerable magnitude. We *study*, Jack; study every race we come in contact with, try to understand why they do what they do, or have done what they've done, even try to imagine what they might do in the future. We want to know why the throbbing light creatures of Proneus travel their solar system putting an end to all disease, famine, and the like. Or why the Kodommo of Soldon III find it necessary to annihilate half their planet and enslave most of whoever is left. This is our existence."

"Then you'll be . . . watching me?"

"You'll be under observation by our particular study group during a goodly portion of your journey. We don't interfere—"

Something happened. The Old Guy flickered, and through the wall behind him I could see the U.S. Grant Hotel, although kind of dimly. He looked around, then seemed solid again as he turned to me.

"What's wrong?" I asked.

"The field is dispersing. No time, and oh, so much more to talk about. Jack, tell me, do you want to know more or not?"

He was flickering again. "Yeah, sure."

"Then meet me tomorrow morning."

"Where?"

"I have the coordinates." He shoved the finger in again. "Camp Pendleton Marine Base, Stuart Mesa Road, top of the big hill, near the eucalyptus tree. It's the Starting Point. You know where that is?"

"Sure, I biked it a hundred times."

The bottom half of him was gone. He reminded me of an albino Cheshire cat. "See you later, Jack," he said in a voice that came from somewhere else.

"Wait a minute! I don't even know your name."

Only his face was left. He curled his mouth. "You can call me the Old Guy," he said, then was gone.

CHAPTER 2

Starting Point

The kid with the blaster nearly became unglued from it when he ran into me. "Hey, asshole," he yelled above Guns 'N Roses' "Move to the City," "watch where you're goin'!"

People were glancing at me as they crossed Fourth Avenue. I suppose I came off weird, even for southern California. I mean, walking around sort of dazed in blue Cannondale bike shorts, a Descente road jersey, and a San Diego Padres baseball cap, *that* might warrant attention. So I got the hell away from there as fast as I could.

If I did drugs there might have been a simpler explanation for what just happened to me. Assuming it *had* happened. With everything back the way it was, I had trouble convincing *myself*. Then I thought, Hey, I've always been open-minded about it, never doubted Betty and Barney Hill or Whitley Strieber or anyone else who said it was real, so why not? *I* had met a visitor, and he was up front with everything, and he'd made me one awesome proposition! And since inquiring minds like mine just had to know, there wasn't any way I would turn it down.

Okay, so I went ahead with my regular outing in the big city, haunting old bookstores and thrift shops and stuff. But it wasn't the same, because I kept thinking about the white room and half expected it to pop up on the next corner. I finally left early in the afternoon, long before the traffic started pouring out of downtown, and hardly remembered the ride up to Del Mar, except for running through the gears a few times—*twenty-one* of them. That was all I could find.

Here's a thought: It's the eve of the most amazing, historic, monumental happening on the planet, a journey on a mountain bike through space, time, God knows where else. How do you, the soon-to-be intrepid explorer, spend that last night?

I did my laundry. Trust me, I had to. Then I thought about stopping the mail, the paper delivery, changing the Titanic tape on the answering machine (*Jack's not in, leave your message and I'll*

7

see that he gets it just as soon as we reach port). What about my theater date with Paula Kaufman Friday night?

Scenario: "Hi, Paula, listen, I'm not going to be able to make it."

"Why not?"

"I'll be zipping around the Pleiades for a while, then I plan on sucking a few grapes with Aristotle."

"Right. Jack, the next time you have an urge to call me—control it!"

I liked Paula Kaufman. That would have to be rethought.

Anyway, I decided that I shouldn't have to be concerned about any of it—except the laundry. In the first place, maybe the Old Guy didn't have it in mind for me to just up and leave tomorrow. Maybe the planets or time lines or whatever weren't in the right alignment till next Tuesday morning at eleven-sixteen. Or even if I did go, shouldn't I be able to return to the exact time and place?

There's this old *Star Trek* episode where Kirk and Spock follow McCoy through a time portal to Depression-era New York. They have to prevent the good doctor from interfering with Joan Collins getting run over by a truck (Joan Collins?). If she lives, the Nazis win the war, there's no space program, ultimately no *Enterprise*. Well, Kirk pulls it off (not without falling in love with the lady first; like, what else?), and the three of them return to their own time. When Scotty sees them pop out of the portal he comments that they just left, when in fact they'd been there for over a week.

That's why I figured, no problem. I could tour a couple of galaxies, observe every day of the Thirty Years War, and still be back in time for Paula Kaufman.

This was getting crazy. I had to sleep on it. Maybe by morning the Old Guy and his pals will have erased all memory of this, or I might figure out that I had dreamed the whole thing.

But no way. I awakened at five fifty-six, the same time I always used to, four minutes before the alarm got me up for work. Orange juice, vitamins, a couple of bananas for a potassium fix, that was all I could handle. Almost squeezed Preparation H on my toothbrush. More nervous than I thought.

Sunrise surfers exulted in the day's first waves as I pedaled up the coast to Camp Pendleton. This part of Old Highway 101 was great, especially so early in the morning. The surf at Tamarack Beach in Carlsbad was awesome. Couldn't help slowing down through there.

But where Carlsbad ended, Oceanside began. Cyclists hated that. Over the years Hill Street had been reclassified from an obstacle course to a demilitarized zone. Hunting season was year-round for anything on two wheels.

Scenario: Two young males in a pickup truck.

"Hey, Bud, see what I see?"

"Bike rider at two o'clock, Earl!"

"Fifty points if he hits the sidewalk face first."

"Shit, Earl, I got two hundred comin' if I put him through the window of that 7-Eleven!"

"Aww-right!"

It wasn't so bad this time. Took some side streets, got through the worst of it okay. At a little before eight I was pedaling up to the main gate of Camp Pendleton, at Oceanside's northern edge.

I don't know why I think they should recognize me. Some of the sentries were ones I'd seen before, I would bet on it. But whether they did or not, it was always the same.

Sentry: "Doyouknowthebikeroute*sir*?"

Me: "Sure do."

Sentry: "Haveagoodday*sir*."

Me: "You too."

If you tell him no, he'll explain every mile to you. Once heard him doing it for some riders. A minute and a half without inhaling or using a single punctuation mark. It has to be done, no question. Make a wrong turn out there and you end up on a gunnery range in the middle of a war game with a 155mm howitzer ripping holes the size of swimming pools around you, or with the treads of a main battle tank about to convert your high-tech very expensive bike into a coffee table–size piece of modern art.

There was no one else on two wheels going in either direction; didn't think there would be too many on a Thursday morning. Camp Pendleton was a great place if you liked isolation. Farther in you might get buzzed by a Cobra or Huey helicopter, passed by a convoy or watched by guards with M16A2 rifles on the perimeter of a camouflaged encampment that looks like a bunch of ordinary hills. And along the first few miles your only concerns are a skunk crossing the road that you don't want to get pissed off, or the swarming flocks of swallows from the mud condominiums under the Santa Margarita River bridge (a Hitchcockian scene that I enjoyed).

The hill up to the top of the mesa was not incredibly steep, but went on for half a mile. Average riders worked hard; novices died. It was a great stretch if you were coming in the other direction. I didn't mind it now as much as in the past, especially looking down at the scrub-filled ravine on one side or the salt flats on the other. Never got tired of seeing stuff like that.

At the top of the mesa, near a lone eucalyptus, was the edge of what used to be flower fields. Quite an awesome sight biking past it in the spring. Now, most of it had been leveled, and base housing was going up. Progress.

I thought, So what if the Old Guy doesn't show up? I'd get back on the bike, ride up to San Clemente or Dana Point, kill some time, and turn around. Probably would have made this ride tomorrow anyway. Then I could do tomorrow whatever I would have done today . . .

The Old Guy appeared while I was making myself crazy with all of that. He came from the other direction, riding an old black Schwinn World ten-speed. Not too well, like a kid who was just starting to get the hang of it. He didn't exactly *look* like a cyclist either, dressed in tan Dockers, a Chaps by Ralph Lauren crested rugby shirt, and a pair of Reebok low-tops, no socks. He did have on a yellow Bell V1 Pro helmet. At least he wasn't all in white.

"Halloo! Jack Miller!" he called, tried to wave, nearly fell off the bike. "Glad you came. Saves having to do it all over again. I knew you were the one!"

He was off the Schwinn now, trying and failing to put down the kickstand, finally laying it in the scrub. Even when he was talking to me his eyes were on the Nishiki. His expression was like one on a guy sitting in his beat-up Pinto looking at someone's Jaguar XJ6, which had just pulled alongside.

"So, that's it," he went on. "A beautiful host for the Vurdabrok Gear."

"Which, by the way, I can't find," I told him.

"No, of course not. But you will, Jack."

"And this Vurdabrok Gear will open doors through space and time?"

He shook his head. I swear something rattled inside. "Oh, no, the Vurdabrok Gear is only the first step. What it does is allows you access to the *mhuva lun gallee*."

"The *what*?"

"The *mhuva lun gallee*. Vurdabrok himself named it. Our words, of course. Actually it's a rather lengthy phrase. Unlike your language, where you use so much to say so little, ours is an economy of sounds."

"What does it mean?"

"*That* question I was prepared for. Gave it a lot of thought. Trimming it down to basics, *mhuva lun gallee* means Ultimate Bike Path. Vurdabrok used to ride it all the time. Didn't invent it or anything, because it's always been there."

"Just what is it?" I asked.

He shrugged. "That's . . ."

". . . part of the half I wouldn't understand, right? So make it simple."

"You ride along it on your bike," he began.

"I figured that."

"It goes on in either direction, never ending—at least no one ever traveled it far enough to find out. You don't know how fast you're moving, perhaps slowly, or a thousand miles a second. But it's a ride like no ride you've ever taken. And there are things to see, Jack, wonderful things all along the way!" He stopped for a moment and stuck a finger in his ear. "Doors, passageways, gates, portals, openings into . . ."

"Time and space?"

"Yes—yes to both! But those are just *words* to help you label things of which your understanding is so impossibly small!"

"You don't say." I was a little pissed off. He didn't notice.

The finger remained in his ear as he blurted out, "Dimensions, Jack! Another *word*. Other worlds are everywhere you can imagine, and in places that you cannot!"

"How do you know . . . where you're going?" It sounded like a dumb question. "I mean, are these gates marked or something? Are there exit signs?"

He pulled the finger out and straightened his head. "You *don't* know, not at first. Vurdabrok said it was trial and error for the longest time. But he also said that when it happens, traveling the *mhuva lun gallee* becomes the easiest thing. In a way that makes it less of an adventure than when you first start out."

"So you'll be watching this whole thing," I said. "That's what you started to tell me yesterday."

"Yes, a small but highly interested study group. We'll be observing you—most of the time."

"But not all of it?"

He shook his head, and this time I *know* something rattled.

"Not every step of the way. There are at times diversions that warrant our attention."

I leaned forward and looked at him like a customer does with a used-car salesman when he's trying to get the *real* scoop on a vehicle the huckster had been touting. "I won't be in any danger, will I?"

The Old Guy shrugged. "Not on the *mhuva lun gallee*, no, not likely. But in so many other worlds? Yes, Jack, there *will* be danger. I suppose you could even be killed."

Shit, I knew there had to be a catch.

CHAPTER 3

The Ultimate Bike Path

It didn't seem to bother the Old Guy too much, what he had just told me. He was battling with that smile again, doing okay, except for looking a little smug. Maybe it was supposed to be that way.

"What'd you think, Jack," he said, "this was going to be a cycling tour of the Puget Sound? The Rosarita Beach–Ensenada Fun Run? It's *real*. And with anything that's real, there's risk."

"Guess I just never got around to thinking about it."

"But the risks aren't as great as you might imagine," the Old Guy went on. "First, you'll have your Nishiki and the Vurdabrok Gear. You can exit any world that way."

"As long as I can get to the bike."

"Second, while the study group is watching, your danger will be minimized. We won't knowingly let you die. But we *will* wait as long as possible for you to get out of the situation by yourself. It's important that our subjects make use of their own resources and capabilities. And it will be significant to you in another way."

"What do you mean?"

"We can save you two times, no more. After that it's over, and you'll never hear from us again. Assuming you've come to grow fond of the journey—all of our past subjects have—you won't find that to your liking."

I turned, walked away from the Old Guy, and stared across the construction site. For the longest time I just thought. You know, even with the possibility that I might not come back, I was still excited about it. The Ultimate Bike Path! A chance to be the first—maybe the *only* one—on my world to make this journey!

Sure, I was a half-decent biker. I could ride a century in a day, handle some rugged hills, do stuff that others couldn't. But did you ever notice that no matter how good you may think you are at something, there are others who can make you feel like a wimp? Someone can do *two* centuries in a day in almost the same time as your one. Or jog twice as far, twice as fast, whatever. Unless you

13

had the commitment of an Olympian or a triathlete, you just had to be content with your own personal bests.

No, I wasn't about to let this go by. I looked at the Old Guy. "When do I leave?" I asked him.

It was the absolute best smile he'd done so far. His whole body moved like a dog shaking off water from a bath it didn't want to take. He made some kind of sign to the heavens. Then he pumped my hand, and I felt a low-voltage charge of electricity run through my arm.

"Now, Jack, you can go *now*," he said. "But we have to do this right. The first thing will be for you to ride the Ultimate Bike Path, to get the 'hang of it,' as you say. Then, I want you to return to this place and time. It's important you know how to do that."

"How will I recognize the way back?"

"As soon as you enter the *mhuva lun gallee*, look behind you. There will be a moment before it's gone. No matter which way you travel, you'll see it again—often, in fact—because it is *your* place and time, and therefore strong. When you see it the first time, go through. Just remember to shift down out of your Vurdabrok Gear immediately, as you must do upon entering any world. But don't touch it while riding the Ultimate Bike Path. Do you understand all of this?"

"I suppose it'll make more sense when I'm there," I shrugged.

"All right then, let's—"

A rider came over the hill, stared at us, nodded. We nodded back, and he went on his way to San Clemente or wherever. At the same time a pickup truck drove past in the opposite direction. The Old Guy shut his eyes and concentrated hard.

Then he looked at me and said, "No other bikers, and there won't be any traffic for at least three minutes."

"How do you know that?"

"Never mind. Now look." He pointed at my right thumb lever. "For the Vurdabrok Gear, you shift that up."

"Can't do it," I argued, trying to force the lever. "See?"

He shook his head. "Only when the bicycle is moving fast."

"How fast?"

"Ideally, free-fall; off a cliff or building, or—"

"No way!"

"You'll get used to that sometime," he muttered, "but what an inconvenience until then. All right, the next best thing is to go downhill."

"This hill?"

"Of course, why do you think I had you meet me here?"

"But there are steeper hills around."

"Not quite as long, though. Besides, this road is on a perfect parallel plane with the Ultimate Bike Path, and that makes access all the more easy. Get on, Jack. You should leave before there are any observers."

I climbed on the bike. The legs felt rubbery; I tried to ignore that. The Old Guy ran behind as I slipped into the toe clips and started pedaling.

"Remember to look behind you as soon as you're in," he called. "And don't shift out of the Vurdabrok Gear until you come back!"

"Wish me luck," I said.

"Luck?" The middle finger went into his ear. "Luck? I don't understand . . ."

"Never mind," I told him, and was off down the hill.

This had always been my favorite part of the Camp Pendleton ride. Usually you're on your way back from a long run up the coast, you're tired, and your car is waiting for you on San Rafael Drive on the other side of the main gate, three miles away. It was an exhilarating end.

So now I was racing down it, thinking I wasn't even going to make the bottom. It was weird, but it didn't bother me. I leaned forward, streamlining my body to lessen the wind resistance. A quarter of the way down I pushed on the lever. Nothing. I started pedaling and tried again. Halfway down, I felt it give a little! Thirty mph on my bike computer. Thirty-one. I pedaled furiously. Wind whistled past me. Three quarters of the way down; 31.5 mph. I pushed up as hard as I could. Thought it would snap, but no, it went all the way, like the Old Guy had said.

"*Holy sh*—!" was the unfinished supplication I left behind on the hillside.

The first impression was of everything being white, like the crazy room where the Old Guy had first spoken to me. It was a glaring light that didn't last too long. Then, I felt like I was pedaling through water . . . at least what I thought it might feel like, never having ridden along the bottom of anyone's swimming pool before. That was briefer than the first impression—I think. Couldn't really tell how long or short *anything* was here.

But I was definitely aware of bursting onto the Ultimate Bike Path. Previously there had been a weird, uncomfortable silence, but now I could hear sounds, so many different kinds that not one dominated. And I wasn't *hearing* them in the way we were used to, but rather *through* my body, like vibrations.

Instinct told me to keep my eyes straight ahead. But I had to follow the Old Guy's instructions. I suppose he'd bring me back if I couldn't find the right gate. Yeah, but why go out of my way to show him I was an idiot?

So, keeping a firm grip on the handlebars, I turned around to look at the closing gate. The first thing I realized was how quickly it was falling behind. Maybe I'd waited too long! Concentrate, Miller, look at the gate. Try to do this right!

It was about the size of an ordinary door, maybe even narrower. There didn't seem to be anything solid or substantial about it, more like a deep blue, floating mist that expanded and contracted, like it was breathing. The part that was "closing," or filling in, had the distinct shape of a bicycle and rider. In the bottom right corner—and only there—the mist sparkled, like sunlight reflecting off a rippling lake. There was a distinctive pattern to it, seven tiny pyramids, each spinning on its own, but all of them revolving around an eighth, which was stationary. Wait, I could see *one* other pyramid, even smaller, segregated at the top of the portal, just to the left. Noticing that, I stared even harder. But I couldn't see anything else, not before the passageway to my place and time in the universe (*that* was a heavy thought) fell from sight.

When I turned and really started looking at the Ultimate Bike Path, I was amazed how I'd been able to pull my attention away from it in the first place. The Old Guy's *mhuva lun gallee* was . . . a tunnel, I guess, because I could see rust-red "walls" on both sides, which curved up to something overhead that must have been a "ceiling." It didn't look *that* far above, and the walls weren't a great distance from me, so it wasn't the size that made this place so awesome. The gates, that's what it was. One after another, on the left, the right, no consistent pattern. Some were like the door I'd come through, most were incredibly different. I was able to get a good look at every one, because—this was weird—even though I was still pedaling and could feel my forward momentum, it seemed that I would come to a dead stop in front of each gate. Just for an instant, before it—or me—whizzed past, but enough. Here was a small circular one, black, with bright yellow streaks pulsating like strobes. Over there a watery green one shaped like Florida with a Stetson hat. Then an isosceles triangle with fireworks from a thousand state fairs on a thousand July Fourths exploding inside it. Another shaped like the profile of Elmer Fudd's head with the hunting cap on, alive with spurts of flowing, yellow-white molten lava.

The fat tires on my mountain bike had to be touching *something*, I suddenly realized, looking down. There was a fine mist, its color the same rust-red as the tunnel. Through it, the "floor" seemed to be solid, but not smooth, more gravelly. What was really strange was that I should've been able to hear—or feel—the tires rolling over the surface. It was like two hundred pounds of bike and me weren't there.

Maybe we weren't.

Back to the gates: As quickly as each came and went, I was able—for that moment—to sense it with a profound awareness the like of which had eluded me for all these thirty-four years. From one of the small black circles I felt this warm, safe middle-of-the-featherbed feeling, while an Elmer Fudd cast a foreboding shadow that flooded me with anxiety—or in other words gave me one hell of a case of the willies. These two were extreme; all the others were in-between. But you know, not even the worst of them scared me off. In some ways every one drew me irresistibly, summoned me to enter and see what was beyond. And I'll be damned if that wasn't exactly what I wanted to do. The lure of the *mhuva lun gallee* was undeniable! At least that would make the Old Guy happy.

But I couldn't leave yet. This was a quick round trip back to Stuart Mesa Road. I wasn't ready. There was more the Old Guy had to tell me. So okay, get the hang of it, which I was already starting to do, then find my doorway and exit the Ultimate Bike Path just long enough to learn the rest—

There! That's the right one! No, check it out: same shape, but only *six* spinning pyramids, and one on the top right, not left, and—look at that—another small one just outside the circle. Not mine at all. Close . . . or was it? Where would that one take me?

Didn't matter yet. The important thing was that I could tell the difference. And when the next similar one showed up, I turned the trick even faster. A mere novice on the Ultimate Bike Path and already I was beginning to figure it out!

Now I was really turning onto the sight of the passing gates, and the feel of the sounds that came out of them. The silence of the spinning tires was still weird, but I suppose in time I'd get used to that, too.

Which made me think of my cadence. It was a slow, steady one, hardly any effort pushing the pedals, even in the Vurdabrok Gear. I couldn't shift down, not here. But I could speed up without working much harder, so I tried it, at the same time fighting to keep my thumb off the shift lever.

You know what happened? I felt like a stone shot out of some giant slingshot, and in the first few seconds it really freaked me out! Black circles and Elmer Fudds and pyrotechnic triangles and blue doors flew past me in one psychedelic blur. Now *that* scared the hell out of me, and—I swear—for an instant I thought I'd wet my spandex. Just what I would have needed the study group to observe.

But before I consciously slowed down, it occurred to me that riding this way on the Ultimate Bike Path was incredible: the ride down Stuart Mesa or the Torrey Pines hill near Del Mar carried to some geometrically lofty number! So what if I couldn't tell a time portal from a space portal from a whatever? This was great! And to be honest, I still wasn't pedaling *that* hard. What would it be like going a little faster . . .

I decided to stop playing around. The important thing now was to get back to where the Old Guy waited. Just a little slower on the pedals; hardly anything at all, but enough. Now I could see each gate again. Among the already familiar shapes was a new one, an iridescent snowman with long skinny needles sticking out of it. For a while they seemed to dominate, then there weren't any at all.

The gate back was suddenly there, on my right. I was as sure of it as if there had been a sign with an arrow saying CAMP PENDLETON EXIT. Turning toward it without thinking, I began pedaling fast. For a moment the bike felt like it wanted to resist. Then it grabbed hold of the rough surface, and I was hurtling the short distance (actually it turned out to be longer than I thought) toward the misty blue door.

Scenario: Study Group observing Jack Miller on the Ultimate Bike Path.

Study Group Old Guy #1: "Then he's able to recognize the correct door back to his place and time?"

Study Group Old Guy #2: "Yes, he's a good subject. You selected well."

My Old Guy: "Thank you."

Study Group Old Guy #1: "But what is that sound he's making?"

Study Group Old Guy #2 (Covering ear holes on some part of his *body* or whatever.): "Yes, what is it?"

My Old Guy: "The motivation for the sound is the gate he approaches, which at the moment he perceives as solid. The sound itself is common on his world and is called a scream."

CHAPTER 4

What's Behind Door Number One?

I shut my mouth as soon as I realized that the mountain bike was again speeding down the Stuart Mesa hill. The Old Guy knew I'd come out near where I went in. He was waiting for me at the bottom, on the Santa Margarita River bridge.

Wait a minute, what about the Vurdabrok Gear? No, I wasn't in it anymore. Must've shifted down as soon as I hit the blue mist. Damned if I remember doing it.

"Welcome back, Jack," called the Old Guy, pleased with his poetic prowess. "So, what'd you think of the *mhuva lun gallee*?"

I didn't answer him right away. First I looked over my body, then the bike. Next I glanced up the hill, then turned to him. "I feel kind of weird," I said.

"Like your head's filled with air and floating above your shoulders?"

"Yeah, that's it exactly."

"Don't worry, everything's cool."

Everything's cool again. "That's easy for you to say."

"It'll pass quickly, and after you've done it a few times you won't even notice a thing."

He was right—about the first part. My head seemed to settle down on the rest of me. I shook it now; didn't before, thought it might wind up in the river or something.

"Actually," I said, "that was a great ride. The Ultimate Bike Path is incredible!"

"Then you want to go back?"

"You know it!"

This was the best smile I'd seen on him yet. "Way to go, Jack!" he exclaimed. "Now, you have some questions?"

He knew I did. "All these different . . . places I'll be going to: What if one isn't exactly suited for me? I mean, the atmosphere is methane gas, the surface molten lead, something like that. It's a good chance I wouldn't be too glad to be there."

"No problem, Jack." He waved his hands. "Not too many gates

along the *mhuva lun gallee* summon you to inhospitable worlds, and you'll know them before you enter."

"Then it'll only be Class M planets?"

"Class . . . M?" His middle finger came up. I grabbed his wrist gently.

"Never mind. You answered the question."

"But while you'll always be able to breathe and perform other natural functions, there is one area where some help will be useful."

The Old Guy held out his palm. There was this round silver thing, like a power cell from a digital watch, only smaller and flatter. While I was looking at it, he suddenly reached around and stuck it against the back of my neck. He did it so fast, there was no time to react. I felt this burning, condensed in one tiny spot, but really hot. It didn't last long.

"What'd you do to me?" I snapped, touching the spot.

"That? It's the UT5. Our best model. Far superior to all those before it."

"UT5?"

"Universal Translator. You'll hear anyone—or anything—in your language, and they'll hear you in theirs. Trust me, Jack, it's tough making oneself understood out there."

"I suppose."

"For example," he continued, "The Workedos of Bablubor communicate by means of short flatulent bursts through their anal orifice, mixed with high-pitched nasal whines."

"Can't wait to have a nice chat with them over dinner," I said, and the Old Guy nodded, so I figured he believed me.

"Yes, well, so you see the importance of the UT5?"

"Makes perfect sense to me."

"Good. What else?"

"Will I ever get over thinking those gates are solid?"

"In time you'll wonder how you ever saw them that way!"

"I felt like a real schmuck coming through."

"A what?"

"Never mind. You said that you'd be able to pull me out of trouble twice."

"That's right."

"So in case you're *not* watching, what do I have to do to get your attention? Say a magic word? Jump up and down and wave frantically? Yell 'Hey, guys, I'm in deep kaka, pull my ass out of here'? What?"

"Actually, none of those." He reached into the saddlebag of his Schwinn and pulled out something that looked like a large copper-colored coin, the size of a silver dollar, on a skinny chain. "Here."

He tossed it to me. I looked it over. One side was blank. There was a stamping on the other, an animal's horned head, I figured. Don't know what kind, wouldn't even guess, it was so ugly.

"This amulet is called the Bukko, after the animal," said the Old Guy. "If it becomes necessary, rub the left horn vigorously with your thumb. The second time around, do it to the right horn. And Jack?"

"Yes?"

He hung the Bukko around my neck. "The Bukko is my own personal property, and I value it highly. Don't lose it, and don't let anybody take it away. There are civilizations that will consider something like this a great prize."

"That makes me feel great," I said, tucking it inside my shirt. "Okay, I'm ready."

"One last thing, Jack. It's *real* important."

"What's that?"

"On worlds other than your own there are no limitations to your actions or behavior. But in Earth's past you can't be anything more than a visitor; an observer, like us. We are bound by even greater laws of the universe that prohibit us from such interference. If we were not effective enough to prevent you at the time you acted, then we would rectify it after the fact. But in the meantime you will forever relinquish the privilege of traveling the *mhuva lun gallee*, and would risk losing . . . even more."

"That sounds like a threat."

"Like I said, it's important. What's done is done on your world. It has to stay that way."

I shrugged. "No problem."

"Please, Jack, you're not convincing me."

"Okay, what might happen?"

"To be technical would be to get into the half you wouldn't understand. This is a vague analogy: You're riding along the *mhuva lun gallee* when eight portals suddenly draw your attention at once. Their pull is strong. You enter all of them at the same time, in pieces . . ."

"Okay, I got the message, don't tell Lincoln to skip the theater, the play sucks, or the Indians that Peter Minuit is ripping them off."

"Good boy, Jack," he nodded. "Off you go then."

A Nissan 4X4 passed on its way up the hill. Two young flat-topped marines had the volume control of their stereo set on Fry-Your-Brains. A trio of elderly bikers followed in the same direction, while a lone jogger enjoyed the downhill part of his run. This was rush hour on Stuart Mesa Road.

"Should I wait?" I asked.

The Old Guy shrugged. "Better to wait at the top."

I started off. "See you."

"Good luck, Jack," he said, tapping his head. "I looked it up."

The three riders had been halfway up the hill while I was still on the bridge. I rode as slowly as I could without falling off, but eventually passed them. They were walking their bikes. There were two women and a man, and from the way they moved it seemed like they would be on the hill forever.

"Need any help?" I asked.

The man grimaced. "We'll make it, sonny. Just don't have legs like you do anymore."

"You don't have *anything* like he does anymore, Walt," said one of the women.

"Shuddup, Muriel," he responded.

I got away from there quick.

A bus bound for the Outer Camp roared past while I waited on top. No one was around now, so I started down. It was 8:23. There was some resistance from the wind. I pedaled fast. The Vurdabrok Gear yielded slowly. I pushed harder, and it went all the way . . .

I was back on the Ultimate Bike Path. It didn't seem as much of a shock getting there this time. I began a steady cadence, something between the two I'd tried before, slow enough to catch a glimpse of each gate.

The pattern was different. There were mostly isosceles triangles on both sides, broken occasionally by an Elmer Fudd. Watching the continuous run of fireworks from the triangles was impressive. But I didn't have the urge to ride into one.

After a while the iridescent snowmen dominated, and when this was done the random pattern resumed. I kept passing all the gates, maybe because I was still getting used to it, but more likely because I was scared shitless about going through. If you think the blue mist that looked solid was unnerving, what about exploding fireworks and molten lava?

But they can't hurt me, they're just doors. Okay, so pick one. A black circle with the throbbing yellow lights, on the left.

I turned the bike toward it. There was no sensation of it summoning me, but on the other hand I didn't feel any resistance. As I got closer the streaks of light began to look like sharp-edged bands of metal. I would be sliced going through them, like a rye bread. But you know what Conan's girlfriend says in the movie: "Do you wanna live forever?"

Actually, yes.

So I screamed again. Sorry, Old Guys in the study group.

But I went through, give me credit. And this time I remember shifting down, just as soon as the yellow streaks (which *didn't* slice me into rye bread) were behind. The mostly dark gate was instantly gone, and I was blinded by some incredibly bright light. Shutting my eyes tightly, I tried to brake. The bike was moving fast, and I went into a skid. Instinctively I pulled free of the clips and thrust one leg out. My foot touched a surface that was solid, but slick, like ice. I couldn't look at it, but somehow I found a foothold and regained control.

I tried opening my eyes again, but this wasn't like coming out of a movie theater into daylight, where it takes a few seconds to adjust. This place was just too bright! So much for the Old Guy's idea of "hospitable." Then I remembered my sunglasses, in the seat bag. I put them on, and in a moment had a look at the first place I'd chosen.

Through the Gargoyles, everything around me was a pale shade of yellow: The "ground," some nearby hills, a distant range of mountains, and like the surface all of it appeared glassy, polished but not translucent. Even a cluster of something nearby that resembled trees was made out of the same stuff. Neat-looking, but weird.

The sun filled up half the sky. Seemed like the surface temperature should have been 800 degrees or something, but it was a cool light, comfortable. It reflected off everything, and even with the glasses on I was still bothered by numerous bright flashes. This place was a Sylvania Quality Control inspector's worst nightmare.

Starting tentatively I pedaled across the surface, which was level for a considerable distance. The fat tires held, as long as I kept it in a straight line. I had a hunch that exploring this place wasn't going to be too . . .

Something moved, over by the "trees." I couldn't make out what it was with all the flashing. Pedaling toward the cluster, I saw it again. It was darting between the vertical formations. When I was a few yards away, it froze. I could see it clearly now.

In the coastal tide pools there are thousands of these slug things called sea hares. Big ugly creatures with two sensors on top that look like rabbit ears. You get a sea hare pissed off, it squirts purple ink at you. That's what this thing in the cluster looked like. It was thicker than the average sea hare, and about a yard long. You couldn't really tell one end from the other, because there were sensors on both. It was dark brown, so you could distinguish it against the background.

It was watching me. I got off the bike, stood still for a moment, then took a few steps toward it. The thing reared, spun around like a top, finally began to run (or slither, crawl, whatever) across my path in the direction of some hills. It left a trail of slimy stuff behind.

"Momma, Momma!" I heard it say.

That's right, it talked! Or communicated, or something. I couldn't accept that at first, so I just stood there and watched it. Speedy thing, actually.

The UT5, of course! If I could understand it, then it should be able to do the same. I started to follow.

"Hey, stop," I called. "I won't hurt you."

"Momma, Momma!" it said again. "Help! There's a monster chasing me!"

"Wait a minute, I'm not a monster." I was rather indignant. "Come on, slow down, let's talk about this."

But it kept on moving. I couldn't catch up, even though I had rubber soles on my Avocet bike shoes. Also, I was walking with the Nishiki. No way was I going to leave it anywhere.

Still shouting for its mother, the thing disappeared between some hills. It was simple to follow the slime trail, but the path grew narrower, making it hard to fit through with the bike.

"Come on, you little creep," I muttered. "I'm only trying to be friends."

Then I turned a corner, and the thing was waiting for me. Next to it was another one, three times the size. I stopped.

"See, Momma? I told you it was an ugly scary monster!"

The big one reared. I looked up. "Why are you frightening Metthustroovakee?" it said, or at least the last part is what I *think* it said.

"I wasn't trying to scare the kid, just talk to . . . him. I'm a stranger here, in case you couldn't tell."

"You can talk to my mate," Momma said, twisting around. Then her head (I think) turned back toward me. "It's not that he's any smarter than me," she explained, "but he shouldn't be as sickened looking at you as I am."

Thus spake the nine-foot slug-thing.

Momma's slime trail was wide. I couldn't help stepping in it as I followed them. A couple of minutes later we were out of the hills. There was a "village," or someplace where a lot more of these things congregated. Many of them were even bigger than Momma. You don't want me to describe what the numerous intersecting slime trails looked like, do you?

There were no dwellings on the surface. Some of the things were emerging from gaping holes. Momma made her way toward one of them.

"Wait here," she said, and I stopped—happy to oblige. Dozens of the things were turning toward me, staring with eyes that must've been somewhere on their twin ends. I heard whispers.

"What is that awful thing?"

"Disgusting!"

"Where did Yoniaristakkaloo find it?"

"My momma didn't find it." That was Metthustroovakee. "I saw it first and brought it to her."

"You should have left it there."

I had an appropriate gesture in mind for these warmhearted folk. But not having limbs, they probably wouldn't have understood it anyway.

When Momma returned, her mate was following. *Big* son of a gun. Momma nodded in my direction.

"That's it over there, as if you couldn't tell," she said. "Excuse me, I think I'm going to be sick."

She slithered off to their hole. Poppa looked over the bike and me.

"Why don't you go away now?" he said. "Nobody wants you here."

"Gee, you could've fooled me," I replied. "What's the problem, anyway? I'm a stranger here. I only wanted to—"

"Every thousand years or so a life form such as yourself comes through," he muttered. "Let one stay and who knows what'll follow! Besides, you wouldn't like it here. No food for you. We eat our own trailings."

Just as he said this I glanced at a bunch of the things nearby. That's what they were doing! Sounded like a hundred old toothless Bill Cosbys gumming Jell-O.

"And you couldn't sleep here," Poppa went on. "At night the surface turns into dry ice. You'll stick to it and it'll rip off your flesh if you roll over."

"Great planet you have here," I nodded.

"And we won't tolerate you trying to eat any of us!" Its outer skin rippled. "We can protect ourselves. Wanna see the stuff we use?"

A hole started to open on its underbelly. I held up one hand. "You made your point. I'm outta here."

Poppa nodded. "A good thing too. You're starting to make me nauseous."

"Any hills around here?"

He swung to the left. "Try that way."

I started to walk. A murmur of satisfaction followed. Turning, I said, "Hope to see you all next time through. I'll bring everybody a gift . . . nice box of Snarol."

Leaving them to contemplate that, I climbed back on the bike and rode out of the village. "Sorry, Old Guy," I said to the weird sky. "That was crude, I know; but they really pissed me off!"

The glassy surface suddenly sloped down. Holding the handlebars tightly, I inched over to the thumb lever. The downhill speed became unreasonable, considering what was under my tires. Writing off my first experience along the Ultimate Bike Path as brief and uninspired, I shifted into the Vurdabrok Gear.

CHAPTER 5

Averill and His Cart

Something passed me on the Ultimate Bike Path. It was going in the opposite direction. I wasn't surprised. After all, this was some great universal artery, right? And since it was arrogant to think that many others—or *any* others, for that matter—looked like us Earthers, it was just as presumptuous to suppose that every "bicycle" had two big wheels with spokes, derailleurs, and Vetta gel seats.

The thing that passed looked like a giant turtle in a miniature wheelchair. That's the best I could do, only seeing it for a couple of seconds. The top of its pea-green, severely curved shell was about five feet above the ground mist. I couldn't see a head anywhere. The wheels of whatever it rode on were small, parallel but spaced narrowly apart. In retrospect I couldn't say whether the conveyance was under the rider or part of it. I did try to get its attention with a wave, but nothing happened, and it was gone.

So I forgot about it and started contemplating my next port of call. This time, no black circles with laser bread slicers. That's not to count them out forever, but after the last trip why ask for it? There were a lot of others to choose from, and after a few moments I settled on an Elmer Fudd.

This gate actually *wanted* me to come through. I could tell that the instant I turned toward it. The sensation wasn't anything like being sucked in by a vacuum cleaner or dragged on a conveyor. It was more in your head, a suggestion . . . an impulse, maybe.

Whatever, there I was barreling toward what looked like the caldera of Mount St. Helens. The gate was so wide that I couldn't miss it, so I closed my eyes. If I couldn't *see* molten lava cover my body, I reasoned, there wouldn't be anything to worry about.

Damned if it didn't work. The sound of rushing air grew louder, but that was all. I shifted down. Two seconds later it became still, and I opened my eyes.

Just in time to run the bike into a thornbush.

This was the Mother of all thornbushes, ten feet high and

double that around. I was thrown over the handlebars head first.
Brittle branches cracked as I fell, leaving me on a bed of the sticky
brambles. But they weren't as bad as they could've been. I walked
away wearing lots of scratches, but nothing that I couldn't live
with for a while . . . so I thought.

The bike was all right. Some thorns were stuck to the tires, but
no way were these hairlike tips going to puncture the rubber.
Brushing them off, I looked around.

There were lots of trees—sort of gnarly pines and a greater
number of something that looked like a stunted sycamore. Though
for the most part these trees were green, the thick grass that
covered a lot of the surrounding countryside was blue. Not
Kentucky bluegrass blue, which isn't really blue, but *blue*. L.A.
Dodger blue, IBM blue. It was disconcerting at the least.

Walking the bike, I found my way out of the trees. It took a
while. Nowhere else did I see another thornbush. That figures, I'd
hit the only one.

This wasn't Earth, unless it was *way* in the future, and
something really radical had happened. Like two suns? The nearer
of the two, directly overhead, was dull and looked like a pumpkin.
You could stare right at it. Not so the other one, sitting barely
above the horizon. It burned intensely, despite appearing so small.
Had it been any closer to this world I probably would have been
approaching medium rare. As it was, the temperature felt just
right.

I finally came across a hard dirt path and started riding along it.
There were trees on both sides, but at a distance. Behind them
were hills, not awesome ones, but interesting, lots of yellow and
white patches on the slopes. The fact that this road ran right down
the middle of the valley made it clear there was some form of
intelligent life around. Hope they didn't leave slime trails.

I wasn't feeling too great. Maybe it was the passage, the fall,
whatever. First, I felt weak, and had some trouble pushing on the
pedals. A lower gear took care of that for the moment. But there
was this weird feeling in my body, like a low but steady charge of
electricity passing through. Two places it was most noticeable
were my toes and earlobes. My head hurt, too. I took off my
helmet and fastened it to the rear rack, but left my Padres cap on.

Nothing appeared on the path during the first hour. Not that I
was burning up the distance or anything. I doubt if I'd even gone
four miles, and most of that was at the beginning. Lower gears

didn't help after a while. Whatever had started messing up my body was spreading. I barely had a grip on the handlebars, and moving my legs was an ordeal.

Finally, the bike and me toppled over. I should've gotten off before, when there was still some feeling left, but I waited till now. What a jerk. I broke the bike's fall, took a cut on the shin from the rear derailleur, didn't feel a thing; same for a road rash on my left arm. Truthfully, I would rather have been standing there screaming in pain; I could at least relate to that.

But this was . . . nothing! My legs were numb. Same for my arms below the elbows. I could still feel some of that weird tingling, although there weren't too many places left. Soon they'd be gone, and I would be totally paralyzed.

Not that I could do a hell of a lot now. By twisting my shoulders I managed to work my way out from under the bike, then rolled a yard away. With even more work I dragged myself to a nearby boulder and pressed my back against it. Good timing too, because—other than in my earlobes—the tingling was gone.

Let me tell you this without hesitation: I was scared shitless. The thing that bothered me most was that it was heading straight for the brain. As soon as my ears went numb, as soon as I couldn't move my mouth or blink my eyes, that's it; Jack Miller becomes history on some nameless planet. Great.

And even after time had passed, making that scenario unlikely, I still found myself coping with something other than a positive outlook. I mean, was this some temporary anomaly, or was I doomed to live in a dead body forever? If that was so, it could be a very short *forever*. No one was around to help; no food, no nothing.

Then, revelation! I looked up. (Why always *up* I have no idea.) "Hey, Old Guy," I shouted, "you and your buddies *must* be watching. Since I just started this trip I'm still a novelty, right? Well, as you can see, I have a slight problem. Wait, don't overreact! I'm not pushing the panic button yet. In fact, I can't push *any* button just now. Ha ha. But I'll stick it out, see what happens. I would appreciate it if you'd stay tuned in, you know, in case something with seven rows of nasty teeth decides to walk over and chow down on my face. I'll holler loud, okay?"

That helped a little; not much. My body, my dead body; Jesus, I was scared! Okay, Miller, cut the crap. Concentrate on other things. Yeah. The bike, what about the bike? *Rugged 100 percent*

Tange chromoly monostay frame. It was fine. So, how about the road? I could look up the road, down the road, move the head a bit either way. Nothing coming, nothing I could see or hear, anyway. Somebody will. Roads don't grow, they have to be put there.

The pumpkin sun seemed to move as I watched it. I don't know how much time passed, but before long it was nearly down. The other one, which I hadn't been able to see for a while, was now almost overhead. I could feel its heat on my face; a little uncomfortable, but not intense. The brim of my Padres cap helped.

Actually, I *was* concerned about the appearance of any native fauna. I mean, how long do I wait before bailing out? The beastie might not want to devour me, maybe just lick my face or take a leak. Maybe it would be better to stop worrying until it happened.

A lot of hours must have passed, because by now the smaller sun was on its way down. Funny, it seemed as if I had lost some time. Then I realized that even with what was going on, I had fallen asleep. Swell.

On the other hand, maybe it was for the better. It got my mind off things, and it let enough time pass for—someone to be coming!

"Thank you, God; thank you, Study Group, whoever," I said.

The sound was still too far off to see who or what was making it. I think it came from "down" the road, to my left, the direction in which I'd been going. A clattering sound, that's what it was, and a less frequent but consistent squeak, like a door moving on a rusty hinge. Undoubtedly, something man-made.

Sounds carried well here, because it was one hell of a long time until I could see anything. Before that happened I started hearing a weird sound. It was like the howling of a sick, dying animal, really pathetic. But when I recognized it as words, I knew someone was singing.

"Tiny Tim lives," I muttered.

The fellow coming my way was humanoid; the appropriate number of arms and legs were in the right place. But he was a little . . . different. Picture this: Jonathan Winters with fire engine–red hair is caught in a cider press, gets squashed to half his size, then has his arms stretched until they span eight feet. That's what was coming up the road, wailing in agony.

Behind him was the source of the clattering and squeaking,

something that looked like an ore car, only bigger. It was made of wood, and rolled along on four big wheels. This was weird: *nothing* appeared to be pushing or pulling it. The squashed gnome (who by the way had on a one-piece purple outfit that reflected light, it was so shiny) was a couple of yards in front of it, and I couldn't see any kind of harness or tow rope.

> *"The fair Amelia, oh, did shiver so,*
> *From favors offered in the snow,*
> *Till I swore to her I'd never go,*
> *So we summoned her brother, the village runt,*
> *Who sharpened axes dull and blunt,*
> *Said he, 'My sister is a—'"*

"Yo!" I called when he was still ten yards away. "Over here!"

I'm sure he saw me, but damned if he didn't keep singing and moving at the same slow pace. The expression on his jowly face said that he was angry at being interrupted. There, now I felt positive he was looking at me. But that didn't speed him up.

So I waited; like, what choice did I have? From how they came out, I'm sure the Translator was having a devil of a time with his words. Not that I cared about *what* he sang; it was the off-key falsetto that made me wish I had hands to cover my ears.

Then, a couple of yards away, he stopped looking at me. "So, what's this?" he exclaimed. His voice, naturally, was basso profundo.

The object of his attention was my Nishiki Pinnacle. He stood over it, poking around with his foot, like making sure an animal was dead. Behind him, the cart kept rolling. I thought it would flatten him and was going to yell when he suddenly slapped himself on the rear. The cart stopped.

"I *never* saw anything like this before," he whined. "What sort of thing is it? I want to know."

"Come here and I'll tell you," I said.

He stared at the bike a few more seconds, finally started my way. For some reason he circled me, and at one point was upwind of where I lay in my useless body. That's when I caught the first whiff of this would-be stunted savior. I nearly died.

It was like a dairy farm I often biked past in the San Pasqual Valley. I swear, that's how bad it smelled! Why couldn't my olfactory nerves be paralyzed? The little humanoid was clean enough, didn't look like he'd just rolled in the slops or anything. But it *had* to be coming from him!

"So, tell me," he said, stopping a few feet away.

"Tell you what?" I sounded strange, since I was holding my breath.

"That thing!" He practically jumped off the ground. "What *is* it?"

"Aren't you curious about anything else?" I asked.

"No. What is it?"

"It's a bicycle; twenty-one-speed Nishiki Pinnacle mountain bike, if you really want to know."

"What does it do?"

"You ride it. That's how I got here."

"Show me."

"Ah, now's where it gets good.. Sorry, can't do that."

His mouth formed an O. It was bright red inside. "What do you mean you *can't*? I said I wanted you to, so you'd better!"

I moved what I could on my face. "See that? It's all I can do. The rest of me is dead. It just happened earlier this—"

"You didn't by chance . . ." He looked at me sidelong. "Naaah, impossible. Not the Bush of Turttek."

"A big thornbush? Sits in the middle of a wood? Little sticky brambles? I ran into it back there."

"You *ran* . . . ?" He started to laugh. It was an infuriating titter. He went out of control, fell on his back, grabbed his toes and rocked like a hobby horse. I had a gut feeling I wasn't going to like this guy.

"How about letting me in on the joke?" I said dryly.

He sat up and tried to compose himself. "The only Bush of Turttek for six valleys in any direction, and you run into it! I don't even think the giant wartworm, which hides from its enemies by sticking its head up its anal canal, is *that* stupid!"

And this was my only hope! I was getting a little worried. "So the Bush of Turttek paralyzed me, right? Okay, when does it wear off?"

He wiped his eyes. "I don't think it does. At least, I'm not sure anyone ever recovered from the Bush of Turttek."

I rolled my eyes back. "Swell."

"That's a fine-looking thing," he said, staring at the bike again. "I'd like to take it back and present it to Mosconi. That'll score a few points. But I know Mosconi, he'll say, 'Nice, Averill, what do you do with it?' And I'll say, 'You ride it,' and he'll say, 'Show me,' and I'll say, 'I can't, don't know how.' Then you know what'll happen?"

"Who cares?"

"Ooh, he has a terrible temper, Mosconi does! So I would try to do a good thing for him and wind up with some punishment. Is that fair, I ask you?"

"Listen, Averill—"

"How'd you know my name?" He looked at me suspiciously.

"You just said it."

"Oh. What's yours?"

"Jack."

"Odd name."

"Thanks. What about someone who can help me? You must know a doctor or something."

"Doctor?"

"Yes, doctor! Medicine man, physician, sawbones, shaman! Someone who heals the sick."

Averill nodded. "That would be Hazel the Healer. Lives alone in the hills, mixes all kinds of strange stuff. We avoid her, unless there's some *real* need. I can give you directions."

"Oh, great," I snapped, "and how do you think I'd get there?"

"I forgot." He shrugged, turned, and started walking away. "Can't do any good here," he muttered. "Be dark soon, have to get back."

"Hey, you can't leave me here!"

"Why not? Too much trouble otherwise. I didn't know you a few minutes ago, and I'll forget you soon."

"Averill, wait! We can make a deal!" I was getting desperate. "Listen, I have an idea."

He stopped. "What kind of deal?"

"If you take me to Hazel, and she cures me, then I'll be able to ride the bike again, right? So then I can show you, or I can show this Mosconi. Either way, you'll score a lot of points with him. What do you say?"

I'd pushed the right button. He turned and looked at me. That squashed Jonathan Winters face was even more twisted as he contemplated what I'd said. Then he came closer. I sucked in air and held my breath.

"You'll teach me good enough to show Mosconi?" he asked.

"Absolutely."

He glanced at the bike. "I'll be able to do it?"

I tried not to look at his tree-stump legs. "Sure, no problem."

Now you and I know that I wasn't about to give my bike up to this little creep or his bad-tempered boss. So sue me, I'm an asshole. But he was going to leave me here! If the situation had been reversed, I would've taken him anywhere he wanted to go. That's why I didn't feel so bad doing it.

But actually, I could play it out. Once I was okay I'd stick him on the bike, let him fall on his head a couple of times. With his disposition he'd get mad and forget the idea then and there. That was a definite possibility.

"Okay, I'll do it!" he said emphatically. "But you'd better be right." He stuck out a hand. "Here, let's shake on the deal."

"Sorry, can't."

"Oops, forgot." He picked up my left hand, pumped it vigorously, then let go. It smashed against the boulder. Must've hurt like hell.

"Well, let's see," he went on, "I'll have to get you and the . . . bike into the cart." He backed away. I took a breath. He knelt by the bike, touched it, and said, "This won't be any problem."

Averill turned, bent over, and stuck out his rear end. He slapped one cheek firmly. The bike stood up. He slapped the other cheek. The bike lifted a few inches off the ground. It wobbled, but stayed in the air. He shook his rear, and the bike rose to a height of three feet. Now he started walking. The bike followed. It was actually on a collision course with the side of the cart. But before that could happen, Averill practically did a somersault. The bike leaped up, floated above the open cart for a moment, then fell as he turned his butt away. I expected a crash or something, but the noise was barely audible, sort of muffled.

Then he was walking toward me, impatiently fumbling around in a pocket of his jumpsuit. He pulled something out, but palmed it, so I couldn't see what it was. With his other hand he started poking around my body, even snapping the elastic on my bike pants.

"I don't suppose . . ." he began. "No, didn't think so. Well, this will work."

The thing in his hand was flat and triangular, made of bronze or something. After moving me around he pressed it in my crotch. I don't know how, but it must've stuck.

"Now for you," he said turning around.

"Wait a minute!" I exclaimed. "Is this going to—?"

He hit himself. I floated up and straightened out. My toes dangled half a foot above the ground. He started walking. I followed two yards behind. As we got close to the cart he smacked his rear again. I rose higher. Now I could see down into it.

The cart was a third full with shit.

My beautiful mountain bike was buried up to the top of the chainwheel. It might've still been sinking; I wasn't sure.

"Yo, Averill!" I cried. "What is this—?"

"Great load, huh?" he said proudly. "Lots of fuel to get from that. I may only be a Second Apprentice Dungmaster now, but just you wait. Found this ravine in the Mirjiret Hills where a big pack of jof jofs do their dumping. Nobody else knows about it. Mosconi will really be impressed!"

He was a Second Apprentice Dungmaster.

I was directly over the cart now. He spun around.

"Averill!"

I fell into the cart of jof jof shit.

CHAPTER 6

Which Hazel?

Screw you, Old Guy, and your buddies. Screw the Ultimate Bike Path. This wasn't what I signed up for! I mean, look at me! Up to my armpits. Lucky I didn't sink under altogether. What a way to go. Enough, I want out!

No, wait a minute. Think it over carefully, Miller. They might be able to pull me out of here, but what guarantees they can get my body working again? This is a local problem. The only way to solve it might be with a local cure. Okay, so keep your mouth shut and wait it out. Really, is it so bad being stuck in shit and totally paralyzed?

"Did you land all right?" Averill looked in over the side.

"Yeah, nice of you to care," I muttered. "What if I sink more when we start moving?"

"Shouldn't be much chance of that," he said. "But if it happens, scream loud. With any luck I'll hear you."

A few seconds later the cart lurched forward, then started moving steadily along the road. With the first jolt I sank a little deeper, but now I must've been stuck firmly, because even the bumpy ride didn't make matters worse. Not that I was lulled into a false sense of security. This particular situation wasn't conducive to *lulling*.

So could it have gotten any worse? Sure, why not? My head started hurting again. It wasn't one of those real throbbers, more like a dull ache. But it was uncomfortable.

So *now* could it have gotten any worse?

Averill started singing again.

More bawdy tunes about Amelia. Hell of a girl she must be. Fortunately it didn't last long, about ten choruses. After it was quiet for a minute, I almost asked him *how come*. But I figured that might set him off again.

Then the cart stopped moving. I expected him to look in, but he was a no-show.

"Dark already," he said, sounding far away. "See how much you held me up?"

Considering where I was, I hadn't paid attention to the sky turning dark. But it had: not black but an incredible deep blue with clusters of bright stars everywhere you looked. Another time I might've been impressed.

"Why'd we stop, Averill?" I called. "What's the plan?"

"What do you think?" He sounded more distant. "Just keep your mouth closed, okay?"

I could hardly hear him. "Averill, what's happening? Averill? Hey!"

Nothing, no response. The little twerp had left me alone! Didn't seem like he'd be coming back soon either. A whole night stuck like this. Swell.

The first thing I tried to do was fall asleep. But I was probably trying too hard, because it didn't work. So then I thought I'd better do something to keep from freaking out. Recite the states and their capitals. Sing all of Springsteen's *Born in the U.S.A.* album. Hum Beethoven's Seventh Symphony. List the current batting averages of the Padres.

Memorable lines from some of my favorite movies. That sounded good.

"They'll see, they'll see and they'll know, and they'll say, 'Why, she wouldn't even harm a fly.'" Mother Bates, the last line in *Psycho*.

"I heff no son!" Laurence Olivier to Neil Diamond in *The Jazz Singer*.

"You are a stench in the nostrils of God!" Ernest Borgnine in *Deadly Blessing*.

"Make me a sergeant, gimme the booze." Jensen the drunk in *Them!*

"I am your father!" Darth Vader to Luke Skywalker in *The Empire Strikes Back*.

Three yellow moons rose over the edge of the dung cart. You could see them move, that's how suddenly they were there. Two were tiny, the third a little larger. They were positioned like the eyes and nose of a happy face, waiting for the smile to be drawn. I started on movie titles with *moon* in them.

Teahouse of the August Moon. From the Earth to the Moon. Brother Sun, Sister Moon. Destination Moon. Cat Women of the Moon. Shine on Harvest Moon. Black Moon Rising . . .

I heard a sound.

Not close by, but the night in this valley was so deathly quiet that anything carried. Something moving along the road. Maybe it was Averill coming back. I was going to call out, but didn't. If it *was* him, why bother? And if it wasn't . . .

Tuning into the sound, I listened intently. Pebbles crunched under footfalls; not ponderous footfalls, but short mincing ones. Two at a time, followed by something being dragged over the gritty road surface. A half second of silence, then it would repeat.

Mince-mince-draaag. Mince-mince-draaag.

Real close now, making me ver-ry nervous. I held my breath, which was stupid.

Mince-mince-draaag. Mince-mince-draaag.

It stopped. I could hear it breathing. A subdued guttural growling punctuated by a sound you would make if you flapped your tongue real fast against your lips. Then, two *mince-mince-draaags*, and it was at the cart.

Snuffling, going around all four sides. Couldn't wait to see what it looked like when its head came up over the edge.

Actually, I could.

Then it sneezed. Considering what it was smelling, that was no surprise. Tell the truth, I'd gotten so used to the jof jof dung that I didn't notice it anymore. But the whatever-it-was, even with a keen sniffer, couldn't have detected the fresh meat inside.

Another sound now, something liquid hitting the side of the cart in a hard steady stream. Sneezing again, it moved away. Two dozen or so *mince-mince-draaags* later, it was quiet again.

I wanted to sleep, couldn't. This was really getting to me. Think of something, keep the brain busy. Old ballplayers with colors in their names. Bill White. Pumpsie Green. Vida Blue. Mordecai "Three Finger" Brown. Boston Blackie. Red Schoendienst.

Boston Blackie. I was losing it.

Mince-mince-draaag.

A second came, did exactly as the first. Now it was one after the other, sometimes a few of them together. It went on all night.

Fortunately it was a short night. The three little moons went up, then down, and even while they were still in sight the pumpkin sun rose. Stars faded; the dark blue sky folded over into a weird coppery overcast. Ten minutes later the last of the creatures was gone.

A while after that Averill's head appeared over the edge of the cart. Scared the hell out of me, because I hadn't heard a sound.

"You're still here," he said, disinterested. "The hoorklas didn't rip you to shreds."

"No thanks to you, creep," I muttered.

He ignored that. "Let's go then. The day's wasting already."

The cart rolled forward. Averill was quiet for the first couple of minutes, then resumed his falsetto singing, this time about someone named Lizzie. *Her* exploits would have made Amelia blush. But I fell asleep and missed most of the lascivious saga.

I only woke up because the cart was being jolted hard. The first thing I noticed was that the big pumpkin sun hung almost straight overhead. The sky was less dull, and it was warmer, which meant that the other sun was also up. This was about the same time of day I had arrived here yesterday.

When I'd run into the Bush of Turttek.

The dung cart wasn't on the valley road anymore. I saw tall rock formations close on both sides. Whatever we were on now couldn't have been much of a road at all.

Averill was puffing hard and whining as he spoke: "So, not answering, huh? Maybe you're dead in there. That would be okay. I could dump you out and start back down."

"It would be appreciated if you didn't."

"Ah, so you're still around."

"I was sleeping. Where are we?"

"On the hill trail, almost to Hazel the Healer," he said. "This is not easy, you know."

"I'm grateful to you, Averill, I really am."

"Humphh. You'd better be more than grateful when this is all done."

He stayed quiet after that, except for some grunting and an occasional native expletive. The uphill road grew worse. I was on the verge of one hell of a headache. But a short time later the dung cart jarred to a stop.

"Well, we're here," Averill grumbled. "Can't say I'm too thrilled about coming anywhere near that reclusive witch."

"You watch your tongue, wartworm," a woman's low, sultry voice warned, "or I'll squash you down so far that Mosconi will use you for a place mat."

"Oh, er, hello, Hazel," said Averill nervously. "I didn't see you there."

"No doubt of that. What do you want?"

"Nothing for me, to be sure. It's—"

"The stranger in your dung cart," she interrupted. "What happened to him?"

"He ran into the Bush of Turttek," Averill told her.

"You're kidding! Not even the three-toed imbecilicus ninipal—"

"No, he's not, ma'am," I called out. "I'll explain later. But can you help me?"

"Yes, I told him you might be able to," Averill said.

"I suppose. But he won't come into my house that way. Put him in the stream first."

"You mean . . . ?" Averill swallowed hard. "*That* stream?"

"Is there any other here?" Hazel asked peevishly. "Go ahead, I'll be with you."

A few seconds later Averill's Jonathan Winters face appeared over the front of the dung cart. He glared at me, probably thinking silent curses for the trouble I was causing him, then turned around and slapped his rump.

The jof jof dung must have set like mortar. I didn't emerge as easily as I'd gone in. Averill strained, wiggling from side to side. Then he turned around in a circle. I did too, and started coming out like a corkscrew. Once my feet dangled above the mess, he stopped working so hard.

I was clear of the cart now. No sign of Hazel. Straight ahead, just beyond the top of a rise, was a meadow, lots of yellow and white flowers on top of tall stems rising over an expanse of Dodger-blue grass. Round pinkish animals grazed in the distance, things that looked like sheep. There was a cottage, a neat-looking little building right out of *Hansel and Gretel*, with a stone-lined well in front.

On the left, just within my limited range of vision, was a stream. Narrow, but it flowed swiftly, especially as it started down the hillside after twisting across the meadow. There, now I could see it better, because Averill turned me toward it. I still couldn't find Hazel the Healer.

The stream was twenty yards from the dung cart. Halfway there I heard Hazel's voice from behind, so close that it startled me.

"No offense, stranger, but you really smell awful," she said.

"None taken," I replied. "If it was the other way around I would do the same. Anyway, I don't have much choice."

"I'm sure of that."

"Listen, ma'am—"

"Hazel."

"Yeah, Hazel. I hate to have you talking to the back of my head, but there's nothing I can do. Couldn't you come around?"

There was a pause before she said, "In time." Now she spoke to Averill. "Put him right there, wartworm. You see where I'm pointing?"

"Yes, yes," the Second Assistant Dungmaster muttered. But as I floated past I could see his expression was one of concern.

What was the story here?

I was over the middle of the stream. The swiftly flowing water was clear. I could see all the way down to its sandy bottom. Averill lowered me in. It was probably nice and refreshing. On the other hand the temperature could be forty-eight degrees and I might go into hypothermia without even knowing it.

The water was up to my chin. I was able to get my tongue into it and lap some, like a dog. Cool, but tolerable. The rapid flow was rinsing away layers of jof jof dung. That was good.

"What about it, Hazel?" asked Averill after about fifteen seconds.

"Not yet. Put him all the way under, then spin him around. Stranger, hold your breath."

"Okay," I said. Although I couldn't see the little man, I could almost hear him shrug.

Underwater now, spinning around rapidly. This was surely getting off the rest of the jof jof dung . . .

Something big and dark glided through the water below me.

I couldn't see what it was, it went by so fast. Still spinning, I noticed another. What was Hazel the Healer up to?

My head broke the surface. I had stopped turning and was again faced away from the pair on shore. Sputtering, I managed to say, "Hey, folks. I'm not alone in here!"

"I'm bringing him out," Averill said.

"Not yet," Hazel said.

Ten more seconds. Another dark thing glided by. Looked like a torpedo.

"Really, I'm clean enough," I warbled.

"Hazel—!" the little man cried.

"Okay, now."

Averill must've jerked his butt high. I rose like a missile fired from a sub. My bike shoes were a yard above the water.

The three gaping mouths full of razor-sharp teeth that followed half a second later snapped at nothing, then went under again.

"Holy shit!" I exclaimed.

"Take him to the cottage," Hazel said calmly. "The door to the restoring room is open. Sit him up in the chair. Just be sure *you* don't go inside."

"Why not?" Averill asked indignantly.

"What do you think? Of course, if you'd like to bathe in the stream first . . ."

"I'll stay out!"

"Thought you would."

Averill turned me around slowly. I still couldn't see Hazel. This time, as he led me toward the cottage, I wasn't aware of her behind me.

The little man was grumbling again. "So much work, besides the humiliation. This better be worth it!"

The front door of the gingerbread house was closed, but another on the side was open. Averill stopped in front of it. I kept going. He made a face as I floated past. Although the doorway was big enough, I hit my head on the top. The squashed creep did that on purpose.

It wasn't a bright room, not much chance to look around as I sailed across. Right into a sort of artsy contoured chair facing the opposite wall—a mirror, from top to bottom, side to side. I wasn't thrilled to see myself so helpless, or watch the way I crumpled onto the chair, my legs at an odd angle.

Averill knew what I was thinking. "Sorry, can't help," he called from the doorway. "Hazel won't let me in. I'll be at the cart, getting the . . . bike out and looking it over."

"Give it a good cleaning too, okay, pal?"

Shouting something that the Translator had trouble with, Averill slammed the door. Even darker now, but I could still see most of the small room reflected on the mirror wall. Not much, really, shutters covering two rectangular windows, a shaggy rug over half the wood floor. No furniture, other than my chair.

But lots of shelves on the side walls, narrow ones, lined with little round and oval jars, vials and phials filled with colored liquids, square tins and matchboxes and capped white tubes that looked like PVC pipes.

Hazel the Healer's tools of the trade. Potions? Witches' brews? What was *really* in there? Eye of wartworm? Flared nostril of hoorkla? Concentrate of imbecilicus ninipal kidney?

I didn't want to know.

The shutters opened when Hazel came in. Not that the room became blindingly bright or anything, but I could see better. She was right behind me. I stared at her in the mirror wall.

Hazel the Healer was gorgeous.

Tall, long black hair, a face that belonged on the cover of next month's issue of *any* magazine. She wore this blue filmy thing, not so much a dress but layers of gossamer material wrapped around, thrown over, whatever, most of her dusky body. They clung perfectly, and hid very little.

"You don't look comfortable," she said. "That wartworm Averill took poor care in your landing."

"It's . . . fine. Can't feel a thing, remember?" I was gasping like an idiot in the presence of this woman.

"You will, when the feeling returns."

"Then why don't you straighten me out?"

"Sorry, I can't," she said mysteriously. "Let me find the proper cure."

She walked to one of the shelves. Glided, more accurately. Looking around, she took off a round jar here, rejected a tin there, grabbed a couple of phials. She had everything she wanted now and was mixing them together.

"I know Averill and his people," she said. "You must be paying him a good price to bring you here."

"That's for sure."

"But what about *my* price? We haven't discussed that yet."

"Sure, anything. I don't have much, but—"

"One kiss. I'll settle for that."

"What?"

"You heard me."

I stared at Hazel in the mirror, tried not to smile. "That's *all* you want?" I asked.

"It'll do. Ah, ready. Now keep your eyes closed while I give it to you. It's . . . part of the cure."

I watched her glide toward me, a phial of green liquid held between her long, slim fingers. Then I did as I'd been told. When she tilted my head back, I opened my mouth. Her touch on my chin was like . . . sandpaper. I swear. Almost took a peek.

"Keep them closed," she warned. "And . . . there!"

The stuff tasted like oversweetened Gatorade. It was grainy. I made sure every bit went down. Hazel backed away.

"You can open them now," she said. "It won't take long to work . . . what *is* your name?"

I looked at her in the mirror wall. "Jack Miller. Listen, Hazel, are you sure . . . ?"

Something was happening. A sitting-in-the-jacuzzi kind of warmth began running through my body. Inch by inch, feeling was coming back.

Most of me hurt like hell.

My hand, from Averill dropping it against a boulder. Various bruises from where the bike had fallen. My legs, from being twisted in this chair. And my crotch, from that damn levitation disk!

But I wasn't complaining, mind you. Glad to be alive again, which I was in less than a minute. The first thing I did was remove the disk.

The second thing I did was turn around to face this wonderful mixer of potions.

"Hey, Hazel, thanks a—!"

Remember the Wicked Witch of the West in *The Wizard of Oz*? Remember how ugly?

Multiply that by ten.

Hazel the Healer was a shriveled-up crone. She wore something black and shapeless from her neck to her ankles. Part of her angular face was covered with tufts of fur. Her nose stuck straight out a couple of inches, then jutted sharply down, ending in a point. She might've had two eyes (or more, for that matter), but only one was open. Her hair looked like a used S.O.S pad. Under a shadowy mustache her lips were gray, puffy.

"You're welcome, Jack Miller," she said in the same sultry voice.

I looked at the mirror wall. The goddess in blue gauze, the woman-to-die-for, was still there. I shook my head and turned back to Hazel.

"No," I said.

"No what?" Hazel asked.

"I mean, no, don't bother to explain. Probably wouldn't understand anyway."

She raised a rough-skinned hand and pointed a bent finger. "Try and get up, but do it slowly."

Good advice. My legs felt like string cheese and almost buckled. After that I was okay.

"It won't come back, right?" I asked.

Hazel shook her head. "Not a chance. Now, don't you think it's time you paid up?"

I knew she'd get around to that. "Oh . . . yeah." I glanced at the mirror, shrugged wistfully, and started toward her.

Actually, how bad could it be? When I was a kid there seemed to be an endless procession of aunts and great-aunts at our house. Every one of them had a mustache. You not only had to endure a kiss but a nasty pinch on the cheek. So what? I survived them and usually wound up with a dollar from Auntie Whoever for being such a good little trouper.

That's what I kept telling myself as I approached those sickly-looking gray lips, already puckered (I think) and waiting. I closed my eyes, swallowed hard, and kissed Hazel the Healer.

It was okay, really. There was even this sort of nice flowery scent about her. I almost looked, but didn't.

"We're even, Jack Miller," she said afterward. "You'd best not challenge the Bush of Turttek again. And you don't have to explain what happened. I saw your . . . thing in Averill's cart, and I understand."

She had a real knowing look when she said that. "Speaking of Averill—"

A noise from outside was followed by this frantic blustering. Hazel shrugged. "We'd better see what the wartworm has gotten himself into."

I followed her out of the restoring room. Down the road, Averill lay on his back next to the Nishiki, kicking and flailing. Besides removing my bike from the dung cart, it looked like he actually *had* cleaned it.

"Blasted pile of junk!" the Jonathan Winters gnome bellowed as I helped him to his feet. "I jumped up on the seat and it rolled forward a little, then wouldn't do a thing and fell over!"

"You should've waited for me," I scolded, looking the bike over. "Anyway, you're supposed to use the pedals to make it go. That's these things here."

"Very well, lower the seat so I can reach them."

"But it only goes down a couple of inches. Sorry, Averill, it won't work."

"You *knew* that," he bellowed, "and still told me that I'd be able to ride it?"

"Uh, I forgot . . ."

"You *vambo*! You son of a *sodweel*!"

"Tell me, wartworm," said Hazel, ignoring his histrionics, "what sort of load are you bringing back to Mosconi this time?"

"Oh, a third of a cart, even a little more," he bragged. "Not counting what came off on him and his bike. A good load for the short time I was out."

"Are you sure?" Hazel asked. "It looked like more to me. You should check."

Averill climbed up a wheel and peered into the dung cart. His moon eyes widened.

"Full! It's full!" he exclaimed. "No Second Apprentice Dung-master has *ever* brought back a full load in less than *ten* days! Oh, what a moment it will be!"

Hazel looked at me and blinked (winked?) her eye. "One can never foretell the nature of a gift that will make one happy."

I grinned. "Guess not. Thanks for getting me off the hook."

"Now, wartworm, take your treasure and go," Hazel said. "You've no more business here."

"Right away, right away!" He jumped down from the wheel, shuffled along the road, and slapped his rump. The heavy dung cart lurched forward, then rolled easily behind him on the downhill trail. He was already into a bawdy ballad.

I looked at Hazel. "Guess I'll be going too."

She shook her head. "You're tired, are you not? Hungry, right? Those strange garments of yours are still wet, aren't they?"

"Yes to everything."

"Then you'll stay until morning. Not in the cottage, of course. See that grove across the meadow? An area has been prepared for you there. You can even bathe at your leisure in the pond; nothing alive in it. And the hoorklas won't bother you. Good-bye, Jack Miller."

"Won't I see you again?"

"Perhaps not."

The bent woman turned and started toward the cottage. I watched her for a few seconds. You know, looks notwithstanding, she was okay.

"Thanks for everything, Hazel," I called, but she went inside without glancing back.

Walking the bike, I crossed the meadow to the small ring of trees. A couple of the nearest sheep things looked at me, snorted, and went back to their grazing.

The trees were the same stunted sycamores I had seen around the Bush of Turttek. Within them the grass was only a couple of inches high, and there were hardly any flowers. A straw sleeping mat had been rolled out. Next to it was a tray with bread, fruits, cheese, and a stone pitcher containing something thick and yellow.

Hazel had mentioned a pond. It was a couple of yards away from the sleeping mat. Real small; I could only get into it standing up. Which I did, after I spread my clothes out to dry. It was warm. I stayed in a long time, then let the small sun dry me as I attacked the tray. Everything tasted great, especially the stuff in the pitcher, sort of like egg nog.

Was I relaxed, or what! I laid on my back, looking up past the treetops at this world's odd-colored sky. Even with the small sun going down I still felt warm and comfortable in the grove. Pretty soon it all caught up to me, and I was asleep.

What a great dream I had during the night! The goddess in blue gauze glided through the trees, right over to where I lay. She didn't say anything, just knelt beside me and . . . Well, no need getting *that* descriptive, it was only a dream.

In the morning there was this faint, pleasant scent that I remembered from when I'd kissed Hazel the Healer.

I felt great; rested, not as sore as yesterday. There was still some food, which I finished. My clothes were dry.

Enough of this world. I was ready to move on. Beyond Hazel's cottage the trail rose sharply for a couple of hundred yards before topping a ridge. It was steep enough for my purposes; just hope it wasn't too clogged with debris.

I watched the cottage as I passed, didn't see anything. Now I was on the hill. It was even steeper than I'd guessed. Defining a yard-wide corridor down the middle, I tossed dozens of rocks off to either side and filled in some of the worst holes. Quite a while to reach the top, but worth it.

Using a tree for balance I slipped into the toe clips. Pushing off, I hurtled down. This *was* steep. A quarter of the way and already approaching thirty mph. My thumb reached for the lever.

"Come again, Jack Miller."

That sultry voice. Hazel the Healer stood along the side of the road, on my left. Her blue gossamer dress and long hair fluttered in the gentle morning breeze. I smiled . . .

. . . and shifted into the twenty-second gear.

CHAPTER 7

Cowboys and Indians

The doorway back to Stuart Mesa Road beckoned. The Old Guy probably figured I wasn't going to take it. But do you know what he did? This was cool: Just over the misty door was a sign with thin letters printed in what looked like yellow neon. It said GOOD GOING, JACK! and was signed O.G.

That made me feel good.

Even though I wasn't going back to Camp Pendleton, I still didn't feel quite ready for another excursion. So I rode the Ultimate Bike Path for what I guessed was half an hour (the clock on the bike computer was still frozen at 8:23), enjoying the silence of the spectral straightaway and the kaleidoscopic spectacle of the passing doors. Didn't see any other riders the whole time.

I was ready to choose. Each gate snapped to attention before me as I slowed the Nishiki. The one I finally picked was similar to the doorway home, except that there were six tiny pyramids revolving around two that were larger, and stationary. No other hidden ones. With my eyes open, I penetrated it; felt like Mary Poppins jumping into a chalk picture.

No thornbushes this time, no glossy surface. A country road, not paved, but firm; easy going for a mountain bike. Gently rolling farmland on both sides; everything so green! An agreeable temperature. Probably late spring; the tops of distant mountains— plenty of mountains—still wore cones of white.

I was back on Earth. Where—or when—I had no idea.

Just up the road was a building; or maybe more than one side by side. I was too far away to see. Closer, coming toward me, was a small herd of cows, urged along by a plain-looking girl of about seventeen. She was dressed in a red-and-white dirndl and bonnet; her long hair was braided. I said hello and stepped aside as she passed with the cows, but she was shy and barely nodded at me.

Dirndl. Europe. These mountains were probably the Alps. But that covered a lot of ground.

Just before the cluster of buildings (there *was* more than one), a road sign announced LAMBACH, KM 5, and LINZ, KM 50. Never heard of Lambach . . . No, wait. Mozart subtitled a symphony with that name. Linz too.

Mozart. Austria. I was definitely in Austria.

The widest building was a tavern. It was flanked by a sausage shop and a sugar bakery. I stood at the window of the latter, staring hard at mounds of tortes, almond buns, and croissants.

A man in leather shorts and a forester's hat came out of the sausage shop. He looked at me, then the bike, thought about saying something, decided against it. With a nod he started up the road toward Lambach and Linz.

I went into the tavern. No one was there. According to a clock on the wall it was not yet ten. Too early for the crowds. Magazines and newspapers were scattered on tables and bench seats. I looked at one of the papers. It was fresh.

The date below the masthead was Saturday, May 23, 1896.

"Acch, but I didn't hear anyone come in! What can I get for you?"

The innkeeper was fat and jolly, with a white walrus mustache. He rubbed his hands together while waiting for my answer. I thought about ordering a beer, then wondered what he would say when I paid for it with a 1988 series one-dollar bill.

"Nothing, thanks. Or maybe a glass of water, if you don't mind."

"Of course, of course." He brought me a glass, looked me over as I drank it. "You're just passing through Hafeld?" he said.

Hafeld. "Yes, on my way to . . . Vienna."

"Acch, but where else?" he chuckled. "You're sure I can't get you anything?"

I handed him the glass. "Positive. Thank you very much."

He followed me outside. The bike caught his attention. He scratched his head.

"I'm an inventor," I told him. "Trying out something new. Not bad, but it'll never replace the horse."

Austria. 1896. Nothing significant that I could think of. Nice friendly tradition-steeped country. The junior Strauss was still waltz king, except that he would die in a few years.

Okay, so it was a nice diversion. The alpine landscape could take your breath away. I could almost see the edelweiss blooming on the higher meadows. So enjoy it, Miller, because your next port of call might be the battlefield at Gettysburg on the wrong morning.

People were working on the farms. Children either helped the adults or played by themselves, sometimes climbing over the fence to continue their games on the road. Two elderly people went past; I overtook another milkmaid with a larger herd.

One farm was rather attractive and idyllic. I stopped along the side of the road for a better look. The fields were softly rolling hillocks. There was an active little brook that flowed past an orchard. The small farmhouse, with its snow-shedding roof, was a picturesque building nearly hidden by the trees.

Three boys of about seven or eight were playing in the nearest field. One, in pursuit of the others, wore something on his head. As they came closer I saw that it was a band of feathers. The kid had on a makeshift Indian headdress.

"Otto, Edmund, where are you going?" he called. "We've hardly begun to play yet."

"We don't want to play with you anymore, Dolfie," Edmund said. "When you're the Indians you always win, and when you're the cowboys you win also!"

"I can change—" Dolfie began.

"And you play too rough besides," Otto added. "I hurt my elbow."

"Acch, what babies!" Dolfie exclaimed, waving a carved toy pistol. "I'll play by myself then."

He ran around, not hyperactive but enthusiastic, gunning down imaginary enemies. Otto and Edmund climbed the fence near where I stood. Instead of running off they became interested in the Nishiki.

"Good morning, sir," they said, bowing slightly. Polite little guys.

"Hi, fellas. Problems this morning?" I gestured across the field.

"Our mothers say we have to play with Dolfie," Otto said, "because we're neighbors and it's the right thing to do. But we don't like him!"

"Always the cowboys and Indians, cowboys and Indians!" Edmund added. "Only once in a while is it soldiers!"

"He's as grumpy as his father," Otto said, "who is stung all the time from the bees that he keeps."

"Actually"—Edmund laughed—"Momma told me Herr Hitler is so old that he might as well be Dolfie's *grand*father."

Both boys were chuckling. I looked at them. "Who was that you said?"

"Herr Hitler? He owns this farm."

"Let's go, Otto, before Dolfie comes back."

The boys scampered away. I stared at the lone figure in the field.

Dolfie.

Beekeeping.

Austria. 1896.

The kid playing cowboys and Indians was Adolf Hitler.

Hey, Study Group, really testing me, huh?

Just a kid, like kids all over the world; running, playing, not concerned about many things, having a good time . . .

A kid who would be responsible for the deaths of millions of human beings.

Look at this neat farm. Nine acres. Incredible countryside. The kid's having a ball. But the family would move from here soon, wouldn't it? Move and move and move. Different towns, different schools, less freedom for a boy whose early ambitions were to be an artist and work in the church.

Why'd you keep moving, Alois and Klara? Didn't you know? Couldn't you tell that your son would grow up to be the most awful person who ever lived? Alois, couldn't you have given as much time to the kid as you did to your bees or your buddies at the tavern?

Dolfie was a hundred feet away, firing in all directions at the pony soldiers who were attacking his village. Sometimes I got in the line of fire.

American Indians. Let me tell you what happened to the American Indians, you little bastard . . .

What's going on inside your head? Some Wagnerian opus resounding through it? Does Siegfried and Wotan and Alberich mean anything to you yet?

Farm. Animals. Goose-step.

The kid was closer to the road. He fell to his stomach in the soft grass, rolled over once, dodging imaginary bullets. His gun empty, he unslung an air bow and fired arrows at an alarming rate.

Not fast enough though, is it? Line them up and shoot them by the hundreds. Hang them by the thousands. Gas them by the millions and burn the bodies so they don't pile up. Make sure you get all the gold fillings first.

Fifty feet away, back on his feet, having as much fun alone as with Otto and Edmund. Not even curious about the mountain bike.

I'm a writer too, kid. Never did anything like *Mein Kampf*. I have to say, at least you tried to *warn* them. You tried to give them a look inside your sick mind, tried to tell them what you'd do to the world if you were king.

If.

Twelve years of your Third Reich, twelve years of crushing all the little guys and standing up to the big guys. Scared the hell out of them, too. Gave the world a few bad dreams. But it could've been worse, could've been a Thousand Years, like you'd predicted.

Dolfie was twenty-five feet away. I clenched the handlebars tightly; would've liked it to be his throat. That's it, I could kill him. Hop the fence, strangle the shit out of him, whap his head against a tree for good measure. But you'd bring him back to life, wouldn't you, Old Guy? Because that's the way it has to be.

Because that's the way it *was*.

Wouldn't he stay dead in *some* time plane? This was crazy. If I did it, I'd never be able to travel the Ultimate Bike Path again. It would be worth it, though. Personal gratification. But for how long? Enjoy it for a moment, then wind up like hamburger meat in a Cuisinart. That's what would happen, right?

Why did you have to bring me *here*? It's not fair.

Dolfie was fifteen feet away, still fending off bad guys. I pointed a finger at him. "Hey, kid."

He looked up. "Yes, sir?" As polite as Otto and Edmund.

"Bang, you're dead."

He took the cue. Good little actor. Falling to the grass, he clutched at his chest and made all kinds of moaning sounds as he rolled around.

I biked away from the farm in Hafeld, leaving Adolf Hitler in his death throes.

CHAPTER 8

Gimme a Break

"But, Jack, you can't blame us for *that*!"

"Oh, yeah, wanna bet?"

I was leaning on the railing of the bridge over the Santa Margarita River, looking down at the murky water. A male egret was preening in the reeds, trying to hit on a female; the long-necked lady could care less.

"Jack, you're being irrational." The Old Guy tried a shrug; the upper half of his body rippled like a spastic belly dancer. "The number of gates along the *mhuva lun gallee* is infinite. Your selection—*yours*, Jack—is totally random." He pondered a moment. "Luck of the draw, I think you call it. You might have appeared along a road where an eight-year-old Mahatma Gandhi or Martin Luther King was at play."

I turned and glared at him. "Do you *know* who that little creep was?"

He nodded. "We absorbed all of your world's history. Yes, that was quite a bad one. But all the more reason to be proud of yourself for the restraint you showed. The others in the study group complimented me, but I told them the credit is all yours. They wanted you to know that."

This time *I* shrugged, making sure he saw how it was done. "Yeah, well . . ." I looked back at the river, where the male egret seemed to be making progress.

"Jack, will you be returning to the *mhuva lun gallee* now?"

I glanced at my watch: 8:28 and some seconds, and moving right along. You have no idea how *normal* it felt to see time passing.

"Not just yet," I told him. "I need a break."

"A . . . break?" His finger started for his ear. I held up a hand.

"Yeah, a break, a time-out, interlude, *caesura*, recess, breather, *entr' acte*. You got it?"

He lowered the finger. "Oh, I understand. When do you think you'll be ready?"

"Saturday morning; early, like seven. Too many riders later on. Will you be here?"

"Do you need me to?"

"I guess not."

"Then you're on your own. We'll be observing, of course. Good-bye, Jack. Have a nice . . . break."

He climbed onto the Schwinn and wobbled off toward the traffic light at Vandegrift Boulevard. I watched him for a while, wondering where it was he went. Did he get sucked up (or down), or did he just wink out, or did he fade away as a pillar of glittery stuff, like in the *Enterprise*'s transporter? But none of the above happened before he turned the corner.

I could have followed him; after all, it *was* the way home. But I was no more ready for that than I was to be back on the Ultimate Bike Path. Just last weekend I'd finished my newest literary masterpiece, *Mutant Bats of Krimmia,* and had sent it off to Izzy McCarthy, my agent in New York, on Monday morning. Between books, I always bulked up on my riding. And there was something about a *normal* bike ride, along *normal* paths, with time passing *normally,* that appealed to me at the moment. For the third time that morning I started up the Stuart Mesa hill.

In the ten (real) minutes that passed since I last saw them, Muriel and her bunch had progressed another mile along the top of the mesa. I gave them a wide berth, waving as I passed. Behind me, a chain reaction of bumping bicycles nearly deposited the senior citizens into the turkey mullen and scrub. Subsequent expletives from Walt would have embarrassed any marine on the base.

Having ridden this route so often I almost always ran into someone I knew, and usually joined, for some portion of it. (There was this one in particular named Gina, from San Juan Capistrano . . . but that's another story.) But it was dead on the base, and later through San Onofre State Park, and I was glad, because I needed time alone to vacuum out my brain.

A nine-foot slug named Yoniaristakkaloo.

Averill, a Second Apprentice Dungmaster.

Adolf Hitler.

Yeah, I definitely needed this ride.

But my body had other ideas and started bitching shortly after

I left the north end of the state park. Some sort of cosmic jet lag, I suppose. In any case, my goal of Dana Point Harbor, another dozen miles up the coast, was not going to happen. I turned around in front of the twin round concrete mounds of the San Onofre nuclear power station (known to many as Dolly Parton Park) and started back.

Oh, did my body complain loudly! And if I wasn't out of it before, get this: I'm racing down the hill off Stuart Mesa, not even *thinking* about the Vurdabrok Gear, only about my car on San Rafael Drive less than three miles away. So I start working like crazy to get there.

Halfway, I remember that I'd ridden up from Del Mar. I still had over twenty miles to go.

Thank you, Mr. Jacuzzi, Mr. Whirlpool, whoever. There was a pool and spa for all the townhouse-style condos in the neighborhood. I rode directly to the frothing caldron. Leaving on everything but my shoes, I lowered myself into the hot water, which merited some weird looks from a couple of swimmers. At that point, being a spectacle was the least of my concerns.

Twenty minutes later, when the screams of my muscles had subsided into low moans of agony, I went home. The light on my answering machine was flashing, but no way was I going to worry about it until I'd stood under the shower for as long as the water stayed hot.

While doing this, I thought about the possibility of having brought back some deadly alien bacteria from either of my first two stops. Maybe I'd begun the spread of some virulent superflu, like in Stephen King's *The Stand*. (*Most of North America dead, film at eleven . . . we hope*.) But if I *had* caught something, wouldn't I have infected Austria in 1896? And if that had happened, wouldn't the kid called Dolfie . . .

Enough. I could get myself crazy without that. Finished and semi-dry, I rewound my tape. The first message was from Izzy McCarthy, my agent, who was chock-full of good news. Yeah, he'd received *Mutuant Bats of Krimmia* that morning, had a chance to read a few pages, thought it was the "same old crap" (his words), and therefore should be salable. Even better, my current publisher was going to do a third printing of my "big one," *Tree Men of Quazzak*. And even better than that, after four months of sitting on it, they were finally going to make an offer on my next-to-last project, *Wasp Women of Naheedi*. Izzy sounded ecstatic.

Now, lest those of you who are not writers think this is pretty nifty, let me assure you otherwise. The first two printings of *Tree Men of Quazzak* had sold less than thirty thousand paperback copies. Financially, you could do better on welfare. And my publisher, although I know you've heard of them, is not exactly a Bantam, Berkley, or Pocket Books. They are prone to a few errors in judgment (not in my case, I hope). Like a few years ago, when the romance novel craze was at its peak, and dozens of them came out every month, and it was hard to be original? My publisher created a new line called *Nunswept*, in which the lead lovers were Catholic clergy, either already fallen or on their way down. It was discontinued after three months, for a number of reasons.

So for the longest time now I've asked Izzy when he would find a bigger and better house for fantasy, like Del Rey or Ace or DAW. In time, he always tells me, in time. Until then, be happy with what you have, it's more than most.

Actually, I *am* happy. I make up stories in my head, which only a few people can do, and I put them on paper, which most can't. They get read, and once in a while I receive a letter—or get told face-to-face—how much this story or that one was enjoyed. And for every one of those there might be a hundred, or a thousand, who enjoyed them just as much, found some diversion for a day or two from *my* words, and that's kind of awesome, when you think about it.

So when friends, or my mother, wonder about how I exist, what I do, and tell me to get a life, get a job, get real, whatever, I ignore them. Because I *have* a life, and it's rewarding, more so than when I was a purchasing agent and worried about whether the secretaries and their bosses liked the new coffee service, or whether everyone thought the toilet paper was soft enough.

My mother. The second message was from her, and that *was* cause for concern. Mrs. Rose Miller Leventhal of Pompano Beach, Florida, *never* called long distance on a weekday unless it was before eight in the morning or after five at night. Even though she left a stock message (*Jackie, it's your mother. I'm fine, could be better, but I'm fine. Did you find work yet? Try the civil service, they always need good people. What about grandchildren, Jackie? I'm sixty-seven, not getting any younger. You don't have to call me back, I'll hear from you in two weeks around.*), I decided to find out what was going on.

But not until after the rates changed, no way. *Jackie, you own stock in Ma Bell or something?* she would say. *Ma, there is no more Ma Bell*, I would answer. *So you want to support NBC or Sprite?* she would counter. *Ma, that's MCI and Sprint*.

I was born in White Plains, New York, the only child of Rose and Henry Miller. No, not *that* Henry Miller, who wrote more books in his life than my father ever read in his. Dad was an unimaginative bean counter for a firm in Manhattan's garment district, faithfully commuting into the city for three decades. He died of a massive heart attack when he was fifty-six, and I was eighteen, three months after learning that his two-pack-a-day habit of over forty years had rotted his lungs and left him with incurable cancer. I have to say, for such an uncreative life, he went out in storybook fashion. He died in Yankee Stadium during the fifth inning of a game in which his beloved Yankees were whipping the pants off the hated Red Sox. Pictures of my uncle Jerry doing CPR in the aisle behind third base made the eleven o'clock news, not to mention the early editions of the *Post* and *Daily News*.

Fifteen months later, Rose Miller—mah-jongg queen of White Plains—married a recent widower from the Bronx named Tobias Leventhal (everyone called him "Tobe," which made me think of the guy who directed *The Texas Chainsaw Massacre*), ten years her senior. *Jackie, it's terrible to be alone*, she said, *and worse, old and alone*. She was fifty-three, then. Two years after that, when Chainsaw retired, they moved to Florida. By that time, I was long gone to California.

The third and last message on my machine was from Phil Melkowitz, my best buddy, erstwhile roommate, and fellow wage slave at the same company, where he was still gainfully but miserably employed. We were supposed to ride together Saturday, and he was checking to see if we were still on. Saturday; I'd forgotten that. On the other hand, I could hit the Ultimate Bike Path at seven, go off on a month's worth of adventures, get a good night's sleep somewhere, and still be back at 7:01 to . . .

Both of us dated Carol Delaney in college. Either of us could have married her. I won; I think. We could have been the perfect yuppie couple, except she grew up after we graduated, and I never did. Peter Pan, she used to call me (God, I hated that!). The divorce was mutually desired, and amicable—sort of. No alimony or anything; hell, she made more than I did back then as a contracts administrator, and was undoubtedly doing even better now. She'd moved back to Denver, her hometown, nearly five years ago, which was the last time we'd communicated. I would guess that by now she was remarried with 1.7 children.

Anyway, you probably noticed I've been keeping my brain well occupied for the past few hours. Now, it was time to deal with the reality (or un-) of what had happened on that hillside in Camp Pendleton. Part of me still wanted to believe it was all some kind of weird dream, but I couldn't, not with this crazy damn coin hanging around my neck. So I decided to deal with it in the best way I knew how, by writing down everything I remembered about the three jaunts, as well as the Path itself. Yeah, it could actually turn out to be a hell of a narrative. Hey, I might have the means of breaking away from the publishers of *Nunswept* yet!

Six minutes after sitting down on the comfortable chaise lounge out on my patio, I fell asleep.

The jangling phone roused me from my coma at five-thirty. Phil Melkowitz, who lived about a mile away, had just gotten home from work and was checking in to confirm Saturday. Now I knew Phil as well as anyone in the world, and there is no way he'll get up early on a non-work day, especially having a hot date with his friend Jennifer King the night before. To him, even nine is "rooster time." I could see the whole universe and still get back to Del Mar by then, well rested. We confirmed the ride.

Eventually I got around to calling my mother, though not before I had downed a can of Coors Light. Chainsaw Leventhal, one of the most uncommunicative people I've ever met (Ma loved that), answered the phone. No, she wasn't home, out playing mah-jongg. No, she didn't call for anything important, said she thought of you when the arthritis in her elbow began kicking up. She'll call you in two weeks around, so don't waste any money on Ma Bell.

Chainsaw related all this in about seven words and a handful of musical wheezes.

I always wondered what my mother had against the phone company. Their employees had families too, didn't they?

Another call brought dinner to my door twenty-three minutes later in a flat box that looked like a big domino. Afterward, I finally started writing about my first encounter with the Old Guy, in the weird white room at Fourth and Broadway. Not exactly being in high gear, the words came slowly, which wasn't my usual style. But you know, as I recounted that meeting, and thought about what followed, I got excited. I don't mean jump-up-and-down-we-just-won-the-Super-Bowl excited, or the-Berlin-Wall-is-down-and-world-peace-is-imminent excited, but I actually started thinking about being back on the Ultimate Bike Path. Hell, that didn't take long!

But I was still tired, and no way was I going to make the eleven o'clock news. So I caught the start of a ten o'clock newscast on an L.A. station (people in L.A. have to watch the news earlier so they can get to sleep and be ready for their two-hour commute the next morning), made sure I hadn't infected the planet, and turned in.

This time, I slept long past 5:56 A.M.

My condo is a great place if you're a writer and you need quiet to work. The common walls on both sides are well insulated; even if the neighbors engaged in stentorian bouts of domestic violence, or turned Megadeth up a few decibels on the CD player, most of the noise would be filtered out.

The neighbors I had did neither. Mrs. Leana DeMutt, a widow in her seventies, spent as much time away traveling as she did at home. I usually kept an eye on her place, and she brought me back souvenirs from wherever she'd been. When she was around, Mrs. DeMutt entertained different men nearly every other night. She was an attractive woman for her age. These guys always walked a lot slower on their way out than when they got there.

My other immediate neighbor, Maury Khazuti, was co-owner of a Middle Eastern restaurant in La Jolla, which kept him away most of the time. When he was around, Maury mostly listened to pan flute music and played Nintendo. I got to know him over the patio fence, thought he was an okay guy. But most people didn't take to Maury, probably because of this hangdog scowl that was frozen on his face. Some folks in the neighborhood called him Rootie, which I thought sounded tacky.

I spent most of the day writing down what had happened to me, and got more excited about doing it again. It was past three, and I was putting it on my hard disk, when Paula Kaufman called.

She canceled our date for that night.

She canceled anything that might have happened for the rest of our lives.

Seems her old boyfriend, a guy she'd lived with for two years, had come back to town, and they'd had lunch, and he still loved her, and when she saw him it was like bells and whistles and Tchaikovsky playing as they ran barefoot toward each other in slow motion across a rippling meadow, and he was flying her to San Francisco for the weekend, and I'm sorry, Jack.

Makes a great story, doesn't it?

Bells and whistles and Tchaikovsky . . .

I might've heard bells and whistles and Tchaikovsky with Carol, at the beginning.

Maybe it was just bells . . .

I wonder what it feels like.

Why not head up to Camp Pendleton and get back on the Ultimate Bike Path *now*? What was there to stop me?

But I had told the Old Guy tomorrow morning, so he wouldn't be expecting me to leave now, and his study group wouldn't be watching. And if I was in mortal danger on some god-awful world, they wouldn't be around to pull me out.

So what?

Bells and whistles and Tchaikovsky . . .

I decided to wait until the morning. Phil Melkowitz could use my theater tickets tonight. He and Jennifer had only planned on going dancing after dinner, and these were tickets for one of the most popular shows in the city, and they'd cost me a few bucks. He'll impress the hell out of her.

I spent Friday night playing Super Mario Brothers with Rootie Khazuti.

CHAPTER 9

A Practical Cat

As advertised, the Old Guy was nowhere to be seen on Stuart Mesa that morning.

I had driven up; why not? Left my car on San Rafael Drive. Whatever happened to me this time, I wanted a quick way home when it was over.

Even at seven there was a surprising amount of bike traffic. (It was 7:08, actually; sorry, best I could do.) I pretended to fuss with a tire near the eucalyptus tree while a lone rider and a couple of small parties headed north. My first run down the hill was aborted when a group of thirty or more, most in the same orange-and-white jerseys, came at me in the opposite direction.

You know these guys: You're riding along, doing a steady cadence, when they suddenly hum past you like you're standing still, eyes transfixed on the road ahead. If they're coming the other way, forget about them calling a greeting, waving, or even nodding. I often pondered over the motivation for their intensity and finally decided that, see, this incubus-demon rises from hell and warns each of them, *You'll ride from Oceanside to Mission Viejo and back again, and you'll do it as fast as you can, and you'll never lag behind the group, otherwise I'll rip out your mother's heart and rape your kid sister*. That *has* to be it.

I almost didn't make it the second time down, but for a different reason. A nasty headwind suddenly gusted up, and I mean it was *strong*. I pedaled like crazy, my thumb futilely exerting pressure against the lever. As the bottom of the hill came nearer I decided that this, too, was a washout. But it slipped into the Vurdabrok Gear, and suddenly I was . . .

. . . bursting through the misty blue door onto the Ultimate Bike Path.

Nothing about the *mhuva lun gallee* made me uneasy this time; I was glad to be there. My plan was to ride along the rust-red tunnel for a while (or at least what I estimated to be a reasonable period of time, there being no way to measure it), then choose a gate, or maybe let it choose me.

Skipping the first bunch of gates wasn't hard, because with a few exceptions they were all Elmer Fudds. Eventually they became random, except for a brief stretch of the iridescent snowmen with the needles. None of the gates as yet seemed to beckon, which was okay, because I was enjoying the effortless ride.

Ahead, I saw another rider.

The fact that I was rapidly narrowing the distance meant that I was going a lot faster than the other person . . . being, whatever. I slowed down, and it took a few moments to lick the fear that I was going to topple over sideways. Once that passed, I pulled up alongside my fellow traveler.

She (definitely a she) was, for the most part, humanoid; my first impression was that she had escaped from a road company production of *Cats*. With whiskers, a dark button nose, and triangular ears, she could have passed for Jennyanydots, Rumpleteazer, any of them. But the rest of her—*nearly* all the rest of her—was decidedly feminine: full red lips, incredibly captivating indigo eyes, long, luxurious black hair. A gray, one-piece garment hugged her lithe body and endless legs. Her breasts were either very small or well contained. I said *nearly*, because of her feet, which were disproportionately wide. On them were black, medium-high heels, oval in shape, practically round; you know, like Daisy Duck's feet.

So what was she riding? It looked like one of those scooters that kids used to make decades ago out of a wooden crate, a two-by-four, and some old street skates, except the "box" part was silver, metallic. The cat-girl sat on top of it, her legs dangling on both sides, not a comfortable-looking position. Every few seconds the Daisy Duck shoes clicked against the box, like an equestrian trying to urge a tired horse along. I had no idea how this made the thing go, but obviously it did.

I was afraid of startling her, but she took my sudden appearance in stride. "Hello," I said, "going my way?" (Now how's that for being original? What a schmuck!)

She glanced at me with those wonderful eyes; her lids fell. Slowly, almost reverently, she tilted her upper body forward in what I had to assume was the standard greeting of her people. She remained that way, L-shaped, for a few seconds. The Daisy Duck shoes never missed a beat on the box.

Snapping up suddenly, she turned those eyes on me again. "The question is without significance," she said in a deep, purring voice.

"Huh? What question?" I asked.

"You wanted to know if I was going your way. Since we are traveling next to one another, that answer is obvious."

Her voice, emanating from *those lips,* was turning me on. "Yeah, well, it . . . I was only trying to start a conversation."

She twitched her nose; the whiskers moved up and down. "By speaking to me, you *did* start a conversation. It was not a matter of *trying.* You either start a conversation or you don't. To say you're *trying* to do it is also without significance."

I wasn't exactly sure what she was saying, even though I liked the way she said it. "So, you think I'm illogical or something." I grinned as I gestured at her pointy cat ears. "Maybe you're a Vulcan or something."

She didn't do a Mr. Spock-cock of the brow, but she did open her eyes wider. "A Vulcan? No, but you're close. I'm a Vulvan."

"A . . . Vulvan?"

"That is correct. I won't presume you've heard of my world, since I realize that many travel this path. More than likely I've no prior knowledge of yours."

"I'm from Earth," I told her.

She blinked and nodded. "Yes, I was right; never heard of it."

Trying to ignore the indifference in her words, I held out my right hand. "My name is Jack; Jack Miller."

She looked at the hand. "What is this for?"

"It's our customary greeting." I shook my right hand with my left. "See?"

"Oh." She raised her right and and shook it with *her* left. "For economy's sake you may call me Hormona."

She was Hormona of Vulvan. That made sense, I guess. I put my hand down.

"Yeah, well, nice to meet you . . . Hormona."

Her indigo eyes absorbed the Nishiki. I was almost envious. "What do you call your go-thing, Jack-Jack Miller?"

I smiled. "For economy's sake you can call me Jack. And the go-thing is a bicycle."

She nodded. "Interesting."

"So, Hormona, how long have you been riding the Path?"

"Since time is frozen here, that question is—"

"—without significance, right. Okay. Have you been through some of the gates?"

Her sleek black hair bounced when she shook her head. "I'm not interested in exploration, only recreation and solitude, both of which this provides. Ours is a crowded world, and one is seldom alone." She gestured toward the right wall, where the iridescent snowmen were appearing again with more frequency. "The gate to my place and time on Vulvan is almost here, and I must return."

If those eyes or those lips or that body weren't enough to drive me crazy, I became aware of this seductive flowery scent emanating from her. Faint at first, but growing. I tried to shake it off.

"Uh, do you have family on Vulvan?" I asked.

That puzzled her. "Family?"

"You know, parents, brothers, sisters, husband, children . . ."

Now she got it. "We are all . . . family on Vulvan. It is unimportant who our progenitors and siblings are, and we take no permanent mates. As for small ones, I have personally yielded more than fifty, for that is my task."

"Your . . . task?"

"Yes, I am a Reproductor."

Hormona of Vulvan was a Reproductor. I guess that made sense too.

The flowery scent was definitely stronger.

Her body suddenly stiffened. The red lips parted, and a pink tongue moistened them. Those unbelievable indigo eyes-to-die-for grew dreamy, and something like a smile cracked through her staid demeanor.

Hormona was turning herself on without any outside aid.

The flowery scent was overpowering, like an invisible aphrodisiac. I suddenly realized how uncomfortable spandex bike pants could be. I squirted water from my bike bottle down a very dry throat, then into my face.

Hormona's body shuddered; she made soft mewling sounds. Even with this going on, the Daisy Duck shoes didn't miss a beat.

The killer aroma wafted past, and was gone. Her body eased, and her face reassumed its sober facade. She had satisfied herself.

Glad *she* had. Sorry to be crude, but I would have loved to jump her feline bones right then and there. Can't stop along the *mhuva lun gallee*, right?

She turned those eyes on me again. "The metabolisms of Reproductors are such that we find the need to be invigorated quite routinely, even when we're not performing our assigned tasks."

Invigorated. God, I would have loved to *invigorate* . . .

"My people have no difficulty in accepting off-worlders," Hormona went on. "Would you like to come to Vulvan with me?"

Oh thank you thank you greater powers on high for reading the thoughts of poor frustrated souls like me!

"Yeah, sure, okay," I managed to croak out.

A world full of sexy feline females who were assigned the tasks of Reproductors and who craved invigoration with clockwork regularity and who probably had lips and eyes and bodies and aphrodisiac smells like the one riding next to me . . .

Hormona was no longer riding next to me.

She'd fallen back, and was now angling toward one of the iridescent snowmen on the left. "Sorry," she called, "but while being invigorated I lost track of the gates. It came more suddenly than I'd anticipated."

I had slowed nearly to a stop, but there was no way I could cut back to the gate. "What should I do?" I exclaimed.

The Daisy Duck shoes were rapping faster against the silver scooter. She was near the portal. "Don't worry, you'll come across it again," she said.

It suddenly occurred to me that the iridescent snowmen with the needles sticking out of them looked *exactly* the same. "How will I know which one?" I shouted.

Almost gone now. She pointed at the laserlike needles. "The one to my place and time on Vulvan has seventy-three thousand four hundred and ninety-two of those. Good-bye, Ja—"

Seventy-three thousand four hundred and ninety-two needles. All I had to do to reach a world of invigorative Reproductors was find an iridescent snowman with seventy-three thousand four hundred and ninety-two needles sticking out of it.

Last night, Paula Kaufman.

Today, Hormona of Vulvan.

I was having a lousy weekend.

CHAPTER 10

The Gods Are *Definitely* Crazy

Do you *really* think I was going to try to look for a gate with seventy-three thousand four hundred and ninety-two needles? Even if I *could* take my time in front of each one, which I couldn't, the enormity of the task would have made cleaning the Augean stables seem like picking up after a miniature poodle. Maybe, had I thought of it, I could've asked Hormona to tie a yellow ribbon or something around the snowman's arm . . . Yeah, right.

Okay, Miller, you were victimized by some cosmic glitch, and there's nothing you can do about it, and the whole thing's over, so leave it alone and go on your merry way.

Damn!

I stayed on the Ultimate Bike Path for a while. My first goal was to get away from these snowmen, because they were really depressing me. I pedaled faster, until they became a blur, and before long the rust-red walls were dominated by two gates. The first was the familiar isosceles triangle with the exploding fireworks; the other was one I'd not yet seen. Looking at it should have struck an amusing chord, because it was all ripply and resembled Bart Simpson's head. But there was something ominous about these gates, a throbbing force from each that seemed to say, *Hey, buddy, we really don't want to stop you from coming in here, but you oughtta know that if you choose one of us, you're gonna wind up in some really deep shit.*

Yeah, thanks for the warning; I'll pass right now.

Okay, intrepid explorer, enough screwing around. Pick a gate and get on with the exploits that will assure you a place in history.

I pedaled toward a kinder, gentler isosceles triangle; even managed to keep my eyes open as the fireworks burst around me . . .

. . . I shifted down from the twenty-second gear and squeezed the brakes.

This skinny guy—a teenage kid, eighteen or so—stared at me, wide-eyed, dropped to one knee, and tilted his head forward.

Behind him, stunted greenish-brown hills rose uninspiringly before a range of granite mountains, the tallest snowcapped peaks of which disappeared into amoeba-shaped gray clouds. Weird-looking things. Most everywhere else, a cerulean blue sky was visible. Standing here, in these foothills, I had a pretty good view of this broad, fertile-looking valley, webbed by tributaries. The valley stretched to an even more impressive mountain range in the distance. A single apricot-hued sun, not hard to look at, floated straight overhead, which should have made it high noon here. It was cool, too cool to be shirtless, like the kid was. All he wore was a brief, wraparound *skirt* (or something) and a pair of sandals that had been woven from reeds.

The kid was still kneeling, his eyes down. He was trembling, too, and I don't think it was from the cold.

"Hey, what's happening?" I said. "Talk to me."

He glanced up. "Is it permitted?"

"Sure, and so's standing. Why not?"

He got up slowly. "Usually it is only the Farseeing Ones who talk to gods."

Farseeing Ones. The UT5 must've had a ball with that. I . . .

Gods. The kid thought I was a god.

"Why are you so sure I'm what you think I am?" I asked.

"You appear from nowhere, sitting atop that . . . thing. Your garments are different. What else can you be?"

My first instinct was to pooh-pooh the whole thing. Then, I thought, Hey, a *god* to a whole tribe of unenlightened people! *O Great Jack-O, we are your servants. Here, see the throne we have built for you. What is your pleasure, O Great Jack-O? Food? Wine? Which of our wives or daughters would please you, Great One?*

Then, there was the other side of godhood, the old turn-the-water-into-wine and cure-my-leprosy stuff: *Our crops are thirsty, O Great Jack-O, please make it rain,* or *A fifty-foot tall Whatever has emerged from its cave and is approaching the village, intent on crushing the heads of all the males and dragging off the women, as is its way. Take care of it, will you, O Great One?*

Right.

Okay then, a compromise of sorts. I looked at the kid and smiled.

"Well, you figured me out, didn't you . . . ? What *is* your name anyway?"

"Kimbal," he said, accenting the second syllable. "I am Kimbal, son of Kraztik and Wistilla."

"Yeah, I knew that, just checking to see if you're a truthful fellow. Okay, I *am* a god, but I've chosen to let no one but you know of my coming, not even the Farseeing Ones, because . . ."

He dropped to his knee again. "I was right!" he exclaimed. "Oh, I was!"

I motioned him back up. "This will have to stop, Kimbal. That's what I wanted to tell you. I will enter your village not as a god, but as a weary traveler from a far land. You will introduce me as Jack, from Del Mar. Then I will see the way your people treat strangers. If I am pleased, I will reveal myself and go on my way. But if I am displeased . . ." I put on my best Richard Nixon scowl and wagged my head. Scared the hell out of the kid.

"Our village of Kamamakama is said to be the most hospitable in all of Murlug," Kimbal said, "and you know, O Great—I mean—Jack, how inhospitable a world Murlug is."

Murlug. "Oh, yeah, that's for sure. Well, on to Kamamakama."

"Uh, Jack, should you not shed your god's clothing first, and leave the . . . thing behind?"

"I'm testing you, Kimbal, and so far you're doing nicely. Of course I can't go like this. Is there somewhere safe I can conceal my . . . thing?"

"Yes, a cave, over there. I'll cover it with brush."

"But unfortunately I have no other clothes."

"That is not a problem." Kimbal unraveled his skirt. An identical one was underneath. "I wore two, for it was cool today."

I looked at his bare chest and arms, covered with goose pimples. "Right. Where'd you say that cave was?"

Wearing only the Bukko, the skirt, and my bike shoes, freezing my ass off, I followed Kimbal, son of Kraztik and Wistilla, toward the most hospitable village on Murlug.

It wasn't any great distance to Kamamakama, probably less than a mile, and most of it downhill. But the way there (I wouldn't dignify it by calling it a path) was strewn with rocks, rent by animal burrows, and choked with these fleshy, purplish-green vines, which at first scared the hell out of me, because I thought they were snakes. I stepped along gingerly, and was doing okay; not Kimbal, though, who must have come this way a few times before, but kept stumbling, or getting tangled in the creepers. Nice kid, but what a klutz.

One good thing about descending was that it kept getting warmer, and on the valley floor it was comfortable, maybe just a bit humid. I started having second thoughts about cruising into the village in my Avocet bike shoes, and with the terrain less rugged than before, I took them off. Might as well play this to the hilt. Kimbal stashed them in a sack he was carrying and promised to find me a pair of sandals later.

"Uh, Jack," he said, "before we reach Kamamakama, might I ask you something?"

"Sure; what?"

"This . . . Del Mar I'm to tell people you're from is a place unknown to me. Does it indeed exist?"

"Oh, indeed," I replied, nodding. "It's far to the west, at the edge of the ocean."

"Yes, the Great Ocean!" he exclaimed. "We know of it. But it has always been said the Great Ocean lies to the south."

"Well, Kimbal, now you're the first to learn about the *other* Great Ocean."

"Ah, how little we Kamamakamans, or any who dwell in the Selwok Valley, must know." His eyes shone with interest. "The lands to the west are said to be wild. Is this true of Del Mar?"

"Oh, yes, definitely a savage, untamed place. But those who live there are still my children, and so I look after and cherish them, as I do all on Murlug." I was really getting into this.

Now Kimbal appeared to be puzzled. "But, Jack—you'll excuse me, it's not right to question so much—surely your benevolence does not extend to Atoris the Evil, or any of those who dwell in the terrible land of Areelkrokka!"

I had no idea what in hell he was talking about. "Uh, uh, no way," I said. "That bastard? A thorn in my backside, that's what he is! The gods spit on him!"

Kimbal smiled. "You were testing me again, right?"

I nodded. "Smart fellow. You haven't let me down yet."

"Do the people of Del Mar dress as I first saw you?"

"For sure, many of them dress like that."

"But none ride the . . . thing I saw you upon."

"Oh, no, riding the thing is reserved solely for the gods."

"I thought so. May I ask you something else, or do I bore you with so many questions?"

No, I wasn't going to touch that with a ten-foot Pole, or even two five-foot Czechs. "What did you want to know?"

"We have heard that the Great Ocean has many mouths, with roaring water tongues that devour those who stray too close. Do the people of Del Mar not fear this?"

"Roaring water tongues." *Say what?* "Uh, maybe we call them something else. Can you be more specific?"

Kimbal thought a moment, then raised an arm and bent it at the elbow, curling his hand. "They are said to be shaped like this, and when they lash out . . ." He thrust the hand forward and down.

"A wave!" I exclaimed. "Roaring water tongue . . . that's great. Actually, the people of Del Mar—and for that matter all along the Great Ocean to the west—have learned to tame the terrible roaring water tongues."

"They . . . *tamed* them?" Kimbal was flabbergasted. "But how?"

"Well, see, they take these long, flat pieces of wood . . ."

"Flat pieces of wood," he repeated.

"They sand 'em real smooth and taper one end—sometimes both—to a fine point."

Kimbal's bright, inquisitive face was scrunched in heavy thought. "Taper . . . fine point."

"Then, they wax 'em down . . ."

"What is *wax*?"

"Okay, let's make this easy."

The earth around us was soft; hardly anything growing there, other than a few orange weeds that looked like goldenrod. I found a sharp stick and carved the outlines of a surfboard into the loam. It was about six feet from end to end. Turned out pretty good, actually, for a guy who can't draw a crooked line.

"Now, this is what they look like," I told him. "The people put them in the water, paddle far out, turn around toward shore, and wait."

"For the appearance of the roaring water tongues?"

I nodded. "For sure. And when they come, the people stand on the wood and ride atop the roaring water tongues."

"They are not thrown off, or devoured?" Kimbal exclaimed.

I thought about all my own wipe-outs, but no sense disillusioning the kid. "Nope. They force the roaring water tongues all the way in to shore, where they just break apart and die."

The teenager was awestruck. He pointed at my work of art. "And what do they call this miraculous piece of wood?" he asked.

I cleared my throat and said solemnly, "It's a roaring water tongue depressor."

"Yes, that would make sense. Amazing! The people who live along the Great Ocean are as brave as any I've heard spoken of across Murlug."

Kimbal continued to glance back at the surfboard drawing long after we'd left it behind. It occurred to me that even more than the bullshit I'd just fed him, he was impressed with the outlines of the "roaring water tongue depressor" being left for posterity in the earth; *drawn by the hand of a god.* You know, like all those crisscrossed lines on the Plain of Nazca in Peru. He and his people will probably come back and make this a shrine.

CHAPTER 11

Déjà Vu Times Two

Anyway, it wasn't much longer before we got to Kamamakama. First, we entered this grove of skinny trees with huge, black and yellow fronds that were—surprise—shaped like surfboards. There were chittering sounds, like ground squirrels make, but no animal or bird revealed itself.

A few minutes after entering the trees, we came to a clearing. Kamamakama stood along the edge of a stream; not some mucky brown one like we're used to seeing back home, but a really crystal-clear, sandy-bottomed, *gurgling* stream. You could drink right from it, I was sure of that.

Kamamakama consisted of about forty dwellings, most uniformly small, only a few slightly larger. They were built from the reddish trunks of the local trees and roofed by the fronds, which I would later learn had the texture of rubber, water repellent and impossible to tear. Communal cooking fires were scattered through the village, about one to every five huts. Men and women stirred the contents of large pots, or turned animal carcasses around on a spit. All the males of Kamamakama, from children to elders, were amazingly similar; it was like looking at Kimbal in all the stages from cradle to grave. The women, on the other hand, were markedly different: hair color, facial features, shape and size. The hair on nearly all of them cascaded down below their buns. Now I loved that! Like Kimbal, all the Kamamakamans had bright, inquisitive faces and seemed a happy, peaceful lot. Probably had no enemies here in Happy Valley, or they would've been annihilated a long time ago.

Now this was weird: looking at the crude dwellings, the picturesque stream, the unusual trees behind and the cerulean sky overhead, I was struck with the feeling that I'd been here before. That was impossible, of course, because . . .

No it wasn't. I *did* know this place, because I'd *written* about a primitive village exactly like it. More than once, actually. There was definitely one in *Tree Men of Quazzak*, and another in an early effort of mine, *Blood Roaches of Ibasklar*. Might've been more, too. Oh, not identical, but pretty darn close. Certainly just as weird.

The Kamamakamans seemed little more than mildly curious by my appearance. They waved at Kimbal, smiled at me, in general went about their business. A small, mostly white *dog* (I think) with a black eye patch came out from behind one of the huts and sniffed its way toward us. Its hair was frizzy and puffed up, like someone had left Spuds McKenzie in a clothes drier for too long. The beastie sniffed my feet, chuffed hoarsely a few times, peed on my ankle, and shuffled off. Kimbal thought this was real funny.

"By custom, a stranger must first meet the Farseeing Ones," the teenager said.

We stopped before one of the largest huts. Kimbal knocked twice, and I followed him in. A small window on one side lit the room dimly. The three Farseeing Ones sat cross-legged in a perfect row near the center. They were incredibly old, with scowling faces and foreheads creased by worry lines; looked like Manny, Moe, and Jack after a meeting with their tax consultant. Kimbal nodded at them reverently.

"I bring a stranger to Kamamakama," he said. "He is Jack of distant Del Mar."

"Yes, I know the place," Manny said in a wheezy voice.

Right.

"Show him some of our hospitality, Dumbal," Moe said.

"That's Kimbal," Kimbal told him, guiding me out of the hut.

"Is that it?" I asked.

"The Farseeing Ones must be allowed all the time possible to commune with their wisdom," he informed me.

Shut up, Miller, just shut up. "Yeah, uh, where to now?"

"You'll meet my parents, and then I'll take you to a guest hut. Are you sure, Great One—Jack, that you don't want me to . . . ?"

"I'm sure, Kimbal, I'm sure."

Okay, Kamamakama was a nice place, but I could already tell it was going to be a one-night stand. A chat with the natives, something to eat and drink, maybe a few hours of sleep, then follow Kimbal back to the bike. I could explore some more of Murlug, I suppose, although from what I'd seen of the terrain, even the rugged Nishiki would have trouble getting across it. So, I'd have Kimbal help me clear a slope, then I'd show him how gods disappear into thin air. That should add a bit to Kamamaka-man folklore.

Kimbal's parents, Kraztik and Wistilla, were attractive people who hardly looked any older than me. The red-haired Wistilla was flirting, unless I'd just gone blind, deaf, and dumb. If this bothered Kraztik, it didn't show; in fact, he seemed to encourage it. I'm not sure how Kimbal felt about his mother hitting on a god.

The guest hut was at the perimeter of the village, near the stream. On the way there I noticed the first hints of a gray twilight in the eastern sky, or what I assumed was east. The apricot sun had fallen almost to the treetops, which was surprising, because not that much time could have passed since we came down from the foothills.

"Our village is yours, O Great—Jack," Kimbal said formally when we were standing at the door. "I will return shortly."

I pointed a stern finger at him. "Remember, no one must know."

"Oh, of course! We treat you as we do any other stranger."

He left, and I looked inside. The floor was covered with layers of soft brown furs. Yeah, definitely like in *Blood Roaches of Ibasklar*. Nice clean room, but gloomy and confining, which I wasn't ready for at the moment, so I went back outside.

The Kamamakamans continued to smile at me, but none approached, except for one of the blow-dried Spuds McKenzies, which I frightened off with an evil face before it could leave its calling card. Kimbal soon returned, hand in hand with a girl who redefined the word *cute*. She reminded me of Valerie Bertinelli as a teenager, when respectable older men had felt like perverts because they had the hots for her. They made one heck of a nice couple.

"This is Chatana, she who would be my mate," Kimbal said proudly. "I leave her with you to do as you will."

The girl smiled at me and ran her slim hands along the contours of her body. This wasn't happening, was it?

"Kimbal, I can't—" I began.

"It is considered an affront to refuse the hospitality of any Kamamakaman," he informed me. "And did you not want to see us at our best?"

I tried not to glance at the lovely Chatana. "Well, if you insist . . ."

He left her with me. Their parting look at each other was filled with such caring and warmth that I felt downright guilty about the whole thing. Still, when she turned to me, I sensed no reluctance on her part.

"What is your pleasure, stranger?" she asked.

"Uh, pleasure . . . food, yes, food and drink, because I'm really hungry, and thirsty too."

This was true. As usual I'd left my condo without breakfast, and for all I know I might've been on the Ultimate Bike Path for half a day or more. Without a watch or a normal sun, it's tough judging time out here.

"As you wish," she said, and I watched her walk off, which was a great diversion.

The apricot sun was gone, and darkness was falling rapidly. It was cold again, more so than it had been in the foothills. Kamamakamans were already throwing furs on. Good idea. I went inside and wrapped myself in the thickest one I could find. This time I stayed put.

Chatana soon returned, carrying a woven reed plate and a stone pitcher. The plate was loaded with strips of meat braised with some kind of sauce, which made it look like the roast pork you get in a Chinese restaurant. A boiled vegetable was shaped like a potato but tasted like a carrot. I tried to ignore its bright green color. The stuff in the pitcher was a warm alcoholic beverage; it tasted like a cranberry wine cooler that had been left out in the sun all day.

While I ate, Chatana lit two small torches that hung on opposite walls of the hut, then sat cross-legged in front of me. She seemed to enjoy watching me scarf down the meat, which tasted great. I wondered what it was. In my brief time here I hadn't noticed any herds of animals around, nor could I imagine these wimpy-looking people as great hunters. I don't even think Kimbal was carrying a weapon. Maybe they traded baskets or something for it with another tribe.

Before asking Chatana, I thought: Did I really want to know the source of this meat? What if it came from some disgusting rodent, or a thing that slithered on its belly? Or even poor Spuds and his brothers. Uh-uh.

With Chatana holding her curiosity in check, and me stuffing my face, a weird silence prevailed for a few minutes. When I was done she put the plate and pitcher outside (where it was totally dark now, except for the fading light of the cooking fires), then ran her hands over her curves again.

"What do you wish now, stranger?"

After what I'd been through lately, it was *so-oo* tempting. But in the first place, she was practically a kid, and in the second place . . . I couldn't forget the look that passed between her and Kimbal.

"I'm going to sleep now, because I'm tired. It is my wish that you go back to Kimbal and tell him that you pleased me greatly, and stay with him."

She smiled broadly, threw her arms around my neck, and hurried out. I climbed under the furs, because it was really cold.

Oh, Miller, you schmuck.

Yes, I was tired, but I couldn't fall asleep. I watched the flickering torches, thought about putting them out, but didn't want to throw off the furs.

I sat up when Wistilla, Kimbal's mother, glided into the hut. She was carrying a pair of reed sandals.

"My son told me you needed these," she said.

"Yes, thank you."

"I also understand you are finished with Chatana." She did the same thing with her hands that the girl had done, but more skillfully. "The nights in Kamamakama are cold, stranger. Let me warm you."

"But what about your mate?"

"As you know by now, this is our custom with strangers. As for Kraztik . . . The daughter of my father's brother is also visiting here from a village across the Selwok Valley, and Kraztik has given himself to her for the night."

Yes! That definitely was the right answer. I lifted the furs.

"Catch the lights, Wistilla, will you?" I said.

She was sitting up when I opened my eyes. Streaks of daylight came in through a small window. Dawn. How long had the night been? Fifteen hours? Thirty-six minutes? Damned if I knew.

"What is it?" I asked groggily.

"Oh, no, *they're here!*" she exclaimed. "I must go!"

She stood, wrapped the skirt around her body, and ran from the hut. I really didn't want to get up, because it was still cold, and I was comfortable. But I heard some sort of ruckus outside, and the sound of scraping sandals on the rough ground. Thought I'd better see what was going on.

Shaking off the last of the sleep and dressing quickly, I hurried out. Villagers darted everywhere; even Manny, Moe, and Jack were there. Now get this: The pleasant, wimpy Kamamakamans had transmogrified into grim, determined fighting machines. Men, women, and even kids held longswords, daggers, nasty-looking pikes and maces. Must've had the weapons stashed somewhere. But *what* were they getting ready to fight? Where was the enemy?

They were looking up, so I looked up too.

Huge creatures filled the sky, things with black, membranous wings that spanned over thirty feet. The heads were definitely birdlike, but ugly, with two red eyes peering malignantly over a silver, pointed beak that clattered obscenely, like the tops of two garbage cans being smashed together. The overall appearance was more leathery than feathery. Other, smaller beings rode atop the creatures, though as yet I couldn't see them clearly.

I knew these flying monsters, just like I'd known the village yesterday. Because I had written about them, too. Their counterparts had appeared in *Mutant Bats of Krimmia*, and even further back in *Brain Ingestors of Musi*, which still enjoyed a cult following of sickos who sent me an occasional fan letter.

How weird, to see them alive . . . perhaps getting ready to ingest *my* brains.

"What are they?" I asked of no one in particular.

"The minions of Atoris the Evil," a voice answered, "doubtless up to mischief."

No shit.

One of the clattering bat-birds swooped down, the beating of its powerful wings raising havoc—and dust—in the village. Ducking down as the thing went past, I caught a glimpse of the rider. It was humanoid, but hideous, sort of a malevolent ET *after* Elliot's brother found him all white and decomposing. Before its mount rose, the grotesque thing waved a gnarly fist in my direction.

Kimbal ran toward me, wielding a sword in one hand and a wicked mace in the other. He looked more like a man than he had yesterday. Five yards away, he stumbled over a rock and nearly fell; guess *that* hadn't changed.

"O Great One, the minions of Atoris the Evil attack Kamamakama!" he exclaimed. "Drive them away, please!"

See, I *knew* it! Didn't I tell you that would happen?

"Uh, listen, Kimbal, I was bullshitting you."

He scratched his head, banging it with the hilt of the sword. "Bull . . . ?"

"I'm an ordinary guy, not a god. Just having a little fun, was all."

"But . . . I saw you . . . the thing in the cave . . ."

Another bat-bird swooped down, its talons raking the air inches above our heads. "I'll explain that later. Right now, it looks like you have a problem."

"No, Jack, *we* have a problem." He handed me the sword. "It is also the custom that guests of a village must fight to defend that village when it is threatened. Now do it!"

"But—!"

He hurried off; kind of pissed, he was. Can't say I blame him. I mean, having to deal with a false god when you're under attack by . . .

I suddenly looked at myself: practically naked except for a short sarong, a weird amulet around my neck, and a pair of woven sandals, carrying a sword . . . which by the way was heavy, standing in the middle of a primitive village that was about to be laid to waste by a bunch of Steven Spielberg nightmares riding giant bat-birds.

I'd become a character in one of my own stories.

No way; this was getting crazy. All right, put the sword down, ease into the forest, find my way back to the cave. The surfboard drawing (which would *never* become a shrine now) would point me in the right direction . . .

Another creature, this one bearing three of the pasty little beggars, swooped down. I leaped to the side, one of its claws grazing my shoulder and leaving a nasty scratch. With both hands on the hilt I lifted the sword, its weight nearly pulling me over backward. By sheer accident the sharp edge bit into the beast, severing its foot. Something black and viscous, really gross, spewed from the wound. The thing screeched, then rolled over, which dislodged two of its riders. As it shot headlong into the trees, a great rallying cry rose from the throats of the Kamamakamans, who had witnessed my act. They turned to face the attack with renewed hope.

Okay, what the hell, let's go for it. I faced the two gremlins, who had shaken off the effects of their fall and were coming at me with these dinky knives. Sidestepping the first, I carved him in two. Wistilla appeared with a mace, which she brought down on the head of the other, flattening him to the thickness of second base.

But this wasn't easy, like in the novels. There were dozens of the bat-birds, and hundreds of the white buggers, inundating the village. The turbulence caused by the hovering creatures' wings made standing up and fighting difficult. And the toothpicks those gremlins carried, damn, they hurt! A dozen of them managed to overpower one Kamamakaman, and what they did to him with their teeth . . . *Jeeez!*

I was swinging the sword at three of the devils when another fell out of the sky and landed on my shoulders. It was a bitch trying to reach around and get him off. I expected to feel his teeth in my neck, but the bastard had something else in mind. He grabbed the Bukko in his gnarly hand and yanked on it, which snapped the thin chain. Holding his prize, he leaped to the ground and scampered off.

"Oh, shit, *no!*" I exclaimed, and tried to chase him, but the others were persistent. Half watching, I saw him leap atop one of the bat-birds, which rose up and became lost in the swirl of the others.

There was a barely audible noise, like one of those old, cheap dog whistles. The gremlins immediately stopped what they were doing and leaped atop the nearest bat-bird, all of which flew high above the village, then sped away beyond the trees.

The Kamamakamans soundlessly tallied their casualties. Two were dead, many more injured. If it was any consolation, the remains of over forty little buggers and three bat-birds were fouling up the village.

A subdued Kimbal came over and put a hand on my shoulder (which by the way was bleeding, among plenty of other places on my body). "God or not, Jack, you fought well," he said.

"Yeah, big deal," I replied. "What was it all about? Why did they come?"

"Same reason as always. Atoris the Evil prizes the women of the Selwok Valley."

"Women? I didn't see . . . Did they take any?"

He shrugged. "Four, including my Chatana."

"Jeez, pal, I'm really sorry. So I guess you'll be going with me to get her back, right? I'll do all I can to help."

Kimbal was puzzled. "Why would *you* pursue them?"

I pointed at my bare neck. "Because they stole my Bukko."

"This . . . Bukko, it is very valuable?"

"It is to me."

"Jack, you don't understand. *No one* pursues the minions of Atoris. This is the way it has always been, and the way—"

"Oh, that's bullshit and you know it!" I said peevishly.

"Bullshit again; what does it mean?"

"Never mind. Do you love Chatana?"

"Yes, I do." The defeat suddenly left his face, and he looked grim and determined, as before. "You're right! They did bullshit by taking my Chatana. That is wrong! I will not let them do bullshit again!"

"Good attitude . . . but knock off the bullshit. Where did they take her?"

His voice fell again. "To the terrible land of Areelkrokka, where else?"

"How far is that?"

"Its borders are five mahooganistos from here, but its main city is at least another mahooganisto farther than that."

The UT5 must have had a hell of a time with . . . *that word*, because I felt this prickling in my neck each time he said it. Six mahooganistos. Actually, six of *anything* didn't sound like much of a big deal, but I had to understand it better.

"Come on, follow me."

I led him back through the weird grove, until we could again see across the Selwok Valley. One range of mountains was, by my guess, fifty to sixty miles away. I pointed at them.

"Okay, how far?" I asked.

"Those? Oh, a little less than one mahooganisto," he answered. One mahooganisto.

The main city of the terrible land of Areelkrokka—where the Bukko was headed—was six mahooganistos away.

Are you getting a clear picture that I had a problem here?

CHAPTER 12

A Wild Ride

Scenario: Study Group observing Jack Miller as he contemplates the loss of the Bukko.

Study Group Old Guy #1: "He appears agitated over what happened."

Study Group Old Guy #2: "I should think so. Was he not told how valuable the Bukko is to you?"

My Old Guy: "Of course, but he can't be blamed. It was taken from him in the heat of battle."

Study Group Old Guy #1: "The Bukko is far from him. Shall we look ahead and see what he ultimately does?"

My Old Guy: "No, let's not. Part of this exercise was for us to better understand the meaning of patience. Besides, is not our diversion in *anticipating* his next actions?"

Study Group Old Guy #2: "I *know* what his next action will be. He'll get his bicycle and return to the *mhuva lun gallee*, looking for his own gate." (Inserts finger in ear.) "His people would call him a chicken-shit."

All right, think this out carefully, Miller. Did I really *need* the Bukko? I mean, it's supposed to save my ass, right? But I would have to travel over three hundred miles and probably *risk* my ass a bunch of times just to get it back, and something about that didn't make a whole lot of sense. In addition, according to Kimbal the last fifty miles or so were across the terrible land of Areelkrokka, and I really hated that *terrible land* part. And if I *did* get there, this Atoris the Evil wasn't going to say, "Nice going, Jack, here's your amulet, how about some pizza and beer?" More than likely he'd cut my body up in a thousand pieces to see which one squirms farther.

But what were the alternatives? I couldn't go back and bullshit the Old Guy or his cronies, no way. "Well, you see, it fell into this crevice that the natives informed me runs two miles deep into a molten pool about ten thousand degrees hot, so . . ." They were watching; they *knew* what was going on. And even if I flat-out admitted the truth, what would they think of me? Wouldn't that be a lousy way to represent Earth people? They sure as hell wouldn't want to study *me* anymore.

I *had* to go after the Bukko, if for no other reason than the fact that it meant so much to the Old Guy, and he had entrusted it to me. As I followed Kimbal back to Kamamakama, my decision was made.

"Okay, I'm going," I called out, staring up past the trees. "Do you hear?"

Kimbal looked at me strangely. "I knew that," he said.

The people of Kamamakama were a pragmatic lot. Already they'd lit two funeral pyres for the dead, treated the wounded, begun putting their village back together, and sung some sort of paean to the memory of the women who had been taken. Today's attack was part of life, right? And life does go on.

Kimbal had wavered, especially after his people caught wind of what he planned to do. All this crap about bringing down the wrath of Atoris the Evil, you know. Hell, the guy was bad enough when he was in a *good* mood. Kimbal's final decision, however, was to go. His people were pissed off at me for talking him into it, especially his parents. But in the end it was Wistilla who fixed us up with sacks of provisions and made sure the weapons we took were the best in the village.

Okay, here was the situation: Kimbal had already talked me out of taking the Nishiki. No way could it traverse the rugged terrain. And even if it could, there was this especially nasty mountain range to cross, unless we wanted to take a five-hundred-mile detour. Besides, he had a better idea for transportation and told me to trust him. I was concerned about that.

I really hated leaving the bike. Having it with me at the other end would make this a one-way trip, right? Find a downhill run in Areelkrokka and I'm outta here. *C'est la vie*. I hoped it wouldn't be a one-way trip for other reasons.

Wistilla, Kraztik, and Chatana's parents were the only ones to see us off later that morning. I caught a glimpse of Manny, Moe, and Jack peering out from their hut, but they were too busy communing with their wisdom to offer us godspeed. We started off paralleling the stream, which Kimbal told me twisted in a southeasterly direction. The terrible land of Areelkrokka was due east of Kamamakama; but our first stop, Kimbal said, was a village called Gwonnis, on the far end of the Selwok Valley, where we would find transportation. He still wouldn't tell me what that would be.

The stream quickly emerged from the trees, and after following it for two miles we veered away to the east-southeast. Kimbal hadn't been pulling my chain about not being able to use the bike. Those purplish-green vines I mentioned before were everywhere; so were dense shrubs, and a million varieties of weeds. Countless rifts in the ground, some over two feet across, indicated considerable seismic activity in the valley.

Need I tell you how many times Kimbal fell?

So for the rest of the day we went in and out of forests, crossed rivers and streams, real Sierra Club stuff. Most of the wildlife we saw looked familiar, with a few minor differences. For example, a species of reddish-brown squirrel had a round, black patch on top of its head, which resembled a skullcap. One fat little fellow, sitting on a branch with its paws crossed around a nut, reminded me of my uncle Morty praying in the synagogue.

The people in the villages we passed through were cordial, but exhibited no curiosity over where we were headed. Smiles cast upon us by the young women were unspoken invitations to stay longer, which sounded like a plan. But we pushed on, and when we finally did stop for the night it was in the middle of nowhere, a quiet spot along a wide river that Kimbal told me divided the valley in half.

We'd made twenty or so miles that day (a long day, actually, the apricot sun taking much more time to climb to its zenith than to fall). About one third of a mahooganisto, according to Kimbal. Glad we weren't going to maintain that pace all the way to Areelkrokka.

We forded the river at dawn, and went on. This half of the Selwok Valley was different; less vegetation, fewer tributaries. The villages were more primitive, the people hairier, although still peaceful enough. Was this the kind of place where we would be seeking transportation? Because until now I'd yet to see *anything* in the valley that could be ridden upon, or behind. So far the kid wasn't impressing me.

But that all changed when we reached Gwonnis, which happened about the time the sun was directly overhead; late afternoon, as I now thought of it. Actually, it had been changing for the past couple of hours. Earlier, after crossing this long, boring plain covered with something that waved like wheat but wasn't, the villages changed again and were larger, better constructed. We saw fields of crops growing, and herds of something grazing: large animals, cowlike, except for their heads, which were small, the faces resembling bighorn sheep. Weird-looking beasties.

Gwonnis, two miles away from a pass through the nearest mountain range, was surrounded by some of the most fertile land I'd yet seen. It was large enough to be considered a town. Wide paths (roads, I'll call them roads) intersected at the hub, where diverse people noisily bought and sold goods at a marketplace. A lively street, but not with the sort of carnival atmosphere I might have expected; no dancing dogs, fire-eaters, painted ladies with bells on their toes, nothing like that.

Now, aside from his prowess in battle the other day, you might've gotten this impression of Kimbal as the ultimate country *naif*, Gomer Pyle just off the turnip truck, you know. But I have to say, he handled himself pretty well in the big town. You see, what I didn't know until now was that the kind of transportation he hoped to procure was not the easiest to find. If I understood him correctly, you could say that what we were doing was *against the law*. (Yeah, but so was taking his girlfriend and ripping off my Bukko, so we didn't care.)

After making a few inquiries, we found the guy Kimbal was looking for in a seedy tavern. I waited at the bar, sipping a drink that tasted like cinnamon-flavored dishwater, while he spoke to the rat-faced fellow. When money had changed hands a second time, Kimbal waved for me to follow them outside.

As we walked through Gwonnis a couple of yards behind the weasel, Kimbal said, "He at first denied owning even a single tennapacer. But as you saw, there are ways to deal with the likes of him."

I nodded. "Right. What's a tennapacer?"

The teenager smiled. "It is hard to describe them. You'll see one soon enough. They are rare creatures, found only in canyons far to the north. Possessing them is an offense in every known place across Murlug. Still, there is no better way to travel the vast, rugged distances than atop a tennapacer, so men like this risk the penalties for the rewards."

"Gee, I can't imagine anyone doing something like that," I said dryly, and he looked at me sort of weird, like maybe *I* was the *naif*.

The weasel led us past the eastern edge of Gwonnis. We were still on a road, or at least something that vaguely resembled one, only because the sandals of numerous people had fallen within its general boundaries. It was still pretty rugged; would've caused havoc to the wheels of anything, if anything here *had* wheels. As yet it looked like that most lofty of inventions had escaped the simple folk of Murlug.

A mile out of town the weasel veered off in the direction of some craggy hills. Not having seen another living soul for a while, I was starting to get nervous. I mean, what if there were no tennapacers out here? What if the weasel had some buddies waiting to jump us, take the rest of Kimbal's money and slit our throats? When Kimbal glanced at me and fingered his sword, I knew he was thinking the same thing.

We must've come two miles now, which I hadn't planned on, because my feet were already killing me from the long day. Kamamakama reed sandals had nothing over a good pair of Adidas. The foothills closed in around us, and we studied every possible niche for signs of an ambush. I would have expected the weasel to be casting furtive glances behind him, but all we saw was the back of his knobby head. To tell the truth, I don't think he looked back even once since we left Gwonnis.

"Dealing in tennapacers requires this sort of secrecy," Kimbal whispered. "Still, let us be wary."

One of the mountain slopes loomed on our right when the weasel motioned for us to stop. He walked up to what appeared to be a wall of solid rock. But when he rapped on it three times with his knuckles, there was a hollow sound. A clever camouflage was moved aside, revealing the mouth of a cave, where another weasel stood. Our weasel waved us forward. We hesitated.

Grinning a grin of rotted teeth (what else?), our weasel said, "We may be the scum of the land, but we are honest scum. What kind of business would we have if word got around that we robbed and murdered our customers? Now get in here."

It hadn't occurred to me until the moment I crossed the threshold how awful a closed-in cave containing some kind of animals would smell. Compared to this place, Averill the Second Apprentice Dungmaster (probably promoted by now) bore the aroma of the perfume counter at Nordstorm's. Kimbal showed only mild displeasure; I tried not to gag as we followed the weasels.

There were twelve stalls, each occupied by a tennapacer. Surprise, it was déjà vu again. In every book I'd ever written, from *Blood Roaches of Ibasklar* to *Mutant Bats of Krimmia*, I had created at least one unspeakable monstrosity such as the things before us right now.

A tennapacer looked like a three-toed sloth; not the little guy you see hanging from a tree branch, but a huge thing over fifteen feet long, like the ground-walking mylodon from the Pleistocene Age. Some of its cousins got stuck in the La Brea tar pits and are still hanging around Los Angeles. The tennapacers had elongated skulls with mouths containing *lots* of teeth. Sloths and their ancestors were supposed to be herbivores; I hope these fellows knew that.

Now here's what was *really* weird about them: like the mylodons their trunks were stocky, but instead of proportionately short, robust legs, theirs were long and sleek, like a horse's. No hooves, though, just those three nasty claws at the end of each foot. And something else: What I had first thought was a saddle on their coarse-haired backs was actually a carapace, the kind of protective shell you usually see on an insect. Strange-looking devils, all in all, and getting stared at by their beady red eyes was damned unnerving.

Was *this* the "transportation" we had walked two days to find? I glanced at Kimbal, who was nodding in satisfaction. Yep, guess so.

The first weasel was grinning again. "There, tennapacers, just as I told you. Now let's see the rest of your money."

Kimbal doled out more coins. Both weasels looked at them and nodded in approval.

"We will pick out two of the finest mounts," the second weasel said. "But night has almost fallen, and you know they will not travel in the dark. You can sleep in here until the morning."

Kimbal nodded, but I didn't like the idea. First, these two still might've been planning to jump us. And second, the accommodations inside this cave were not exactly the Ramada Inn.

"Guess I'll sleep under the stars," I told Kimbal.

"Jack, I don't think you want to do that," he said.

But I did, and I went outside, where the apricot sun had finished its speedy descent. Here among the rocks, it was *really* dark. I settled into a niche opposite the cave mouth and dug in my sack for something to eat.

The first throaty roar echoed through the foothills a minute later, followed by another, then a series of god-awful shrieks that sounded like a cat being parboiled.

Ten seconds after that I was back inside the friendly confines of Avis Rent-A-Sloth, where I hardly noticed the smell and had a pretty good night's sleep.

The two tennapacers chosen by the weasels were led out into the morning light with hoods over their elongated heads. These canvas things, held on by drawstrings, looked like feed bags.

"If they cannot see, they will not run," the first weasel told us. "But when the hoods are off . . ."

"Be sure to keep the hoods at hand," the second weasel said, "for when you need to stop. How far did you say you were going?"

"To the terrible land of Areelkrokka," Kimbal told them.

They grinned knowingly at each other. "Then you won't have to worry about making them stop," the first weasel said, "for no man or beast untouched by Atoris the Evil will cross the edge. So, you will not be riding them back. The tennapacers will return on their own."

"What do you mean by that?" I exclaimed.

"If you leave them hooded to await you, they will surely fall victim to some beast. They must be allowed to return."

I was pissed, but Kimbal was calmer. "It's all right, Jack. I knew that. We'll find another way back, don't worry."

The two weasels grinned again. We followed them as they led the hooded beasts to the pass, where they turned their noses eastward. I climbed atop the back of one, observing that its contoured carapace acted like a natural saddle. Stirrups (sort of like crude toe clips) were cinched under the thing's belly, and leather reins encircled its neck. This was the only tack.

We were ready. The weasels pulled off the hoods, handed them to us, and stood back. My tennapacer cast its red eyes back at me, perhaps thinking, Who the hell are you? It then took off as though a ramrod had been inserted in a place where the sun didn't shine.

Later, Kimbal would ask me about the strange sound I made. Jesus, didn't anyone but us Earthers ever scream?

What a ride, I mean . . . *what* . . . *a* . . . *ride!* This was every stomach-flopper at Magic Mountain or Disneyland all rolled together into one daylong thrill. The tireless, long-striding tenna-pacers must've run between thirty and forty miles an hour, and nothing, I mean *nothing*, got in their way. A sheer drop into a canyon? No problem. The damn things went down the walls like spiders! Some sort of sticky suckers on the bottom of those clawed feet, I suppose. Same for going up. That humungous mountain range Kimbal mentioned? We were over it in a couple of hours, the only problem being that we froze our butts off in the snow of the high elevations. Sure, I had extra clothes in my sack, but *no way* would I let go of the reins. In fact, I think the leather and my flesh had become one since starting out, holding on as tightly as I was for dear life. I don't think I stopped being scared shitless, but in retrospect it was a pretty incredible ride.

Beyond the mountains we thawed out quickly across the sands of a blistering desert, then penetrated a forest of towering trees that looked like sequoias. Running full speed toward those wood giants took some getting used to.

Kimbal's tennapacer was a yard to my left, same as it had been for all these miles. The kid looked like he was enjoying himself.

"Do you want to rest, Jack?" he asked.

"Depends. How much longer do we have?"

"We've come a long way. I think the edge of Areelkrokka is near."

"Then let's stick it out."

We left the forest behind and started across a landscape much like the floor of the Selwok Valley, rifts, vines and all. It was amazing that the tennapacers had so far not stumbled and broken one of their fragile-looking legs.

Above, the sun had reached its peak and was on the way down. One way or the other, we would definitely be stopping soon.

It was no challenge figuring out when we had reached the border of the terrible land. First, you could see this brown haze ahead, like when you got on the San Diego Freeway in Orange County and looked north toward Los Angeles. Then, the tennapacers recoiled as though they had run into a wall of foam rubber. They spun 180 degrees on their tails and started back the way they had come.

"The hoods, quick!" Kimbal said.

We covered their heads, and they stopped, but their bodies trembled in fear. Kimbal climbed off first, then helped me, because my hands had cramped sort of arthritically around the reins, and my legs were shaky.

"Over four mahooganistos in a single day!" the kid exclaimed. "Was I not right?"

"For sure," I said, wincing as the parts of me that had been numb for a while came back to life.

We pulled the hoods off the tennapacers and watched them bolt off, doubly motivated. Sure hope they found a cave or something before nightfall. Then we turned to face the terrible land.

CHAPTER 13

Areelkrokka

Okay, I hope you don't think we were *that* stupid. With darkness less than an hour off, there was *no way* we were about to stroll into the heart of everything evil on Murlug and *then* hunt down a cozy place to sleep. Enough time to be brave and reckless in the morning. We found a sheltered spot between some boulders, one of which kept us from having to look at the smog wall. Kimbal got a fire going, and we cooked some of that great Chinese pork.

Over dinner I asked Kimbal, "Once we're in there tomorrow, how will you know where to go?"

"It is said that all paths in Areelkrokka lead to the main city; almost like it draws you in."

"You always call it the *main city*. Doesn't it have a name?"

"Yes, but it is seldom uttered."

"Will you utter it to me?"

"Dohnwana."

"You don' wanna tell me the name?"

"That *is* the name. The city is Dohnwana."

The main city of the terrible land of Areelkrokka was called Dohnwana. Like many other things in my travels, this too seemed to make perfect sense.

"Do you know anything about this place?" I asked.

He shook his head firmly. "It is shrouded in the darkest mystery, even more so than the land surrounding it. There are stories, of course, legends . . . But better you go in without knowing them."

I had a hunch he was right. Still, more knowledge of the layout would've helped. Don't suppose the Auto Club had a map of the place, or listed it in one of their Tourbooks. (Motel 666 in the heart of Dohnwana: "We'll put the lights out for you.")

Time enough to worry about it tomorrow. No throaty roars tonight; beasties seemed to shun the edge of the terrible land. I got some good sleep.

♦ ♦ ♦

In the morning, Areelkrokka was still there. Nope, the whole thing hadn't been a bad dream. I really *was* doing this.

Scenario: Study Group about to stop observing Jack Miller.

Study Group Old Guy #1 (bursting into the . . . room, or whatever): "Come quickly, there is something else of interest you should see."

Study Group Old Guy #2: "But what about Jack? He is just entering the terrible land."

My Old Guy: "Yes, and since he does not have the Bukko, he cannot summon us if there is a life-threatening situation."

Study Group Old Guy #1: "But you *must* see this!"

My Old Guy: "Well, as long as we're not gone *too* long . . ."

I was expecting the terrible land of Areelkrokka to "chill the marrow of my bones," but guess what, it was just the opposite. Hot. Not Las Vegas dry-hot, but sticky-hot, an August-day-in-downtown-Cincinnati-along-the-Ohio-River kind of hot. It sort of hung on you, like a soggy T-shirt.

The smoggy haze filled the air. If it was any consolation, at least it didn't *smell* like Los Angeles, or sting the eyes. Murlug's apricot sun was no longer apricot, more like a burnt-toast brown. I can't even describe what color the sky was.

And everything else around us just sort of *looked* evil. The rocks looked evil, the stunted, gnarly trees, the scrubby weeds (which also smelled bad if you got too close, like old fish in a garbage can), even the cracks in the ground. Evil cracks. I mean, you weren't about to mistake this place for a Japanese tea garden.

We kept on moving east. Don't ask me, I was just following Kimbal. After about two miles we came to our first tributary in Areelkrokka. Surprise, it looked like it was downstream from a factory that took pride in dumping its industrial waste. We paralleled it for a while, and as I watched its sluggish but steady flow, an idea began to germinate. But it soon twisted sharply to the southwest, which wouldn't have done at all.

Another couple of boring miles fell behind us. There were no signs of life anywhere: persons, animals, insects, *nada*. Maybe the only humanoids in Areelkrokka were those mutated ET-things, and they probably lived in the big city, or whatever Dohnwana was.

So of course, just when I thought that was when this guy jumped out from behind some rocks ten yards ahead.

Cro-Magnon type; no, that was being generous. He looked more like something between Homo erectus and Neanderthal. Stumpy, *real* hairy, no clothing of any kind. He carried this enormous club that was shaped like a bowling pin. I don't think he was too happy about running into us.

Kimbal held up his hand in the universal sign of peace and smiled. You know what this hairy dipshit did? He pounded the ground with the business end of the tree trunk, which set off at least a 5.2 on the Richter. Scared the hell out of us.

Then he spoke in an awful croaking voice: "I kill you both and feed your guts to the shlebadoos!" (Or something like that.)

Kimbal's smile faded and he took a step back. But I surprised Fred Flintstone (and myself) by walking toward him.

"Listen, pal," I said, "we don't want any trouble. You let us pass, and maybe I'll find something nice for you in the sack. A Hershey bar, or a pair of nylons for the wife."

He scratched his head (something fell out and crawled away). Then he beat on the ground again; a 5.8 this time, at least. He started hopping from one leg to the other as he swung his cudgel.

"Kill! Kill you both!" he bellowed.

Jesus, did this guy have a one-track mind! All right, I was finished being Mr. Nice Guy. These histrionics were probably empty posturing, as was the way with our apelike progenitors, a form of one-upmanship. Whoever yelled the loudest and meanest won, and the other went away. Yeah, two could play at this game.

Standing like a sumo wrestler, I scowled my meanest scowl and struck a fist against my chest. "All right, enough of this bullshit, you refugee from a Jane Goodall documentary! You flea-ridden hairball! You extreme disappointment to your parents!" I was bellowing stupid things like that, waving my arms, in general making an asshole of myself.

So, you think all *my* posturing sent Fred Flintstone running? It did . . . right toward me with the tree stump swinging over his head!

"Jack, look out!" Kimbal exclaimed, and tackled me to the ground, which winded us both. The cudgel hummed a couple of inches over our heads as the caveman barreled past, his momentum carrying him three yards farther along.

I rose groggily to one knee as he turned. Jeez, was he pissed!

Don't ask me why, but when he charged again I held up my hand like a traffic cop and yelled, "Hey, stop!"

Now *this* you won't believe: Fred Flintstone recoiled, like he had run into a wall, and fell backward, landing on his ample buns. Stupidly, I looked at my hand. Could *I* have done that? Naaah!

But when he got up and charged again, I did the same thing. This time he flew back five feet, dropping the tree trunk as he tried to break the fall. He stared at me with his bloodshot eyes, then stood, but this time sped away in the opposite direction, making a noise like every pissed-off rhinoceros you've ever seen Marlin Perkins running from.

Kimbal, who had watched all this, was staring at me with a mixture of fear and awe. Trying to be cool, I grinned at him.

"Damndest thing, wasn't it?" I said.

"You're sure you are not a god, Jack?" he asked.

"Unless I got ordained or whatever in my sleep, I'm still just me." I shook the hand as though a thermometer was in it; that was going to do something, right? "Come on, we have a long way to go."

During the next five miles we kept a wary eye out for more of the hirsute fellows; but word must've spread quickly through Bedrock that these travelers were not to be messed with, because we didn't see a single one. With the landscape changed, I was pretty sure we wouldn't be encountering the likes of them anymore. Still, our vigilance bordered on paranoia.

There were lots more plants now, most of it a leafy ground cover of an awful purplish-brown color. It spread out in all directions, and in places was knee-high, which worried us. At best, we could step into a crack; at worst, the foliage could conceal some beastie who would like nothing better than to perform an amputation at the ankle. Fortunately, nothing like that happened, and within an hour it had thinned considerably.

We started running into more of those mucky little streams, most of which were narrow enough to jump over. Then, a larger one twisted down from the northwest and seemed to continue on in our direction for as far as we could see (not *that* far in the haze). This is what I had been waiting for.

"Any chance of it flowing all the way to Dohnwana?" I asked Kimbal.

"If it is the Aqapod River, then it surely does. Why do you want to know?"

Even if this wasn't the Aqapod River, it probably emptied into the bigger tributary somewhere along the line. "Because we now have an easier way to get where we're going."

The kid was puzzled. "I don't understand."

"Trust me."

Well, *you* know what I was thinking about. But there wasn't anything around from which we could build a raft, not even a fallen log to float on. So we walked along the river for a few miles, Kimbal waiting for a sudden burst of wisdom or whatever on my part.

Then, this jungle showed up on our left, full of weirdly colored palms and acacias, and a sort of stunted oak tree with a spaghetti-leafed top that looked like Harpo Marx's 'doo. It was even more hot and humid in there, if that were possible. Fortunately, I found what I was looking for near the edge, a tall, reedy plant that was like bamboo, only the color of a rotted carrot. We hacked off about two dozen and carried them back to the river.

By this time, Kimbal was beginning to get the idea. Using long lengths of a tough, skinny vine, we strung all but two of the hollow plants together. A crude job, but not bad, considering my usual mechanical abilities were limited to hanging pictures and replacing the flapper ball in the toilet tank. Pushing off from the bank with the two extra poles, we let a slow but steady current take us downriver. Kimbal was all excited about this.

Yeah, for sure this was the Aqapod River, because other tributaries began emptying into *it*, and before long it was nearly three times as wide. We'd been able to touch the river bottom for the first few miles with the eight-foot poles, but now it was too deep. The water, like everywhere else, had the color of Ovaltine and the consistency of Pennzoil. If anything was alive in its depths, we didn't have a clue . . . .

. . . until now.

Coming around a slight bend, I saw what at first I thought was a large gray rock in the middle of the river. Maintaining our course, we would've barely grazed it on my side of the raft. I got ready to push off with the pole, and that's when I noticed the damn thing was moving! But too late, because I'd already shoved the pole out. It struck the yielding flesh with a sort of liquid *squaarl*. The mound immediately fell under a froth of bubbles that agitated the surface.

"What in hell was *that*?" I exclaimed.

"Nothing of which we would care to make acquaintance," Kimbal said dryly. "We'd better move off quickly, before—"

Too late. The mound broke the surface again, this time rising above it, which enabled us to see that it was only one—*one*—of four similar, knobby protuberances atop the biggest damn reptilian head imaginable. If you really stretched your imagination, you might've said that it looked like a crocodile; only *this* crocodile could have taken out the Pentagon in three bites and then used the Washington Monument to pick its teeth. And worse, this evil head rose thirty feet on a green, scaly neck the approximate thickness of an ancient redwood. I didn't even want to *know* what was still under the water.

The tidal wave caused by this bellowing thing's emergence had pushed us toward the bank, but it was still ten feet away. I paddled like a madman with my hands, Kimbal imitating me. Close enough now, we leaped to the bank and scrambled up.

Two-point-seven seconds later, the monster's teeth turned the raft into something that looked like high-fiber cereal.

Feet, don't fail me now crossed my mind—rather hysterically—as I ran like hell away from the river. I kept expecting a big shadow to fall over me; but the only thing that overtook my ass was Kimbal, who came past like Florence Griffith-Joyner smelling gold and a future in commercials.

Then, the bellowing stopped, and when we glanced back, the thing in the river was gone.

"Well, it was a good idea while it lasted," I said, gasping for air.

After that we paralleled the river at a distance of a hundred yards, which turned out to be a wise move, because more of the fleshy mounds stuck out for the next five miles or so. We were crossing this wide, ugly plain, and I was getting worried, because a range of even uglier mountains was looming ahead. Now I didn't mind climbing or boulder-hopping, but only in their proper place and time, of which this was neither.

We were getting closer to Dohnwana, because I could feel my flesh sort of crawling on me, and it wasn't just the heat, the humidity, or the endless activity since getting up that morning. Still, even with the luxury of the brief river excursion, we'd done twenty, twenty-five miles tops; barely half a mahooganisto. We had at least that much more to go. And the day was nearly over, because the burnt-toast sun was sitting directly overhead.

Our first night in Areelkrokka. Something to cherish, right up there with a proctoscopy.

Kimbal noticed the village before I did. We were on slightly elevated ground, all dry and cracked, when he gestured toward the place, around a quarter mile ahead. No, it wasn't standing along the edge of the Aqapod River; you can understand why. It wasn't near *any* tributary, which wasn't a real shocker either. The water here would have to be boiled, detoxified, and demagnetized— probably a hell of a lot of other things too—before it was fit for consumption by anything, human or otherwise.

This village, amazingly, looked a lot like Kamamakama. It even stood amid a thinned-out grove of trees with the same surfboard-shaped fronds that surrounded Kimbal's village, only these were colored a weird mauve. I didn't see anyone walking around the huts, which got me wondering if they were the abandoned remnants of people who had once thrived here before Atoris the Evil showed up and began screwing with everyone's lives. (I don't know; maybe the sonofabitch has always been around.) Whatever, we weren't about to take the chance of *any* inhabitants of Areelkrokka seeing us cruise by.

"Forget moving toward the river," I told Kimbal. "If anyone's in that village, they'll have a clear view."

He pointed at a denser forest to the northeast. "Then that is our only choice . . . unless we sneak by under the cover of dark-ness."

I didn't like how that sounded. "Let's try the forest."

We swung wide around the village, glancing at it many times. Closer now, we could see it more clearly, and yes, there were definitely people—or beings of some kind—wandering around. Good choice, I told myself.

Shortly after, we were weaving between the trees due north of the village—far enough away, I had thought—when we ran into a woman with a basket.

She spotted us at the same moment and stopped what she had been doing, which was picking these anemic-looking black berries off a ubiquitous, knee-high shrub. Her clothing was similar to what the Kamamakamans wore, though tattered and grimy. She had long black hair that was streaked with gray, and she wasn't particularly attractive. She looked kind of haggard, and while at first guess I would've said she was about forty, it's possible she could've been ten years younger than that.

One thing she had going for her, though, was a nice smile. She wore it now as, putting down the basket, she approached us.

Then you know what she did? She gave us the finger!

"Live briefly, and suffer," she said solemnly, holding the airborne digit out in front of her.

I glanced at Kimbal, who said, "More than likely the formal greeting of her people." He gave her the finger and repeated, "Live briefly, and suffer." I did the same thing, but felt *really* stupid.

The woman was pleased. She lowered her hand and continued toward us. In a sort of monotoned voice she said, "You are strangers, right? We don't see too many strangers in Areelkrokka. Perhaps you are on your way to kick the ass of Atoris the Evil?" (My neck twinged from the UT5 when she said that.)

"Perhaps we are," I said cautiously.

"Oh, that would be a fine thing." There was a bare hint of enthusiasm in her voice. "My people will be glad to share information with you that will be of help."

"About Dohnwana?" Kimbal asked.

"Yes, of course."

Now *that* sounded like a plan. Still, I was cautious and took Kimbal aside. "Can we trust her?" I asked.

"I don't think she is deceitful. We'll stay alert, of course; but if this is true . . ."

We turned back to her. "Okay, take us to your leader," I said, only then realizing how idiotic that sounded.

Her smile grew. She gave me the finger, turned and retrieved her basket. "Come this way," she called.

What the hell; like Kimbal said, if they could give us the lay of the land, we might even have a chance against Atoris. We followed the woman (Yoggana, her name was) to the village we'd been trying to circumvent, arriving there quickly. A few children ran up, smiling and giving us the finger. One old, toothless lady rammed the definitive digit right into my face.

"Live briefly, and suffer," she croaked happily.

"Why do you all say that?" I asked Yoggana.

"It is part of our tradition. Once, long before the time of Atoris, we were a warlike people and had little use for pleasantries."

"When *did* this Atoris show up?" I asked.

"At the time of my fertility, when I was a young girl."

Okay, that couldn't have been too long ago. So in the cosmic scope of things, the archfiend was a newcomer.

Telling us to wait, Yoggana hurried off and had a few words with a man who was about her age. Not a particularly handsome fellow; in fact, you wouldn't have found any of these people in the Faces International catalog. He watched us as he listened to Yoggana, then followed her over.

"This is Rovwik, our leader," she said.

The fellow jerked a really stiff one into the air and mouthed the greeting with a formal sort of military cadence. Not to be outdone, I heaved the finger skyward; I mean, *really* heaved it.

A skinny bolt of lightning rose fifteen feet from the tip, crackled, then dissipated and fell in a shower of sparks. Scared the hell out of the people.

Scared the hell out of *me*.

Oh, shit, here goes the god business again. They were bowing, groveling, all that stuff. Even Kimbal seemed a little less sure of me.

"If what Yoggana told me is true," Rovwik said, "then Atoris the Evil is doomed, for you are surely the one to kick his ass." (Ow, that twinge again.)

As we followed Rovwik to a hut, Kimbal glanced at me and said, "Jack?"

"Yeah?"

"How did you *do* that?"

I shrugged. "Beats me."

So, as the sun over hazy Areelkrokka went down, we were wined and dined (more or less) and told all that these people knew about Dohnwana (not a hell of a lot), which according to Rovwik we would reach tomorrow afternoon, if we followed his instructions. I don't know why, but by the time we turned in for a surprisingly good night's sleep (no, we weren't offered any of their women, mercifully), we actually believed that we could whip this Atoris the Evil.

CHAPTER 14

Atoris the Evil

Rovwik, who would be accompanying us part of the way, was waiting outside with the rest of his people—about fifty or sixty—when we emerged from the shabby hut early the next morning. As a single unit they issued us the customary salute. It reminded me of that scene in *Close Encounters of the Third Kind*, when all the people in India pointed skyward at the source of the five notes. But of course, they were using a different finger.

Rovwik noticed my scowling face. "Is something wrong, Great One?" he asked.

Great One again. "Yeah, couldn't you think of a nicer way to greet people?"

He was nonplussed. "But . . . it is tradition, and all we know! Perhaps . . . perhaps if you taught us a new way, Great One."

Okay, so why not take advantage of this god business for something that wasn't any big deal? I held up my right hand, splitting the third and fourth fingers in the rabbinical benediction sign so familiar to many on my world. "Live long, and prosper," I said solemnly.

Immediately a murmur rose among the people. They *liked* that. Rovwik nodded his approval, and by the time we left the village a few minutes later, the whole tribe was prying apart their fingers and practicing the Vulcan greeting on each other.

If Murlug was a planet in some solar system of our galaxy, can you imagine what an Earth sociologist was going to think when they discovered this civilization centuries in the future?

We probably would've had a devil of a time with those mountains; but Rovwik led us through a pass that was little more than a yard-wide crack, sometimes even narrower. It took a while, but we finally reached the other side, where it was even more hazy, gloomy, overcast, whatever, than before; really gave me the creeps.

The village Rovwik led us to wasn't much farther along. Uneven rows of thatch huts were surrounded by growing fields, which contained a single crop. It was a melon of some kind, but gray and fuzzy, like food you had forgotten about in the back of your refrigerator, then found months later. The people here, without exception, wore brown, hooded robes. I found out it was because they all looked like Pruneface in *Dick Tracy*, even the women and kids.

"They raise these fruits for the inhabitants of Dohnwana," Rovwik told us.

While we waited, he talked to one who must've been the honcho. This fellow waved his arms wildly and seemed sort of pissed, which Rovwik had warned us would happen. Rovwik then gave me a sign.

This was the part that worried me. I was supposed to impress the hell out of the guy by doing one of my magic bits. But I didn't have any control over this! I thought about trying to send the guy sprawling, like I'd done with Fred Flintstone. But then, if a bolt of lightning shot out, I would incinerate him. Not the best way to make friends with people.

"What about the tree, Jack?" Kimbal said.

The skeletal trunk and limbs of a long-dead tree towered above the village. Good choice. I jerked a finger at the upper branches. A bolt of lightning far more impressive than the one from yesterday sheared off the top of the tree and sent it plummeting down. The hooded people, as one, fell to their knees and bowed their heads. Great.

"They are yours," Rovwik told me, and started back for the mountains. This was as close as he was going to get to Dohnwana.

Still trying to figure out how I could suddenly do this, we followed the headman across one of the fields. Workers had just finished filling up a giant basket with those hoary melons. I mean, a *giant* basket, the kind Mrs. Kong would have used to do her marketing. A second one stood empty next to it.

"Get in here," the headman said, or actually growled. "They will be coming soon for the baskets."

We stretched out on the bottom of the basket, where we noticed a few knotholes in the sturdy wood. Almost immediately the workers began covering us with melons.

"Hey, is this necessary?" I exclaimed.

"You wanted inside Dohnwana, right?" the headman replied. Did I really?

The melons were heavy, and the fuzz felt awful against my skin, but they kept piling them on. Now I knew what it was like to be a Tokyo subway commuter.

The prunefaces finally left; I could see them scurrying back to the village through one of the knotholes. Kind of unnecessarily fast, I thought, until I heard this odd sound and noticed a shadow falling over the field. Quite a feat, considering how gloomy it already was. The sound, undoubtedly, was made by the flapping wings of the giant bat-birds, those very same creatures that had attacked Kamamakama.

We were about to become airborne in a basket of fuzzy gray melons. Oh, shit.

You have to understand, I don't fly very much. To me, flying ranks up there with oral surgery and bathing in toxic waste. But Kimbal, who I was willing to bet had never been off the ground, seemed all excited about it. Did I really want him to see how much of a chicken-shit I was?

Who cared?

But give me credit, I didn't scream when we were jerked into the air, even though the floor of the basket sagged and groaned beneath us. Nor did I look through one of the holes, not till I was ready. When that finally happened, I saw that we were about a quarter mile above the ground. We were following the Aqapod River, which had narrowed slightly but was still full of those reptilian things. Yep, our carriers were definitely the bat-birds, because I could see one on my side, carrying the other basket. The mutant ET on its back seemed almost bored.

Obviously, we reached Dohnwana quickly. The land surrounding it was black and creepy, like the aftermath of a forest fire. Snakelike things crawled everywhere down there, but we were too high up to see them clearly. And there were more bat-birds in the air, many riderless. Through the gloom, you could barely make out Murlug's small sun overhead.

Dohnwana stood about a hundred yards back from the river. It was an enclosed city, not as vast as I'd expected, but large enough, about the size of your average suburban shopping mall. Vines, crawlers, ferns, and fungus climbed up its walls, as did more of the snake-things we'd been seeing for a while now. The whole aura of it gave me a giant case of the willies.

And somewhere inside that evil place was my Bukko.

The shock of first seeing Dohnwana was lessened slightly by

what we had learned about it from Rovwik and his people. Our basket was deposited on the ground outside the northern wall, dust being raised as the bat-bird hovered for a moment before flying off. Through a higher knothole I could see those snake-things, lots of them, writhing both on the wall and along the base. Not snakes, actually, more like thick, fleshy worms with mandibles at one end. Hideous things about two feet long.

One of them poked its head through a knothole.

Then a second, and a third. Oh, this was great!

Our arms had been pinned to our sides. Now, we tried frantically to move them. But before we could, the worms were pulled out and crushed beneath the four-clawed feet of the white ET-things. A bunch of them had emerged from a door that opened soundlessly on the solid-looking wall. They turned about a dozen of the worms into pâté, and while their kindred fed upon them, the ETs dragged the baskets inside and closed the large door.

Okay, we'd made it; we were in! But we weren't taking time to pound ourselves on the back just yet, not while being dragged along a gravel floor and banged against walls that I don't think were much wider than the basket. I was too busy trying to brace myself to worry about looking out through one of the knotholes; don't think there was too much to see, anyway. The mutants didn't talk the whole time, just made some kind of a grunting noise, which the UT5 must have interpreted as just that, noise.

After a minute of this awful treatment the basket was jerked sharply to the left. The way I figured, we'd just been dragged from the corridor into a room, possibly whatever passed for a kitchen here. The basket was pushed up against a wall. Kimbal couldn't see a thing on his side, but I had a pretty good view.

Yeah, for sure this was the kitchen, because fires burned and caldrons bubbled and ovens baked and all that stuff, and there were aromas, some vaguely familiar and not half-bad, others so disgusting, you wanted to die. They were what I imagined a microwaved rat would smell like after it burst. Half a dozen ETs wearing some sort of white stocking cap (chef's hat? naaah) tended to the food.

The ones who had dragged us in began pulling melons off the top. It occurred to me that we were in trouble here.

But they weren't emptying the baskets, only helping themselves. These ugly fruits must've been some kind of delicacy. One of them sat down with his prize where I could see, and broke the thing open over a bony knee. It cracked, more like an egg than a fruit. The stuff that oozed out of both halves had to be seen to be believed. Imagine taking a jar of *everything* Gerber makes and having a one-year-old mix it all together. The mutant shoved his face into one of the halves, sucked down the mess, then repeated it with the other. He was in hog heaven.

Eventually he and the others left, but more kept drifting in and taking melons. Okay, so we weren't getting crushed as badly; still, if this kept up we would be discovered, and that wasn't in our plans.

The parade finally stopped, and even the chefs drifted out one by one, until the chamber appeared empty. My best guess was that we'd spent four hours in these baskets since the hooded guy told us to get in. Pushing out now through the remaining melons, I heard every joint in my body pop. Kimbal must have felt the same, but he emerged rather stoically.

Ignoring my screaming muscles, I followed the kid toward the door. Halfway there a voice said, "Hey, what are you doing? You're not supposed to be in here!" Weird voice, kind of nasal.

We turned and saw a pasty goblin emerge from between two of the large ovens. The scowl he wore was grotesque and made his face even more malevolent, which was quite a feat.

Putting on my best used-car salesman's grin, I started toward the thing. It was hard to ignore the wicked claws at the end of two spindly arms, but I tried.

"Hiya, pal," I said brightly. "Hey, we must've gotten lost. Can you steer us to the crapper?"

He scratched his head with one of the claws, which must've hurt like hell. "Crapper?" he said. "I don't under—"

I laid him out with a punch to the face, which bruised my hand, because the mutant was mostly bone. He crumpled to the floor like an old skeleton.

"Nice going, Jack," Kimbal said, lifting the body. Before I could ask what he was going to do with it, he pulled one of the oven doors open and threw the thing in. There was a weird popping noise as he slammed the door shut.

Now *that* had taken me by surprise. "Jesus, what did you do that for?" I exclaimed.

Kimbal looked strangely at me. "What else should we have done with it?" he asked.

"We could have tied it up, hid it in a closet or something!"

"And if it was discovered, they would be alerted to our presence. I don't understand you, Jack. We're only talking about a servant of Atoris the Evil here."

He was right; but still, doing what he just did wasn't like wasting them in combat. I had to get used to it, or I wouldn't be worth a damn in Dohnwana.

"Yeah; well, let's go," I said.

We eased out into the corridor. It was hard being stealthy with gravel crunching under our sandals. Moving between the mortared stone walls, I noticed how darkly stained they were in a lot of places. I didn't even want to *think* about what it was.

A door opened suddenly, and one of the mutated ETs stepped (shuffled?) into the corridor. I swung my sword so hard that I nearly cut the thing in two at the waist. Kimbal nodded his approval, then dragged the thing back inside. I'm not sure what he did with it.

The creature's brief scream did not alert any of its buddies. We continued along for another minute, until a noise ahead sent us behind a door and into a dark room. Peering out through a crack, we watched at least a dozen of the things march past. Good call.

When it was quiet again, we started out; but the shaft of light from the corridor illuminated something inside the room, near the back wall; something that didn't quite belong here. Kimbal saw it, too.

"Why, it's like your . . . thing," he said.

Not exactly. This "bicycle" was short, without handlebars. You sat on a round, cushiony *stool* and steered with your feet while pumping two bellows. The tires were big and fat, more like what you'd find on a dune buggy. I studied them, maybe expecting to find a Goodyear or Michelin imprint, but they were perfectly smooth. It seemed so out of place here, especially since I hadn't seen *anything* with wheels on Murlug. I wasn't sure what to make of it.

So let's worry about it later. Back to the corridor, which soon grew wider. The floor changed from gravel to a soft green moss, which also climbed the walls. The silence was unnerving.

Especially when we found ourselves in the midst of people, lots of them, coming out of doors first behind us, then in front. All of them were incredibly beautiful women, and all were in various stages of *clad*, mostly *scantily* and *un-*. In other circumstances, it would've been the closet thing to lecher's heaven; but not here, in the slimy halls of Dohnwana.

We quickly realized they weren't interested in us. Smiling blankly, they formed into two rows and continued down the corridor. Not one even as much as glanced at us.

"Chatana!" Kimbal suddenly exclaimed. "Look, it is Chatana!"

The only thing his girlfriend wore was a smile as she walked past. (Assuming we survived this . . . *God, did I envy the boy!*) Kimbal tried to stop her, but she didn't seem to hear him.

"What has Atoris done to them?" he cried.

"Beats me," I said. "Let's stay close to the ladies. Looks like there might be a party going on."

He didn't know what I was talking about, but so what? We walked between the rows, Kimbal staying close to Chatana. ET-things went past a few times, but we slouched, and they didn't see us.

When the women filed into a big room, we ducked behind a square marble column. Other women were already there, reclining on their knees; forty or fifty, at least. And mutants, only a dozen or so, but *big* suckers, and meaner-looking than any we'd seen before. They were armed, too, with longswords and lances and something that looked like an oversize baby bottle with spikes. Most of them stood along the base of a three-stepped dais, atop which sat this ornate chair, cushioned with red velvet and encrusted with gems. We didn't have to overtax our imaginations to know who it belonged to.

Nothing much seemed to be happening, so we looked around. This was a fancy room, quite a contrast to the slimy corridors. Marble columns, tile floors, satiny tapestries on the walls. Either a thick fur or a brightly colored pillow under each woman, and more surrounding the throne. But none of this could hold Kimbal's attention for long, his eyes returning to Chatana.

A door behind the dais suddenly opened, and Atoris the Evil—*wearing my Bukko around his neck*—emerged. The ET-things bowed their heads to their navels (assuming they had them); the women leaned back and spread their legs.

Now okay, here he was, the baddest of the bad, the honcho of hell, the worst person on the planet, right? You would have figured he'd look like Skeletor, or Darth Vader, or something like that.

Atoris the Evil looked like Lucy and Ricky's landlord, Fred Mertz. Not an exact double, but close enough. He had a lecherous grin on his round, jowly face as he studied the spread-eagled women. His wiry gray hair was done up in a pompadour. This loud, multicolored tunic he wore made him look like a Hawaiian tourist. I had to keep from laughing out loud.

But he *was* evil, make no mistake about it. You could just sort of feel it throbbing in the room. His mutant color guard seemed to thrive on it.

Skipping the throne, he walked to the edge of the top step and clapped his hands three times. Immediately the three nearest women joined him, and they looked real happy about it. They kissed his face, rubbed against him like cats, shoved tongues in his ears, while he did feelies with his chubby little hands. Lifting his tunic, they knelt down and . . .

Well, you don't need a play-by-play of this. Suffice it to say, within a minute they were writhing amid the pillows and furs. Every so often Fred Mertz's grinning face bobbed up through the sea of flesh. Then he dismissed the women, and three others took their place. It started all over again.

When this was repeated a few minutes later, I could tell Kimbal was getting bent out of shape. You see, Chatana was close enough to the dais to be going up there soon, assuming this guy had the staying power, which seemed to be a given. I doubted whether the kid could handle that too well. And if he screwed up . . .

Anyway, that was all taken out of our hands when we felt something sharp jabbing our backs. We'd been so intent on Atoris the Evil that we never saw two of the ET-things come up from behind. They prodded us out into the open, and we moved *real* slow, because I doubt whether they would have thought twice about skewering us.

On the dais furs, pillows, and women flew in all directions as the raging Atoris leaped up and glared at us with furious eyes. "Who dares interrupt my playtime?" he bellowed. "Who . . . *men*? I brought no men to Dohnwana! What do you think I am, anyway? Kill them!"

Hey, no way! These mutants didn't exactly have catlike reflexes. I leaped away as the one behind me shoved his weapon forward. He drew blood, but that was all. I took his feet out from under him, then lopped off his head. (Sorry, that's just where the blade fell, and besides, the heads of these guys came off real easy.) Kimbal, I was glad to see, had also managed to dispatch his guard.

The women had backed away, leaving a wide aisle. On his throne, Fred Mertz was jumping up and down and screaming "Kill them!" over and over. One of the biggest ET-things drew back a long metal bar that looked like a javelin and got ready to heave it. I'm sure he could've impaled both of us with the thing.

I gave him the biggest finger I could muster.

The javelin turned red-hot, but the mutant didn't notice, because he already looked like a lump of Cajun-cooked catfish.

Atoris stopped his ranting, and the room fell silent. He stared at me; I stared back. And in that moment each of us knew the same thing about the other, that we'd both come here from the same place—off the *mhuva lun gallee*. Obviously the bastard had ridden in on the fat-tired "bicycle" I'd seen before.

"How long?" he said malevolently.

"How long *what*?" I replied.

"How long have you been here?"

"A few days."

"I came about twenty years ago."

"Who gives a shit?"

He went on like he hadn't heard me: "I was a criminal on my own world; made a nice living at it, too. But the authorities finally caught up, so I escaped to the Ultimate Bike Path."

(He obviously used his own words for the Path, which the UT5 translated, but I'll tell you, it twinged in my neck like crazy. I'd have to tell the Old Guy to fix it.)

"I wound up on Murlug," he continued, "and soon discovered the immense powers that off-worlders have here. So I turned those powers toward evil, which is much more fun, and if I say so myself, I'm set up quite nicely."

"You lowlife dirtbag, screwing with all these people," I said angrily. "They have lives, they don't want to be stuck doing nothing but humping an old piece of shit like you!"

Fred Mertz was really getting pissed off. "You *dare* talk to me like that?" he shrieked. "I can crush you in an instant! You're too new, and your powers are nothing compared to mine!"

Yeah, why *was* I talking to him like that? He still had the Bukko, and I didn't have a death wish. But I kept it up.

"If you tried to hit on one of these women without controlling their minds, they'd either laugh their heads off or throw up. Boy, they probably hate being *gummed*!"

Now he totally lost it. Screaming curses that almost short-circuited the UT5, he began flailing both arms over his head. Bolts of lightning from his fingers shot up to the ceiling and ripped out huge chunks, which rained to the floor. You'd think this would've stopped him, but he was out of control and couldn't do a thing about it.

"Get the women out!" I told Kimbal.

If this guy was going to get buried, I wanted the Bukko back before it happened. While Kimbal, helped by Chatana, guided the frightened women to the door, I ran to the dais. The mutants were no challenge, because they wanted out also. Hell, they were ugly, but they weren't stupid.

Bolts continued to fly from Fred Mertz's hands (I swear, you'd think he was doing the Monkey) as I leaped up on the dais. The look he gave me was as much fear as malevolence. Dodging a five-pound chunk of the ceiling, I grabbed the Bukko and pulled it over his head.

"Wait! We can be partners!" he shrieked. "I'm not proud! I'll grovel, I'll beg!"

"You know what Arnold Schwarzenegger would say to that?" I asked him.

"Huh? What?"

"Fokk you, asshull!"

I ran from the dais with a wary eye on the ceiling. Kimbal had been less benevolent than me regarding the fate of the mutant ETs. Along with Chatana and a few other women, all of them well-armed, he had carved up the servants of the evil one. Stepping between the bodies, I joined the kid at the door.

"Hey, help me!" Fred Mertz cried as the chunks came down around him.

I looked at Kimbal and shrugged. "Hate to see a guy suffer," I said, and threw *two* fickle fingers at the ceiling.

Atoris the Evil, master of Murlug, autocrat of Areelkrokka, doyen of Dohnwana, was crushed to death.

CHAPTER 15

Thank You, Old Guy

So, what do you think happened after that? Just what you might expect when you've done away with something so *evil*. Sunshine broke through the smog of Areelkrokka, and the Aqapod River looked like the place where Sparkletts got their water, and the humungous reptiles were gone, and all the mutated ETs began dropping like flies, and birds sang, and all that good stuff. As for me, the Bukko was back around my neck, and I must've been kissed by every woman in Dohnwana, so you think I was happy?

Naaaah.

We had one problem: You see, in keeping with the theme of evilness and vileness, Atoris had built Dohnwana in the middle of a mucky swamp. Now, without his powers, it was sinking into the mire. It would take a while; I mean, it wasn't dropping like a stone. But as this foul-smelling mud began oozing up through the cracks, we knew it was time to go. We searched the place, making sure every woman there (women really *were* all he had) was led to safety.

Later, everyone was gathered at the river; it looked like a big communal baptism. Dohnwana was now halfway under and sinking more rapidly. No great loss, that wretched building; it would never have made the cover of *Architectural Digest*. A fitting tomb for Atoris the Evil, I would say.

There were a couple of things on my mind. First, it occurred to me that since the time I'd laid eyes upon Kamamakama a few days ago, this trip to Murlug had been one continuing episode of déjà vu. Change the names and the faces, and I knew this story pretty well. I wasn't sure I'd *ever* be able to write another *Brain Ingestors of Musi* again.

And the second thing was, I wanted to be wearing spandex pants, and a road jersey, and my Padres hat, and be back on my bike again, and *out of here*!

Sure, it was a long way back to Kamamakama, but I wasn't some ordinary *shlub* anymore, was I? High overhead, bat-birds floated aimlessly on wind currents. Their riders, probably creations of Atoris the Evil, had perished, but these things lived, because they were real. Holding up an entire hand this time, I drew one of them down slowly. The beastie even let me pet it, which impressed Kimbal and the women no end.

"Don't tell me," the kid said. "You intend to ride this back to Kamamakama."

"Right on, pal."

"If you don't mind, Chatana and I will go with you. We must let our people know what has happened."

The scores of women had already begun taking charge of their destiny. They would leave this place in four large groups on the way back to their various homelands, where they would resume their lives. Most had only been away a couple of years or less, Atoris preferring them young and fresh. I didn't even want to think about what he'd done over two decades with those who had grown too old. Once again the women thanked me profusely (I liked that!), and I climbed atop the bat-bird with Chatana and Kimbal.

Let me tell you, it was one hell of a ride! The bat-bird was a docile creature and responded well to the reins. We dove low over the fields of the hooded people, then down to Rovwik's village on the other side of the mountains, shouting the good news, although these people had already figured it out, being in bright sunlight. Beyond there, we gave the bat-bird its head and were soon over what had once been the dreaded edge of Areelkrokka.

But the sun was going down, and the day had worn us out; you can imagine. So we stopped to rest, and I tethered the bat-bird.

Kimbal and Chatana were glad to be together again; *really* glad. After dinner I turned in some distance away, although in the quiet of the night I was still within earshot. It was sort of fun listening to them.

Sort of.

The next morning, as the apricot sun peeked over the horizon, we were on our way again. We spread the word to every village we passed; scared the hell out of everyone as we swooped down, but then, what could we do? It wasn't like we were in the Goodyear blimp or something, with graphics on the side. Anyway, the people were pretty happy, once they knew. This was especially true in Gwonnis, where the leaders begged us to come down and be feted like heroes. (Uh, leave the creature out of town somewhere, why don't you?) We respectfully declined.

Deciding to let the rest of the Selwok Valley find out by word of mouth, we sped directly to Kamamakama. After so recent an attack, these folks were ready to kick some ass. Fortunately they spotted the smiling Chatana and Kimbal while we were still in the air, and restrained themselves. You can imagine what kind of nifty reunion followed, once we were down. Even Manny, Moe, and Jack took time from their busy schedules to greet us.

Okay, I could have hung out there a couple of more days, and this time I *would've* been treated like a god, or at the very least, a king. But I was firm on leaving, and that was that. I said my good-byes all around, taking a few seconds longer with Wistilla, Kimbal's mother. She *almost* convinced me to stay, but . . .

So for the last time, I rode with Chatana and Kimbal. It took all of a few minutes to reach the cave in the foothills, where the Nishiki was hidden, on the back of the bat-bird. Their plan had been to release the creature, once this was done. But it had grown fond of Chatana and was like a big, affectionate (ugly) puppy, so they decided to keep it. I convinced them that they could revolutionize travel all over Murlug, become captains of transportation, and they got off on that. Kimbal especially liked the idea of being able to visit the Great Ocean to the west, meet the brave people of Del Mar and see them depress the roaring water tongues.

While I was changing inside the cave, Chatana and Kimbal cleared the worst debris off a steep slope, as I had instructed. I could've used the bat-bird to put me on top, but this was my last few minutes with the pair, so we walked up. Chatana gawked at my weird clothes, and the bike. I didn't say anything about it, but now that they'd been exposed to the wheel, it was possible the enterprising pair could really corner the market for getting around both on land and in the air. It might be fun to come back in a few years and see what happened.

As we neared the top of the slope, Kimbal whispered something to Chatana. Together they dropped to one knee and bowed their heads. Jeez, not this again!

"Kimbal, I thought we already went through—"

He silenced me with a wave of his hand. "We know you're not a god, Jack, but what you've done for Murlug is befitting of a god, and we wanted to honor you accordingly." They stood.

"All of Murlug will know your name," Chatana added, "and sing your praises."

Hey, wouldn't *that* be nifty to come back to!

We were at the top. I pumped Kimbal's hand, hugged Chatana for a few seconds (God, that lucky kid!), then started down, building speed rapidly. Fully aware that I would be adding to the legend of the wonderful visitor from Del Mar who destroyed Atoris the Evil, I shifted into the Vurdabrok Gear and left them gaping at the empty hillside.

It was obviously not the best angle to enter the Ultimate Bike Path, because I nearly ran into one of the rust-red walls before veering away and righting myself. Now I was cruising again, maintaining a steady cadence, each of the now-familiar gates stopping for at least a count of two before whizzing by. It wasn't like being back in my condo or anything, but riding the Path again gave me a sort of secure feeling.

Now detached from my latest adventure, I could look at it more objectively. Hey, considering I was scared shitless a lot of the time, I did pretty good! Got back the Bukko, freed all those people, offed a really bad dude. The Old Guy and his cronies, who for sure had been watching, got themselves a damn good show.

Didn't they?

Scenario: Study Group coming together again after their diversion.

Study Group Old Guy #1: "So, Jack rides the *mhuva lun gallee* again, and the Bukko is around his neck. Then everything turned out well."

My Old Guy (pissed off): "No thanks to us. I feel terrible about leaving him in those circumstances. Had he died, I'm afraid we would have had to break some heavy universal rules to rectify the situation."

Study Group Old Guy #2: "Unthinkable! In any case I had a look into the future of that world, and it seems that Jack's brief time there had a considerable impact. A network of fine roads and highways crisscross Murlug, which has become quite an industrial world. Wheeled vehicles of every kind abound, as do airports for the flying creatures, which carry gondolas of people over great distances. Kimbal and Chatana, his wife, were responsible for this, as well as a theme park called Evil World, built near swampland in Areelkrokka. They have since retired to a resort along the Great Ocean, where Kimbal spends much of his time riding boards atop giant waves. Their oldest son, Jack, is running the business."

My Old Guy (wondering about *boards atop giant waves*): "I'm glad that came to pass, but I still feel badly about abandoning Jack. It will not happen again." (Thinks a minute.) "And so as not to feel guilty, I will do so something for him."

I was still riding along, not in any particular hurry, when I saw the first sign. It wasn't like the time before; you know, when the Old Guy left those few words in yellow neon over the door back to Camp Pendleton. No, this sign was of some glittery silver stuff, kind of insubstantial, that used the rust-red walls between gates as a backdrop.

And I do mean *first*, because there were a few of them in sequence, like those old Burma Shave billboards you used to see along freeways and turnpikes. They don't mean anything until you read the last one, so you get interested in the damn things and wind up creating a twenty-one car pile-up or something.

Anyway, the first shimmering sign said: GREAT PIECE OF ADVENTURE, JACK! WE OF THE STUDY GROUP . . .

That's how it ended, with ellipsis points, those three dots that let you know more is on the way. It wasn't too long before the next message: . . . ARE VERY IMPRESSED WITH YOUR FORTITUDE. TO SHOW . . .

It was weird, watching those letters break apart into nothing an instant after you went past. The third one said: . . . MY APPRE-CIATION, SINCE I AM THE ONE WHO CHOSE YOU . . .

Yeah, yeah, what already? This could get annoying.

. . . KEEP YOUR EYES ON THE GATES AHEAD.

Period. That was it. No more glitter signs. Keep your eyes on . . . What'd he *think* I was doing?

For a while now, most of the gates had been those iridescent snowmen. Seeing a particular one, I suddenly understood.

It had a yellow ribbon tied around some of its needles.

Some of its seventy-three thousand four hundred and ninety-two needles.

I turned the bike rather sharply.

Thank you, Old Guy.

CHAPTER 16

The Source of the Light

Okay, here I am, back on the Ultimate Bike Path again. Well, *sor-ree*, but there are some things you don't want to discuss in any great detail unless you've had quite a few beers and are with your best buddies.

A whole world full of feline females, all of whom looked and smelled like Hormona and who, on the whole, really loved their work!

In the immortal words of a scholarly southern sage: *Yeee-hah!*

Now then, Miller, time for proper decorum. Sitting regally atop the Nishiki, I rode steadily along the *mhuva lun gallee*. No gate appealed to me at the moment, which was okay. I even passed the misty blue door back to my own place and time without hardly a glance. Later, for that; all I wanted to do was ride.

But before long there was a dominant succession of those creepy Bart Simpson heads, and it was really bothering me to stop for a second in front of them. I pedaled harder, and they passed more quickly, but even that wasn't enough.

So for the first time on the Path I *really* began working, and the Bart Simpsons became one long blur. I concentrated on what was directly ahead, scared that I would overtake another rider and send us both toppling to the "ground." (What then? Bread-slicing time?) But just like San Onofre State Park on a cold weekday morning in February, I was the only one pedaling along.

Hey, now *this* was great! A little scary at first, but you get over it. After a while I was kind of sure those ominous gates were behind me, but I continued pedaling fast, because I was enjoying it. In fact, I even speeded up, until I reached a point where up, down, backward, and forward were all sort of the same, which was when I decided to back off. But wow, what a trip while it lasted!

I was right, no more Bart Simpsons. The familiar ones: Elmer Fudds, black circles with bread slicers, lots of Floridas with Stetson hats. Just like with the iridescent snowmen, I had no clue how anyone could tell these Florida gates apart. But after watching them pass for a while, I knew. The hat part very often changed its shape, and there were dots on the state part, like cities on a Triple A map, except these always changed their positions, and they ranged from a few to many hundreds. Hard to figure out, but for sure a lot easier than the iridescent snowmen and their laser needles.

Just then, about two dozen riders passed me in the opposite direction. Now *that* was a surprise. Their conveyances were the closest things I'd yet seen to our kind of bicycles. Each one had skinny racing tires with eight thick gold spokes emanating from a ball-shaped hub. There was something like a derailleur, two curved handlebars, and a narrow, contoured seat that looked like it had been carved out of stone.

The riders atop these boxy-framed bikes were bony and green, for the most part looking like the things Sigourney Weaver had kicked the shit out of in *Aliens*. Except for their heads, which were grapefruit-sized and grapefruit-colored and mostly mouth, a wide, toothy one under two raisin dots that were eyes. Nothing like a nose that I could see, but each of them did have this stovepipe-shaped protuberance on top, which might have been part of their heads, or perhaps the standard riding helmet of their club. They grinned at me as they sped past, these score or more Tom Pettys, waved a bony hand, finger, whatever. At least an incubus-demon from their own version of hell wasn't pursuing them.

Okay, back to the gates. I was leaning toward trying one of the Floridas, since it would have been something new. Almost made my choice, too, when . . .

. . . *it happened*.

Yeah, really dramatic. Amid all these Floridas, a different gate was suddenly there. Not spectacular-looking, as so many were. Smaller, too. It was diamond-shaped and appeared solid white, no exploding fireworks, no revolving pyramids. A simple gate, but irresistible; Jeez, *was it ever!* It beckoned to me as no portal along the Ultimate Bike Path had yet done. In that split second I knew there wasn't any way I could refuse the call. I angled toward it.

(Diamond-shaped, I remember thinking as I passed through the gate. Maybe this was the way to Ray Kinsella's *Field of Dreams*.)

I don't recall shifting down out of the Vurdabrok Gear, but I must have. What was this place? *What was it?* Light, all around me an eternity of light; not soft-white, like from the gate, but brilliant light, a hundred, a *thousand* times more bright, and yet gentle, because you could look at it, beyond it, into it. Not like the endless strobes and flashes in my first port of call along the Path. Not like that at all.

What was this place?

I was standing next to the bike; don't remember climbing off it, either. But what was I standing *on*? A hard surface, cloud-white and flecked like marble, but rough to the touch, feeling similar to sandstone. Pretty deceiving but good for footing, as I learned when I risked a few steps. Wow, where had my equilibrium gone? My head swam, and for a moment it was like speeding on the Path again, when perception of up and down had been meaningless. I was glad when it passed.

No, I wasn't looking *at* light, or *beyond* it, because this place *was* light, and I was *inside* it. Does that make any sense at all? I started walking, found I was on a downhill slope, not real steep. There was no "sky" overhead, only something that was disconcertingly similar to what I walked upon. A "ceiling"? No, too high. On the other hand, sometimes it was infinitely distant, while a moment later it seemed so low that I instinctively ducked my head. Really weird.

And what about the clouds? They were definitely low, these giant puffy footballs, and impregnated with veins of gold and silver, like threads. I touched one as it passed over my head and felt this tingling sensation all through my body; kind of pleasant, actually. The small tendrils of vapor I'd coaxed free almost immediately snapped back to the cloud, as a little kid would run to his mother when something scared him.

Hey, wait a minute, I got it! This was the place the Old Guy came from, right? All this whiteness, the light. Sure, what else? He wanted to see me, introduce me to his pals. Maybe they wanted to have a meeting, a power lunch, something like that.

No, that's not right, Miller, and you know it. This place was something else.

Something special.

I wasn't cold, or hot, or uncomfortable in any way. Just the opposite, I really felt great. Even the cuts and bruises from recent exploits, which had hardly begun to heal, didn't hurt at all. And there was a spiritual healing *inside*, because every fiber of my being was at peace with itself, and part of a greater whole. I suppose this was what achieving harmony or reaching nirvana might feel like, although not being a metaphysical person, I couldn't say for sure.

Whatever, I was prepared to enjoy the feeling for as long as it lasted. The slope leveled out, something I was more able to sense than see, and I continued walking, not having a direction, not needing one, because I was being drawn to my destination, led along, as though the light had folded itself around my heart and was tugging it benevolently. The smile I wore was of infinite placidity. Jeez, this was great!

I continued on through the wonderful light. Somewhere along the way I'd gotten back on my bike and was pedaling slowly, but I could not recall doing it. Even the Nishiki seemed to know where it was going, like it too had a soul, or a manitou, or whatever. I can't begin to guess at how long I rode, because time here—even more so than on the Ultimate Bike Path—seemed a meaningless concept.

The tugging grew stronger, and I knew that I was coming nearer to the core of the light.

Now the smooth-looking, coarse-feeling ground began to slope upward. I shifted down a couple of gears and hardly noticed the change. Seductively overwhelming, such was the power of the throbbing light. I *had* to reach the source.

The hill grew steeper, and I kept on shifting down. Soon I had gone through over half the gears, but the incline continued to fight me. Didn't matter. I would've found a way, even if it was straight up. There was no stopping, no turning back, no way to resist this wonderful, incandescent summons.

Not many gears left now. My legs should have been protesting, as they had been for most of the way up the hill; but just the opposite. They seemed lighter than air, as if they weren't there. I thought that perhaps they'd gone numb, which freaked me out. Uh-uh, not so. A miraculous, pain-relieving warmth was spreading through them, like a generous shot of cortisone. I pedaled all the harder, anxious to reach the summit.

Then, it was there; the core of this fantastic incandescence . . . *the source of the light*. Brighter than ever, and yet you could still look at it. I didn't even consider reaching for my Gargoyles as I climbed off the bike. For an instant I nearly lost my balance, and considering how far I'd come, the trip down would have been a long one. But

I caught myself, and three straining steps later I walked upon level ground, atop the summit, only a few yards from . . . *the source*.

Broad beams of pulsating light emanated in a divine-looking semicircle from this white-robed figure, who sat cross-legged, hands folded in his lap. I first thought him to be a giant, but no, that was more expectation than reality, because I don't think he was any taller than me. The beams of light rose to the "ceiling" of this place, then were deflected, spreading out like a sentient umbrella.

This place. Was it . . . ? Could it be . . . ?

The white-robed being, the source of the light. Was he . . . ? You know.

Shaking now, I put the bike down gently and took a few steps closer. I was on the right side of the source. His long hair and great flowing beard were as pure white as his robe. An ample nose protruded from the hirsute countenance. His brow was creased with the thoughts of millennia. I wasn't even sure he would notice me, but his head turned, and these incredibly blue eyes—deep, all-knowing, and gentle—fell upon my humble self. My knees; yes, I was compelled to fall to my knees, and I continued to gaze at him, seeing the heavy lips part within the folds of the beard. *He was going to speak to me!*

"What the fuck do *you* want?" he said.

O-*kay*, that dispelled the divine illusion. I stood up on legs that were no longer shaking. The beams of light still radiated, halolike, from the guy, but without the same brightness. Those eyes of ultimate wisdom and benevolence squinted as they took me in.

Dumbly I said, "I, uh, just, I mean, you . . ."

"Do you have a tongue, or what?" he snapped. "A waste of my time, that's what it is."

"Time?"

"Yes, time, you know? 'Dost though love life, then do not squander time, for that's the stuff life is made of.' Benjamin Franklin said that, in case you give a shit."

"You know Benjamin Franklin?"

He shook his white mane. "The man's dead, or haven't you heard? But I know his words. I know *everyone's* words, from *everywhere*." He shrugged and muttered, "Come all the way up here for a little privacy and some asshole still finds me."

Hey, divine or not, this was a crock! "Sorry to intrude," I told him dryly, bending over for the bike. "I'm outta here."

"Don't go away mad, just go away," he said.

"Oh, very original." I started for the slope.

"Hey, are you really leaving?" he called.

"Yeah, I'm not gonna stand here and get insulted."

"Sorry about that. 'But we all go a little mad sometimes.' "

"Hey, Norman Bates said that!"

"Good, very good. Come and sit down; we'll chat."

Was this guy a pip? He gives me tons of crap, then invites me over. Okay, I climbed up all this way, might as well find out what was going on. I sat cross-legged in front of him.

"Oftentimes my mouth gets me into trouble," he went on. "As it is said: 'The cesspool of a man's mouth is directly inviolable to the candle's flame on the underwear of a carpenter.' "

Say what? The UT5 nearly short-circuited. "Who said that?" I asked.

"Tinka the Wise, of Pruntor, who else? Very famous words."

Obviously, something was lost in the translation. I stopped rubbing my neck. "Anyway, I'm Jack Miller," I told him.

"Yes, I knew that."

"You did?"

He didn't elaborate. "My name is Ralph Ralph. You can call me Ralph."

Okay. "Yeah, right. Listen . . . *Ralph*, I was wondering—"

"Oh, please," he interrupted, "I hate it when someone calls another by his last name. So impersonal, you know."

This was weird. "Uh-huh. Sorry. Okay . . . Ralph, I was wondering—"

"That's better."

"—what this place was." I gestured all around. "I mean, where are we?"

He glanced around too, apparently puzzled by my question. It occurred to me that he looked just like Charlton Heston as Moses right at the end of *The Ten Commandments*. You remember, where he doesn't cross the Jordan River with his people but goes off to meet his Maker instead.

"Why, we are *here!*" he exclaimed. "Where else could we be?" He thought a moment. "As it is said: 'The place of a man's toes is rooted in the yellow light bulbs of decayed bonsai trees.' "

Ow, my neck! *Jesus!* "Are there . . . others like you around?" I managed to gasp, after the twinging stopped.

"Oh, far too many! Mostly assholes, too. That's why I come way up into this cave, to get away from the great unwashed."

I nodded vaguely. "This is a cave."

"Oh, I hate crowds, don't you?" he went on. "As it is said: 'I would rather sit on a pumpkin and have it all to myself than be crowded on a velvet cushion.' "

I braced myself for the twinge, but nothing happened, and I remembered that those were the words of Henry Thoreau. "But, Ralph, doesn't your world have a name?" I was persistent.

"A name, a name. What's in a name? As it is said—"

Oh, shit!

"—'A name is a washcloth in the back of a chair when the green diarrhea erupts from a frying pan of gold and feathers.' Uh, Jack is something wrong?"

I was holding my neck, gnashing my teeth. "It wasn't that tough a question," I said angrily. "I mean, if you would've said, 'Jack, where are you from?' I would've answered, 'Oh, I'm from Earth.' See how easy?"

"Yes, I know you were from Earth."

Oh, yeah, bullshit! "How did you know that?"

"You knew the words of the famous Earth philosopher Norman Bates. Despite the look of a dullard, Jack, you must be a wise man, and I do respect wisdom. As it is said—"

"No, don't say it!" I exclaimed.

"Why not?" He was puzzled.

"Because your quotes are giving me a big pain in the neck. This damn translator's going to have to be adjusted. So please, Ralph, cool it for now."

"But quoting the great minds of the universe is my reason for being. I can't stop for too long, Jack. It is to me what breathing is to you."

"Then there's no choice, I'll have to leave. I'm talking serious pain here."

"Well, I understand," he said dejectedly. "Shitsticks!"

Shitsticks? "Maybe I'll stop by again some other time, when the UT5 is working."

Those benevolent eyes brightened. "Oh, will you?"

Between you and me, I'd only said that to be polite; you know how it goes. But if you thought about it, Ralph Ralph here could spout the wisdom of *everyone* in the whole damn universe! Pretty impressive. I could learn a lot, assuming the thing in my neck was functional. And despite his bent to rudeness, it was still sort of warm and peaceful sitting near him on this mountaintop inside a cave, or wherever we were.

"Yeah, I promise," I told him.

"Oh, hot damn!" he exclaimed happily. "We will be good friends, Jack, you'll see. As it is said: 'A man must eat a peck of salt with his friend before he knows him.'"

I braced for the twinge, but it didn't happen. Ralph Ralph winked at me. "Cervantes," he said.

I walked the bike to the rim of the hill, where I paused and looked back. The light again pulsated strongly from the source, bringing the cloud-white "ceiling" alive. Despite what I now knew (what *did* I know?), I couldn't help wondering the same thing as before.

This place, was it . . . ?

Ralph Ralph, the source of the light, was he . . . ?

You know.

CHAPTER 17

Reality Time

"Yes, Jack, we were aware of the problems you've been encountering with the UT5. Unfortunately, nothing could be done until you came back."

I was sitting with the Old Guy on the rocks under the Santa Margarita River bridge. Together we were doing a good job of pissing off lots of swallows, which scolded us as they flitted in and out of their mud condos. He was holding this short metal stick, which reminded me of a cattle prod. I was afraid to ask what it was for.

"Can you fix it easily enough?" I asked.

"No need to. Yours wasn't the only UT5 presently failing in field tests. So we simply developed a new model." He stuck a finger in his ear (to look up a word, I guess), smiled, and extracted it. "Violà, the UT6," he said, opening his hand and showing me another tiny power cell.

"So . . . what happens to the UT5?" I asked.

He held up the cattle prod. "We remove it."

Shit, I was afraid of that!

Actually, it wasn't bad at all. He put it to my neck, like they do with those future hypodermic syringes on *Star Trek*, and did something with it (don't ask me, my eyes were shut). There was a slurping noise, like sucking up the end of your drink through a straw, and the UT5 was out! It only hurt for an instant, just like the first time, when he inserted the UT6.

"So, are you going right back, Jack?" he asked as we climbed up to Stuart Mesa Road.

"Not yet," I told him. "As exciting as traveling the Ultimate Bike Path is, I find an occasional need for some . . . reality time, I guess you could call it."

He thought about that a moment, but didn't use the finger. "Yes, I understand. Take your time, Jack; we have other projects to divert us. But speaking for the entire study group, I have to say you are one of the most interesting subjects we've ever observed.

We will look forward to following you again. Er, when will that be?"

"Let's try for tomorrow morning. If anything changes . . ."

"You'll let us know?"

I looked at him. "Are you watching *everything* I do?"

He smiled. "We know when to be discreet."

I thought about the day (or so) I'd spent on Vulvan and hoped that was one of those times. We climbed on our bikes, and he smiled at me again. I gotta say, he was quite the expert at smiling now.

He wanted me to ride off first, so I did. I could see about a hundred yards behind me in the little bike mirror attached to the side of my helmet. When I turned the corner and started up the Vandegrift Boulevard hill, he was still coming. But although I kept looking back, the Old Guy never made the intersection.

Jeez, where did he go? One day, I swore, I would stake out this road!

Anyway, I drove back to Del Mar and was there a little past eight. Now I wasn't exactly what you would call *refreshed*. What I probably should have done after leaving Ralph Ralph and his Electric Light Bulb Arcade was go through *any* gate, catch a few Zs, *then* come back. But I really had an urgent need for reality, and the last trip, despite the long uphill climb, hadn't been *that* draining, thanks to the power of the wonderful light. Besides, when Phil Melkowitz says he'll be over at nine, it's as good as nine-thirty, so I had nearly an hour and a half to rest up.

Surprise, Phil was waiting on my doorstep. The last time he'd gotten up this early on a Saturday, JFK was chasing Russians out of Cuba. Just my luck.

"Started without me, huh?" he said brightly. Jeez, I'd never seen him so wide awake!

"Just up to Encinitas," I replied. "Figured I'd have most of the morning to kill waiting for you."

"So how come you took your car?"

"Uh . . . never mind. I need some coffee."

So, did I even have to *guess* why my buddy was so bright-eyed and bushy-tailed this morning? Yeah, his date with Jennifer King last night had gone just great, and the play was wonderful, and thank you, Jack, and their relationship was getting better, and after the play . . .

And so on and so on.

"Too bad about what happened with Paula," he finally said. "But you know, maybe it was for the better. I mean, she *was* kind of a slut and all."

"Yeah, but a slut's nice once in a while. Besides, how often do you find a woman who likes Pat Metheny, Bruce Springsteen, *and* the New York Philharmonic at the same time?"

Now Phil could be a schmuck upon occasion, but basically he was a good person, so I was a little taken back by his insensitivity. But this gleam in his eye told me that he had something else on his mind, and as we drove off with our bikes in back of his Isuzu pickup, I found out what it was.

First off, I mentioned that we were going riding on Saturday, but I don't think I said where. Guess what, it was up to Orange County through Camp Pendleton! Yep, I was going back again. Well, that was okay. Phil had brought along his older twelve-speed Centurion LeMans with the skinny 25mm tires, which could leave my mountain bike in the lurch if you just blew on it. That's what he used for street riding. When we went off-road, like the desert or something, he switched to *his* new mountain bike, a Nishiki Alien, which cost even more than mine. (That's what it's called, the *Alien*, I swear to God! You think I'd make it up? Would've been one helluva coincidence if that's what I was riding.) Yeah, he had two good bikes, Phil did.

So with his Centurion and my Nishiki in back of the pickup, we started north on Interstate 5. Phil glanced at me, and he had this shit-eating grin on his face to go with the gleam.

"So all right, already," I said, "tell me what's rattling around in that warped brain of yours."

"I'm seeing Jennifer again tonight. Nothing elaborate. Pizza at her place, maybe a Blockbuster video."

"Oh, great, I'm so happy for you. Is that it?" *What* was he getting at.

"You have a date too."

"I have a . . . ? Oh, no, tell me you didn't! Not another blind date! You remember the last one? The medical lab assistant with the black belt in karate?"

"That was a fine-looking lady—"

"She spent most of the evening talking about urinalysis. I was afraid to hit on her, didn't know if she'd give me a blood test or break me in two! No thanks, pal."

He shrugged. "Okay."

We were quiet for half a minute; then, I couldn't stand it anymore. "Who is she?"

"Jennifer's cousin from Iowa, Holly Dragonette."

"Holly Dragonette? You're kidding! Holly *Dragonette*? And she's from *Iowa*, Phil? That's great!"

"Her company's transferring her out here by request," he said patiently. "She's in town looking for a place to live. Holly's twenty-eight, never been married, has a great personality."

"Yeah, they always do. What does she look like?"

The gleam again. "You know how Jane Pauley turns you on? Well, think of a young, outdoorsy Jane Pauley and you got Holly."

"Yeah?"

A yellow Porsche veered across three lanes and cut in front of us. Its bumper sticker read: DON'T LIKE MY DRIVING? DIAL 1-800-EAT SHIT. "I kid you not, my man," he said. "So are you going, or what?"

What do you think? Jane Pauley; oh, wow! "Well, I guess so," I told him, trying to be cool.

"Good, 'cause I already said you'd be there."

That's my buddy, Phil Melkowitz. Kind of like having your mother around, huh?

Anyway, we took our ride through Camp Pendleton up to Dana Point, and I don't need to give you a play-by-play, because it was pretty ordinary. But remember what I had said about needing *reality time*? Well, now I totally understood what I had meant by it. Here I was, riding with my best friend, throwing the usual bullshit back and forth, anticipating a date with a lady from Iowa who looked like Jane Pauley. Nothing monumental or out of the ordinary, like saving an entire world from the forces of evil or running into the sexiest cat-woman in the universe or climbing a mountain of light and meeting . . .

You know.

But it was all of those things that made this so . . . *real*, so special. That's what I mean by *reality time*. Traveling along the Ultimate Bike Path was fantastic, and it would forever set me apart from everyone on the planet. But like some old song said, you can't have one without the other. And right now, I was exactly where I wanted to be. Maybe the Old Guy and his pals in the study group didn't find this too exciting, but who cared?

Hey, let me tell you, Holly Dragonette was *wonderful*. Made me forget about Paula Kaufman real quick. She definitely could've been Jane Pauley's kid sister. And brains? A master's degree in microbiology, going for a Ph.D. would you believe? Loved the outdoors, *especially* biking. We're going to ride later in the day tomorrow, *after* we've had brunch and I've taken her around Del Mar to look at apartments and condos.

I went to sleep Saturday night thinking how great reality time was.

On Sunday I was supposed to meet Holly at ten A.M.

But seven A.M. came first, and for now reality time was over.

CHAPTER 18

Indiana Jones, Where Are you?

This time I biked a *really* long distance on the Ultimate Bike Path. I'm not kidding, I did. Sure, with no way to measure time it was impossible to say just *how* far. But some things you just *know*, and I don't have a doubt in my mind this was the farthest I'd pedaled since the last excursion, when I'd come across the white, diamond-shaped gate, the irresistible one.

Who knows? Maybe it was having this glowing portal on my mind that kept me pumping as long as I did. A chance to go back, sit at the feet of Ralph Ralph, learn the secrets of the universe through the new and improved translator in my neck . . . Yeah, that had a certain appeal. On the other hand, maybe I wasn't ready to hear such things, maybe I needed a romp through the wonders of the *mhuva lun gallee* before my brain could accept the responsibility of bearing such wisdom.

Whatever the case, no gate ever remotely similar to the diamond of light appeared, and I started to get tired. Not physically tired, since the path was easy enough to travel; more like bored-tired. I hadn't run into a single alien rider the whole way, and the gates were all familiar ones. Lots of iridescent snowmen; even saw the one with the yellow ribbon. (The Old Guy hadn't removed it yet, and heck, *I* wasn't about to!) But I didn't plan on stopping there. Reality time still had a toehold on my mind, and I really *was* looking forward to seeing Holly Dragonette in three hours (or three years, or something).

So I decided on a Florida gate, which had been my choice prior to the encounter with Ralph Ralph. They had been scarce for a while but now dominated, along with the isosceles triangles. I skipped a few, finally turned toward one with the fewest dots I'd yet seen. From what I knew about the state, the three largest dots were located around Tampa, Fort Lauderdale, and Orlando. Four others were in the panhandle, the last in the middle of the Stetson hat. I went through with a sound that was like pulling a deeply embedded spoon out of a bowl of Jell-O . . .

◆ ◆ ◆

. . . and shifted down from the Vurdabrok Gear.

Or maybe I shouldn't have, because for a moment it still looked like I was on the Ultimate Bike Path.

No, an illusion, just an instant of disorientation. Sure, this was a tunnel, but not an ethereal one. The only red in the otherwise dirty gray walls were thin, weblike veins, and there were no gates, glowing or otherwise. The Nishiki's fat tires bit into a sandy, rock-strewn floor, an awful surface. I climbed off and walked along the eight-foot-wide passageway, which was dimly lit from somewhere overhead, although I couldn't see the source. All in all, I had a sense of something familiar here. Christ, not déjà vu again!

It had been deathly silent, but now there was a rumbling sound, like a freight train coming through a mountain. I turned and saw this boulder, a *huge* one, filling up nearly the entire shaft. It was ten yards away but gathering momentum as it rolled toward me.

So, can you figure out why this place struck me as being familiar? Yeah, it was a scene out of *Raiders of the Lost Ark*. Only I wasn't Indiana Jones, and this wasn't a movie!

The big rock was bearing down on my ass!

Okay, not panic time yet. I could still outrun it, even pushing my bike along the miserable floor. No way was I going to abandon the Nishiki. There had to be niches somewhere, narrower tunnels, holes in the ground . . . anything! Nope, there weren't, and when I looked back, the boulder had gained a couple of yards.

Up ahead, the tunnel split into a Y. Both new shafts were identical. Now, it was logical to assume that the rock could only go one way, so I had a fifty-fifty chance of avoiding it. Hell, even Vegas won't give you those kind of odds!

I chose the left fork and hurried down it about five yards. Behind, the boulder struck the junction hard, causing the tunnel to shake with something that felt like a 6.4. I let go of the bike, then stumbled over it and rolled a couple of more yards. Stunned, I looked up.

The boulder hung at the junction for a moment, then started along the tunnel I'd chosen. Like, what else?

This shaft sloped downward, which is why I had wound up so far past the Nishiki. For that reason, the boulder was reacting like an eight ball that had just been shot into a side pocket and was now descending into pool-ball purgatory, or wherever they went inside a table. In about two seconds I was going to be transformed into a tortilla.

Let me tell you something about those two seconds. You've heard that business about your whole life flashing before you when you're about to die or get seriously hurt, right? Now I'm not sure I covered the whole thirty-four years, but I do remember some pretty weird shit rattling around.

Like how much punishment my Bell helmet—still on over my Padres cap—could withstand. Imagine what a beneficial thing this could be for the manufacturer: *Sure, the rest of his body you could've wrapped around refried beans and shredded beef, but he suffered no head injuries.*

Another thing I thought about was Roger Maris.

I had been watching the game on television in 1961 when Maris hit his sixty-first home run into the short right-field seats of Yankee Stadium. At least, that's what Henry Miller (my father, remember?) always told me when I was growing up, because who remembers *anything* about when you were that little? I'd been sitting next to him then, and he said I was cheering, just like him. The strange thing was, he never liked Roger Maris before or after, and like most Yankee fans had been rooting for Mickey Mantle, who was neck-and-neck with Maris all season, until the last few weeks. Eventually Roger Maris got traded away, and eventually he died, but his record didn't die, which is what happens sometimes.

Yeah, okay, you're wondering about the Bukko, which I busted my ass to get back from Atoris the Evil. To tell the truth, at first I'd forgotten about the amulet, but it came to me as the tremor threw me down, and I thought more about it in those two seconds. But what could I do with it in *two* lousy seconds? First I had to pull it out of my shirt, then focus on the proper side (not easy, I couldn't even focus on my hand), find the left horn, rub it, wait for whatever . . .

Even so, with one of those seconds ticked off I was frantically groping for the coin, figuring I'd rub the whole damn thing, not take any chances. Then, it occurred to me that the Old Guy and his pals were watching, that they were sharp enough to assess the situation and pull my butt out of here. He had said they would never knowingly let me die.

Right?

They were watching now . . . just like they'd watched my quest across Murlug to retrieve the Bukko.

My hand was down my jersey when the boulder rolled over the Nishiki.

Small consolation, but I didn't scream when it rolled over me. Fear can paralyze, too.

Did I say *rolled over*?

The boulder went *through* me.

Or maybe I went through *it*.

Five yards past, the rumbling stopped; the boulder faded into nothing.

No, I hadn't screamed, but I *had* wet my pants; honest to God, this time! I'd always heard what people did at the moment before sudden death, so I guess it could've been worse. Still . . .

Words appeared on both sides of the tunnel, flashing incessantly. The identical messages said: SORRY, YOU HAVE FAILED TO SURVIVE THE FIRST LEVEL OF *BOULDER!* (*their* italics and exclamation point) AND MUST EXIT THIS MODULE IMMEDIATELY. HAVE A NICE DAY.

Exit this module? What the . . .

A previously invisible seam in one wall appeared, widened, became a door. I stood, picked up the bike, and wheeled it . . . . . . outside?

I was on what appeared to be a carnival midway, with bright colored lights everywhere and hundreds of . . . *people* moving in both directions. More about *them* in a minute. The "module" I'd just come out of (the door had already slid shut) was a windowless building constructed of some sort of smooth, black stone, like all the others lining both sides of the midway. It could have been a really depressing place if not for the numerous "strands" of writhing, bobbing, flickering, gaudy neon; add a cowboy and a high-heeled slipper, you'd swear you were on the Strip.

It was nighttime here—wherever *here* was—either at the moment or permanently. Overhead, the black sky was filled with stars, none in any familiar arrangement. I was looking at them, I realized, through a transparent dome, quite a huge one. And directly above this dome, probably in some low geosynchronous orbit, was a "sign," flashing on and off, proudly announcing: GALAXYLAND, THE MOST FUN AND EXCITEMENT IN THE UNIVERSE!

I was in some sort of cosmic theme park!

Okay, the people, or more precisely the *beings*. About one in six was like you and me; as for the rest . . . hoo boy! Remember the cantina scene in *Star Wars*? Nothing! One family of four looked like Mr. and Mrs. Potatohead and the little spuds, with plastic organs and everything. Two stalks of celery walked hand in hand. There were wanna-be rats with humanoid features, wanna-be humanoids with antlered pig heads, a whole race of shapeless red blobs, like from the old Steve McQueen movie. Ostrich-things walked on nasty-looking bear claws. Nowhere, and I stress *nowhere*, were there beings that looked anything remotely similar to the aliens envisioned by Steven Spielberg, Whitley Strieber, and others. But there were seven-foot fly-creatures, not like Jeff Goldblum in the remake, but more like David Hedison in the original. From a distance the latter's communicating sounded like our trash dumpster on the day before a pickup.

Aside from an occasional nod (I think), few of these beings acknowledged my presence as they walked/shuffled/floated past. Except, that is, for five short ones, all of whom I assumed were kids, even though I could only be sure of two. They had been standing outside the exit to the module and were now around me in a ragged semicircle. There was no doubt I was the focus of their interest.

The two Earth (or Earthlike) kids, a boy and a girl, were about nine or ten. Had to be brother and sister, they looked so much alike; cute kids, too. A second, nearly identical pair (one was slightly larger) resembled frozen turkeys in those tight plastic wrappers, like you get them at the supermarket, only they had these wizened little heads, like owls. The arms and hands were closer to those of a human, but the legs were long and sticklike. From a distance you might mistake them for top-heavy flamingos or storks.

You had to see the fifth one to believe it. Visualize removing a piece of gray lint from your belly button, inflating it to the size of the biggest pumpkin you've ever had on your porch at Halloween time, stick on a head that vaguely resembles Rodney Dangerfield upside down with kinky green hair, add four stumpy legs with cloven hooves, and that's what I had staring at me.

"Ha, only the first exit of *Boulder!* and already the Earther has been put out!" he/it said in a growling-hissing voice. "On *my* first try I made it to the fourth level. Just like I thought, Earthers are a weak lot!" I could already tell I wasn't going to like this kid.

"You be quiet, Pahtui," the smallest butterball turkey said scoldingly in a little girl's voice.

"Yes, Vadera is right," the Earthlike boy added. "We allowed you to come along with us only after you promised to curb your tongue and behave, but so far all you've done is antagonize folks and embarrass us. Therefore, I must ask you to leave."

This was one eloquent little guy! Maybe he was a humanoid adult from somewhere else.

Pahtui pointed a hoof at my right leg, where a slight trickle had escaped the spandex, and chortled (or something like that). He then glared at the boy and said, "I was just going anyway! Who needs to hang around with you weak Earthers!" (So the kids *were* neighbors of mine.) "Or you either!" he snapped at the butterball turkeys.

"Oh, good riddance," the larger turkey said.

With a huffy swish of a tail that resembled a Hebrew National salami, Pahtui trotted into the traffic of the midway. The human kids smiled at me; the turkeys with the owl heads did something like that.

"Sorry about him, sir," the girl said. "We let Pahtui talk us into standing in front of the first exit and making fun of whoever came out. Usually it's only the real little kids . . ."

"Yeah, thanks for letting me know that," I told her, trying without success to conceal the trickle.

"It's probably because we're a little bored," the small turkey named Vadera said, "since we've done most every module in Galaxyland more than once. That's why we let Pahtui talk us into this. It won't happen again."

"My name's Robert Kirby," the human boy said. "This is Jillian, my sister. Krill and Vadera are also brother and sister. They're Deltanians, in case you couldn't tell."

I couldn't, but I wasn't about to let him know. "Hiya, kids, I'm Jack Miller." I shook hands all around, but at a comfortable distance.

"Is this your first trip to Galaxyland?" Krill asked.

"Yep, that's right. It's something I never got around to before."

"Still, the first exit of *Boulder!* . . ." Jillian shook her head. "I don't mean to be impolite, Jack, but how come—?"

"I had to go to the bathroom," I interrupted. "Yeah, that's it. I went in without thinking, and suddenly realized how bad I had to go. Can you point me in the right direction?"

This explanation satisfied them. Vadera said, "We'll be happy to guide you. After our rudeness, it's the least we can do."

"Hey, don't sweat it," I told her. "It was that Pahtui kid who was rude, not any of you."

"It is what you would expect of someone from Centros III, sorry to say." Robert shook his head. "Even though they're now members of the Federation, they are still the rudest creatures in this quadrant of the galaxy. My father says—"

"The . . . Federation?" I said.

"Yes, the United Fed—"

"Wait a minute, don't tell me!" I interrupted. "It's just that, uh, I really have to get to a bathroom."

"Oh, of course," Krill said. "This way, Jack."

With the Deltanians in the lead, Robert and Jillian on either side, we eased into the traffic flow of the midway. No one in this cosmic melting pot, not even the kids, seemed terribly curious about me, my strange clothes, or the Nishiki.

Okay, I was shook up, but wouldn't you be? The thing they called *Boulder!* was obviously a holographic, participatory sort of video game; great if you knew that going in. *But I didn't, and it scared the shit out of me!*

Then, to find out . . . Well, you know it already, right? Not so hard. The Florida gate had not only put me somewhere out in the galaxy, but also way the hell in the future. That's why I'd stopped Robert from telling me anything more, because *I really didn't want to know*. It just seems wrong, I guess.

I don't know . . .

Let's say, for argument's sake, that it's the year 2100. If somewhere in the past they'd come up with ways to give people a nice extended life, then I'm still down there somewhere, an old fart of one hundred and forty-something. Jeez, what a thought! Imagine advertising *that* in a singles newspaper?

But if it's the twenty-fifth century, or the thirtieth century, then I've been dead for a long time, and my grave is down there somewhere in what is now—or what used to be—southern California . . .

Either way, I didn't want to know.

Concentrate first on cleaning up the mess, then concentrate on Galaxyland. Looked like an interesting place, and everyone (-thing?) I'd seen here so far looked like he or she (or it) was having a great time. I suppose even *Boulder!* could be a blast.

We passed the main entrance to the aforementioned module, clearly designated by countless intertwining strands of neon. Lots of kids, human and otherwise, waited to get in; not exactly a summer weekend line at Disneyland, but long enough. Glad I wasn't caught "cutting in." There was a junction here, the entrance to three other modules all within a short distance. I understood *Parachute Free-fall* (no exclamation point), but *Ice Storm on Icora* and *Trouble on Toffarion* would take some explaining. More young ones seemed to be waiting on the latter than on any of the others.

All four of my guides were polite kids; but I could tell that Jillian was bursting at the seams of her silver jumpsuit to ask me something. I smiled and said, "Well, what?"

"Are you from one of the Colonies, or did you come here directly from Earth?" she asked.

Colonies. Jesus! "Oh, directly, for sure. I'm from California. How about you?"

"Robert and I reside with our parents in the South Central Sector, Dome 42 of the Texarkana Quadrant." She glanced at her brother, puzzled. "California? I never heard of it."

"I believe it is part of what they now call—"

"Uh, hey, is that the bathroom over there?" I interrupted. "Yeah, great. Well, you kids don't have to stick around anymore. Thanks a million."

Just past the lengthy module for *Ice Storm on Icora* was Comfort Plaza #4. Among the first things you noticed there were lots of glass coffins with bodies lying in them. *I swear, that's what they looked like!* Really freaked me out, until an attendant with a Galaxyland cap—he/she looked like an eggplant with bowling shoes—came up to me; smiling, I think.

"Do you wish to utilize a sleep chamber, sir?" the eggplant asked.

Sleep chamber. Grab a few quick artificially induced Zs in the middle of the day and you can keep right on truckin'. Would that be a great thing at *any* theme park in America, or what!

"No thanks," I told the eggplant. "Just need to use the bathroom."

The eggplant nodded (I think) and shuffled off. I looked at the kids. "Anyway, like I was saying—"

"We've been discussing things among ourselves," Robert interrupted (quite eloquently, of course), "and since none of us are particularly busy, we would be happy to show you around Galaxyland. Because this is your first time, we will enjoy sharing your reaction."

Was this kid going to be a statesman, or what! Actually, what he just said worked both ways. A lot of the fun for an adult at an amusement park was being with *kids*, seeing and hearing how *they* reacted to all the fun, the excitement.

"Yeah, sounds great," I said. "You can show me the ropes."

"The . . . ropes?" Vadera said. They were all puzzled.

"Never mind. Will you guys do me one favor?"

"What's that?" Jillian asked.

"No more talk about Earth, or the Federation, or anything like that, okay?"

I couldn't help feeling that even though they were kids, they had some sort of vague idea who or what I was. They smiled and nodded.

"We promise," Krill said.

Leaving the bike with them, I walked over to the bathroom. Now notice, I didn't say *men's* room, because I'd already observed there wasn't such a thing. No separate entrances with the universal signs for men and women, no *Ladies* and *Gentlemen*, no *Damas* and *Caballeros*, nothing like that. Just a single door through which *everyone*—men, women, things, vegetables, whatever—passed. Nice idea; maybe a bit radical for my own late twentieth century, but something that will surely work in the future.

There were no urinals on the bathroom walls; no sinks, either. Just booths, dozens of them, like changing rooms at May Co. or some other department store. A few were narrow, perfect for the walking celery stalks, others quite wide, the majority in-between. I was motioned to one of the latter by another attendant, a five-foot-tall dung beetle, who tipped his cap when I offered my thanks.

One great thing about all the booths in this place was that they were totally private; nobody had to see your shorts or your panty hose pulled down around your ankles. My booth was dark, but a soft greenish light came on when I shut the door. Surprise, no toilet, no nothing! The wall opposite the door was a big computer screen; the other walls, and the floor, were built from that same smooth, dark stone as the outside of the modules. I didn't have a clue what I should be doing here.

But this was the glorious future, remember? The screen began flashing a long list headed *Life Form*. At the bottom were instructions to *Scroll for Additional Selections*, which was unnecessary. I pushed *#6: Human, Standard Biological Functions* (as opposed to *#7: Human, Genetically Enhanced Biological Functions*). The screen went blank for an instant, then another list appeared, this one headed *Requirements*. It displayed twenty-two, with more available. *Jeez, how much were we capable of doing?* The first portion of the list looked like this:

> #1:   Defecate
> #2:   Urinate
> #3:   Regurgitate
> #4:   Masturbate
> #5:   Peel Skin
> #6:   Blow Nose
> #7:   Squeeze Pimple

You don't want to know the rest; it gets even more gross, things about hemorrhoids and such. I pressed *#2*, because I really did have to go, even with the accident before. The computer accepted this and asked, *Additional Requirements?* What the hell; I told it *Yes* and got another list that included *Dry-Clean Clothes*, which I punched. Then, *Wash Body, Lower Portion*. I could've also had *Ear Wax Flushed, Toe Jam Extracted, Armpits Shaved*, but I passed.

Now the whole program was entered, and this is where it got good! A square of green light appeared on the floor, telling me to *Place Clothes Here*. I peeled off the bike pants and my soaked jockey shorts, and put them down. The floor immediately . . . absorbed them, or something; happened so fast, I couldn't tell.

Next, two human-shaped footprints appeared. My *marks*, obviously. As soon as I was in position, a silver hose snaked up from the floor. The bulbous end, which sort of looked like Pacman, engulfed my genitals. Scared the hell out of me; thought my next stop was the Vienna Boys Choir. But it was fine, so I did my business, and once done the thing let go gently and retracted to wherever.

Finally, three "arms" that looked more human than robotic gave me one hell of a stimulating sponge bath with something that smelled like perfumed alcohol. By the time they were done, my clothes—all fresh and dry—were back on the floor. As I pulled them on the screen asked, *Any Further Requirements?* This was fun! But I told it *No*, and it flashed the standard Galaxyland salutation, *Have a Nice Day*.

Jesus, of all the sayings to survive the centuries, *why did it have to be that one?* George Carlin was probably rolling over in his grave.

I was in such a good mood now that I would've tipped the dung beetle, if I'd had any idea what the devil to give him. Outside, the Earth kids and the Deltanian butterballs were admiring my Nishiki.

"Come on, gang," I told them, "let's see Galaxyland!"

CHAPTER 19

Galaxyland

Since I was about to have *the most fun and excitement in the universe*, I really didn't feel like hauling the bike around. Nor did I figure on needing anything else, until Robert Kirby told me I should bring along some money.

"Uh, I'm not sure what I have will be any good," I said.

"Don't worry, whatever it is, they'll exchange it."

Okay, he knew best. I slipped my wallet into the elastic rear pocket of my jersey. About fifty bucks, that's what was in there. Didn't seem like much, not here. I mean, if this *was* three or four centuries in the future, and Disneyland was still down on Earth, an all-day Passport would probably cost seven thousand dollars.

The lockers I mentioned before were freebies. I put the saddlebag and helmet in one of them, but left my Padres cap on. (I don't care how far in the future this is. Down on Earth baseball is *still* being played, and Harry Caray is *still* singing "*Take Me Out to the Ball Game*," and Jerry Coleman is *still* screaming "Oh, Doctor!") You locked it by pushing the door with the palm of your hand in a designated area. Now, your handprint was the only thing that could open it again.

"What about the bike?" I asked.

Krill pointed at a blank wall. "You can leave it there, but unlike the locker it is not free. Do you have one unit?"

Nope, didn't have a single unit, I told him. Okay, I could pay him back later. He dug into his pocket (or something) and extracted a small, thin coin. After I propped the bike against the wall, he slipped the coin into a nearly invisible slot. A "hand" popped out, gave me a *counter-coin* (Jillian advised me to keep it separate, since it was the only way I could get the Nishiki back), then took hold of the frame with an iron grip. Weird-looking, but secure. For good measure I borrowed another unit, and soon a second hand held tightly to the removable front wheel. Sorry, but I didn't want to lose *any* of it.

Just the other side of Comfort Plaza #4 was Currency Exchange

#7. Nothing that remotely resembled an ATM here, only a little guy in a circular metallic booth. Did I say *guy*? He looked like a spinach leaf with two eyes and a smiling mouth, arms as thin as a garden hose and hands the size of a first baseman's mitt. Somehow these hands were running dexterously over a keyboard at the base of a big hexagonal screen.

"Can I help you?" he asked in a voice that was partly a whistle.

"Yes, I wondered if I could exchange this for some, uh, units?"

Not really knowing what to do, I'd removed a ten-dollar bill from my wallet. Probably worthless. But would you believe, the spinach leaf's tiny black eyes tripled in size when he saw the picture of Alexander Hamilton. He took it from me with one of his big mitts and held it up to his face.

"Look at the date!" he exclaimed. "Why, this currency is—!"

"He doesn't want to know," Vadera interrupted.

The spinach leaf nodded. "Oh, yes, of course." I was beginning to suspect that encountering time travelers was nothing new to these people.

"So what is it worth?" I asked.

The leaf punched something into the computer and studied the screen. "A collector from Darius IX has entered the current high bid of twenty thousand units for one of these," he said. "Allowing ten percent for our handling fees and profit margin, I can give you eighteen thousand units."

"Ooo, eighteen thousand!" Jillian exclaimed.

"Is that a lot?" I asked.

"Enough for you to see Galaxyland *ten* times, maybe more," Krill said.

Well, it wasn't the fortune I'd envisioned, not enough to purchase my own planet or anything, but it was okay. And if I didn't spend it here, what good was it going to do me back on Earth, late twentieth century? Probably wouldn't even fit the slots at the video arcade in the mall.

"Okay, I'll take it," I said.

That made the spinach leaf very happy. It occurred to me that with this antique bill in hand, the bidding would more than likely get serious. If so, he—or whoever he worked for—would wind up selling it for a lot more than twenty thousand units. Yeah, but that was the game, wasn't it? I didn't mind.

Robert watched closely as the spinach leaf counted out a handful of the skinny coins in a variety of colors, then assured me that all eighteen thousand units were there. I shook one of the leaf's enormous mitts, and we walked back to the midway.

"Which module would you like to try first?" Vadera asked.

"How about . . . *Parachute Free-fall*?" I said.

Now, that choice wouldn't have surprised them, but you know, it sure as hell surprised me. Remember back on Murlug, when I said I didn't like to fly? Well, as much as that bothers me, the thought of *falling out of a plane* is paralyzing. I wouldn't care if they had *ten* chutes strapped to me and an acre of five-yard-thick foam rubber on the ground.

So then, why choose *Parachute Free-fall*, you say? Because it was more than likely a holographic simulation, which meant there was no chance I could get hurt. A safe way, I figured, of overcoming a real bad fear. Besides, you probably also recall how I reacted when the Old Guy told me that free-fall was the best way to slip into the Vurdabrok Gear. Okay, what if sometime I *had* to do it? Might as well be prepared.

Parachute Free-fall was one of the modules we'd passed on the way to the Comfort Plaza. We rejoined the tide of life forms on the midway and were back there quickly. The line wasn't long, but it moved slowly.

I told the kids I'd treat them all to the module with my newfound wealth, which is when I found out something more about them. Turns out that both sets of parents were VIPs, some sort of ambassador or diplomats (that sure explained Robert, didn't it?). They were here for a big meeting at the Galaxyland Hilton Hotel and Convention Center. Accordingly the kids had free rein of the park, every module as often as they wanted. Not surprising they could become jaded.

"So, does that mean none of you will go on this with me?" I asked, kind of nervously.

Krill understood, I think. Maybe Deltanians had some kind of empathic abilities. "If you'd like, I'll make the jump with you," he said.

The jump. I didn't like the sound of that. "Yeah, great," I told him.

"We'd like to watch," Jillian said, "but the attendant will only allow that if it's all right with you."

So they wanted to see a grown man reduced to a blithering idiot. Oh, well. Since the study group was already looking in, what's a few more spectators . . .

"No, I don't mind," I told the girl.

The attendant, another dung beetle, took my twenty-unit coin and checked Krill's VIP pass. We were led into this dark room. Two other attendants—small, scowling humanoids who looked a lot like Averill—strapped these old-fashioned chutes on our backs. An adjustment had to be made for Krill's butterball body. They left, and we heard this hissing sound, probably a door closing. Krill looked at me and smiled.

"This one is fun," he said.

"Can't wait," I replied.

All of a sudden we were inside the huge belly of an ancient B-52, and I was nearly thrown to the floor as strong winds buffeted it. The cargo bay door was open, and the air was freezing. Thick white clouds obscured the ground, except for a few brief glimpses of what looked like patches of farmland—at least a couple of miles down.

No way in *hell*, I decided right then and there, was I going to jump out of this plane! I don't care if the kids thought I was the biggest coward since the guy who shot Jesse James in the back.

"Hey, listen—!" I started to say to Krill when I noticed this gleam in his little owl eyes.

"Here comes the best *paaarr-rrtt*!" he exclaimed.

The plane banked sharply, and we were thrown out into the clouds. No joke, it was more frigid than some women I'd dated. But do you think I was concerned about the weather just then? Uh-uh.

I was falling straight down!

First thing, try not to scream. I tried. Second, grab the ripcord. I grabbed. Third, see what Krill was doing. Actually, who cared?

The frozen turkey kid was a yard away, hands over his head, grinning ecstatically, not even concerned about his parachute. "Don't pull the cord yet, Jack," he shouted through the rushing air. "This is great!"

Yeah, great. Okay, so I didn't pull it, but I didn't let it go either. We were still in the clouds, and it wasn't as bad as I'd thought without the ground rushing up at me.

Two seconds later we fell out of the clouds, and the ground *was* rushing up at me.

I yanked hard on the ripcord, and it broke!

There was this scream down inside me. Yeah, I could feel the sucker being dragged upward, flailing and thrashing frantically, bracing itself against the walls of my throat, clutching at my tonsils, yet hopelessly doomed to pour out of my mouth.

"Uh-oh," I heard Krill warble, which really wasn't what I needed.

Now wait a minute, my brain argued, holding on to the leg of the scream, this was only a simulation, right? I hadn't moved an inch from the middle of that dark room. Say the secret word and an exit sign would show you the way out to the midway of Galaxyland, just like the holodeck on the new *Star Trek* always put your back at the starting point, no matter how far you might've walked, run, whatever, in your fantasy.

And even if I stuck it out, no way would I splatter like guava jelly across the landscape, not any more than I'd been flattened by the boulder (excuse me, *Boulder!*). Yeah, my brain knew all that. But when I saw how close the ground below me was, I discarded all logic and reason, all sense of shame, and got ready to scream my head off.

"Why don't you try the auxiliary chute?" Krill said calmly.

Now he tells me! I reached around back, found the ring, pulled it. The chute billowed over my head; I bounced a couple of times, then floated down gently. For the sake of all my invisible spectators, I flashed a smile into the wind. I touched the ground a second after Krill.

The sky and the farmland vanished, and we were in the dark room again. Our packs were removed, and we were ushered to an exit. There was a sign over the door: *Thank You For Trying Parachute Free-fall. Have A Nice Day.*

The other kids were waiting for us. Jillian said, "You really got into it, Jack. Your expressions of fear were so convincing."

Yeah, well . . .

We crossed the midway to *Trouble on Toffarion*, which must've been one of their favorites, because all the kids said they'd go in with me. While we were in line, a droning voice recited some history. Seems that about a century ago these Toffarion pirates were the scourge of their quadrant of the galaxy. A squad of Federation marines finally went to Toffarion and really kicked some ass.

So in *Trouble on Toffarion* the five of us became part of that squad, uniforms and all, and *we* did some heavy ass-kicking. Armed with beam pistols and laser swords (not the Obi Wan Kanobi kind, these were actually *shaped* like cutlasses), we fought the holographic images of the meanest, ugliest pirates since Blackbeard and his buckos sailed the bounding main. I was *really* into it, more so, I think, than the kids. As advertised, the most fun they had was watching me make a complete juvenile of myself.

After we were awarded our medals (*I Defeated the Space Pirates!*), we returned to the midway. Jillian and Robert excused themselves, something about a function they were required to attend with their parents. They'd rejoin us later, they said. Vadera and Krill were staying with me, which was fine, because I really liked these butterballs.

Our next stop was *Ice Storm on Icora*. In this module you froze your ass off on a planet of ice while trying to return to home base. Struggling through a nasty blizzard, you battled a bevy of Bigfoots (or is it Bigfeet?) and a creature that looked like Frosty the Snowman with fangs and an attitude problem.

I passed on *Earth Voyager*, a sort of roller-coaster ride through the *complete* history of my home world. Vadera and Krill led me to *Comet Adventure*, where you straddled the head of a comet as it hurtled through space. Now *that* was a trip, take it from one who's traveled the Ultimate Bike Path and ridden down the glowing mountain of Ralph Ralph. But again, the Deltanian kids were only mildly excited. I guess "too much of a good thing" is one truism that never dies.

Let me say this about Galaxyland: There's not a place that you or I have ever been to that could touch it. Not Disney World, not Magic Mountain, not King's Island, nothing! Put this place back in our time, and the others would all shut down. You'd have to book admissions a year in advance, no joke.

And you know, at the time we came out of the *Comet Adventure* module, I hadn't learned the half of Galaxyland yet!

CHAPTER 20

Drugs, Sex, and Sickos

We were on our way to a module called *Black Hole!* (yes, with the exclamation point again) when Vadera piqued my curiosity by asking, "Did you also want to visit the Adult Sector?"

"Sure, I guess so," I replied.

"Because you know we can't go in any of the modules with you," the smaller turkey went on, "or even watch."

"Well, in that case I don't have to—"

"I'm sure Jack would want to see the Adult Sector," Krill said. "It's no problem. We'll get together again afterward."

Yeah, I wanted to know too, so I pumped them. Seems like Galaxyland is divided into three main areas, Children's Sector, General Sector, Adult Sector. Not real catchy, like Tomorrowland or Fantasyland, but functional. So far, we'd been in the larger General Sector. In the Children's Sector, little tykes could try *Bug-Eyed Monster Cave, Mr. Bear's Magic Carpet, Aunt Emma and the Space Bunnies,* among others.

But I liked the sleazy ring of *Adult Sector*. It was sort of like saying *south of Broadway* in San Diego, or *Times Square*, period. Definitely worth checking out.

We passed a food stand where everything smelled good, but nothing looked familiar. I treated the kids to lunch. My choice, suggested by Vadera, was something called a blavvawich. It resembled thick, green, day-old oatmeal spread between thin slices of soggy pumpernickel. Not bad, actually, kind of like nutty chicken. I washed it down with a darblend shake, which had the consistency of Testor's rubber cement and tasted like prune juice.

The edge of the Adult Sector was just past a module called *10,000 Fathoms Below*, along a busy portion of the midway. I wondered if all these people would be staring at me as I eased into the forbidden zone. You know, like when you're in Crown Books and trying to innocuously carry a copy of *Penthouse* up to the register? But the flow of traffic into and out of the Adult Sector was heavy, and nobody seemed to think twice about it. Must be my uptight twentieth-century conditioning, I figured.

An attendant whose head was mostly eyes and whose body was rectangular and orange, like a giant box of Tide, watched the life forms coming in, making sure none were underage. I wondered how he could tell with some of these creatures. At least four of his protruding eyes were on Vadera and Krill when we stopped nearby.

"We'll wait for you here," Krill said.

"You don't have to," I told them.

"We don't mind," Vadera said. "Maybe"—she giggled (I think)—"maybe you'll tell us about some of what you saw."

Fair enough. I waved good-bye and joined the flow into Galaxyland's Adult Sector, nodding at the box of Tide as I passed. Nothing much changed here; the black stone modules looked the same, as did all the colorful lights. A sign pointed the way to a Comfort Plaza and a Currency Exchange. There were food stands, and a place where you could buy souvenirs.

What *did* differ were the names of the modules. No *Aunt Emma and the Space Bunnies* here, not even *Black Hole!* The first one I saw was called *Mass Murder Maze*. Past it, across from one another, were *Pleasures of Pantrika* and *Drug Trip*, both of which sounded intriguing. One called *Holiday with Hitler* held no appeal at all, since I'd already met the bastard. Perhaps *Silk and Leather*, or *Turkish Jail* . . .

It was tough to choose! Do I try one with little or no line, or do I assume the popular modules are those worth the wait? For example, *Drug Trip* was really packing 'em in, while only one guy—a sort of walking rice cake—stood in front of *Dismemberment Dreams*. All the other lines were about the same, except for one at *Brothels of Bordellus V*, which was nearly as long as *Drug Trip*.

I finally decided upon the latter, not only because it was clearly popular, but because its line seemed to be moving along more quickly than any of the others. In only three or four minutes I was standing in front of the attendant, yet another dung beetle (they must've had a pretty strong union). The admission, he informed me, was forty units, *double* anything in the General Sector. Sure, I plunked it down, but I thought, This better be good.

The line continued briefly inside the building. Standing there, I saw why it was moving so quickly. First off, there were three doors, all of which—I presumed—were programmed alike. And second, each life form emerged less than two minutes after entering a module. Forty units for under two minutes! If any of them felt like they'd been ripped off, they didn't utter a word. None of them looked angry, either; their expressions ranged from dreamily contented to totally spaced out and disoriented. I was beginning to wonder why I'd chosen this one.

Okay, here was the story on *Drug Trip*, as narrated over a speaker during the short stay on line. At the present time the most popular drug in this quadrant of the galaxy was something called slovor, from Centros III (same place that obnoxious kid Pahtui came from). It's a brownish-yellow, gritty powder that beings use in much the same way that people of my time used wheat germ. You know, sprinkled on ice cream, salads, blended into drinks, that sort of thing. A small amount is relaxing, gives you a nice little high. The problem is, a craving for slovor increased geometrically after you've been on it awhile, until you can't get enough. And then . . .

The purpose of *Drug Trip* was to simulate the hallucinogenic effects of a six-month-long habit, about the limits of an average being before he totally lost it. In the early stages a quick and painless withdrawal was possible, and this was what the module hoped to encourage. There was also a plug for *Drug Trip Jr.*, in the General Sector, which simulated a four-month habit. Hell of an idea, I thought.

Just before my turn came, a purple humanoid female with spidery arms and legs and a face that vaguely resembled Queen Elizabeth II stepped out of a module. She seemed more disoriented than most. After a glance back at the door, she reached into her purse and pulled out a large, transparent packet of what I figured was slovor. She held it up for everyone to see before putting it on the floor, where it was instantly sucked down. A few life forms nodded, clapped, made other weird sounds as she left. *Drug Trip* had obviously worked for her.

My turn. Actually, I was nervous. Just so you know, I *never* tripped out before. No PCP, no LSD, nothing like that. Smoked a joint back in college, nearly threw up. This was virgin ground I was treading here.

The room was as small as the water closet at the Comfort Plaza. Nothing in it but a square foamy pad in the middle, upon which I parked my butt. Almost instantly the room plunged into total darkness, and my stomach flip-flopped from the sensation of being inside an elevator that had just snapped its cable on the fifty-eighth floor and was headed for the sub-basement. Well, that wasn't going to bother me, not after *Parachute Free-fall*.

So what if my stomach was pulling itself up hand over hand and was now halfway along my esophagus?

The descent slowed, and these rings of multicolored lights began spinning around me, I mean *really* fast. Wait a minute; now I couldn't tell if *they* were spinning, or if the lights on the four walls were motionless while *I* was being spun like some out-of-control top. The reason I thought that was because of this dizziness. Maybe if I closed my eyes . . .

But I couldn't close my eyes, because the lids had turned into window shades, and whenever I pulled down the little ring at the end of the cord, the shade would go flapping up, so I had to leave them open . . .

Which meant I was watching when the spinning lights hopped off the walls and came together to form this giant upside-down surgeon who used his scalpel to make a deep cut in my left ankle. I didn't scream, even though the blood was pouring out like a Mount St. Helens lava flow, because the blood was blue, and the *Mayflower* was sailing on it. And on deck a boy pilgrim was raping a girl pilgrim, except the girl pilgrim turned into something big and green and gelatinous and swallowed the boy pilgrim whole, spitting up one of his boots. The surgeon tried to cut the green creature, but when scalpel touched flesh they were both turned into a Volkswagen Beetle–sized pomegranate, which split open with the sound of a toilet flushing and discharged its seeds like bombs, which burst in the air and sent streams of white worms cascading like confetti. All the worms vanished, except for one which fell on the pilgrim's boot and crawled inside . . .

I was spinning like a gyroscope but could still see the mountain of dog and armadillo heads that grew out of the boot and rose a mile high, twisting into the shape of a saguaro cactus, with toothpicks protruding from the eyes of the armadillos, but not the dogs. Mouths yapping silently, the dog heads were shaken off the cactus and plummeted around me, each snapping at my ass or hand or whatever was closer. The heads got up on little feet and came together at the base of the cactus to form a yellow bedpan, which was promptly filled with a red mucus discharge from the holes in the cactus where the dog heads had been. The cactus disintegrated into either a Baby Ruth or a turd, which sprouted thin black arms and a puckered mouth singing a weird three-note tune in the voice of a castrato. The black arms crawled into the mouth, and a scuba diver emerged, leaping fins first into the bedpan, which had sprung leaks in its sides, the discharge forming termite mounds of yellowish-brown slovor, which in turn became a gaping orifice that rose a hundred yards, then snaked down to suck me in . . .

The room was dark, and there was only me, and the foam pad I sat on. I felt a little dizzy, but no big deal.

"Holy shit!" I said, just to say it. Then I got up, because a soft green light had come on and the door had slid open. *Have A Nice Day*, the wall told me.

None of the life forms on line were looking at me, so I said real loud, "If any of you are on that shit, trust me, you'll want off!" Most of them still ignored me, except for this skinny killer whale with parakeet feet, who stuck out his tongue. I didn't respond, since the gesture, for all I knew, could've been his world's highest form of praise.

Wow, if only they had something similar to *Drug Trip* back home! With this kind of education, the Latin American cartels may be reinvesting in coffee for the long haul.

Outside, Vadera and Krill waved to me from where they still waited. They were munching on something that resembled cotton candy, except the color was really wrong. Even though they didn't seem to mind, I still felt weird about their hospitality. Okay, no more than two other modules, then I would rejoin them.

I walked farther into the Adult Sector, passing *Brothels of Bordellus V*, where the line had grown even longer. *Terrorist Torture Tricks* had an interesting ring to it, but *Coroner's Lunch* was a definite no-go. The ubiquitous exclamation point appeared in *Sheila Shows All!* Another long line there, same as for *Nymphets of Neptune*. The only other module along this part of the midway, before it turned sharply to the left, was a well-attended thing called *Psychotic Circus*.

But the one I finally came back to was *Mass Murder Maze*, the very first module in the Adult Sector. Okay, I suppose you're looking askance of me, right? Well, the truth is that, *just like a whole lot of you out there*, I have a morbid fascination for true crime stories. Write a book about a guy murdering dozens of co-eds, or freeway gunmen, or devil-cult sacrifices, and you have a bestseller. I'm talking a *million* copies. So *we* are not alone in *our* curiosity when *we* pick up these books.

This time, Vadera and Krill were gone. No problem: the butterballs were probably getting something else to eat. I waited on a short line, like everyone else eager to dole out my forty units for *Mass Murder Maze*. The object, a voice explained, was to find your way through the maze and emerge unscathed at the other end. Make a wrong turn and you encountered the most infamous mass murderers in the history of the galaxy. Now, you had to get by *them* also to continue on your way. If you got caught, they would do to you whatever it was they did to their victims. At this point your journey would be over, and you would have to exit the module.

Sounds really swell, huh?

The walls of the maze were—guess what?—black, shiny stone, like everything else here. I couldn't tell if they stretched all the way to the ceiling, because *it* was black too. For that matter, I probably wasn't moving at all, but . . .

Okay, I really didn't need to make myself crazy with this. Suffice it to say, this didn't look anything like the bush maze that Jack Nicholson, ax in hand, chases his kid through in the film version of *The Shining* . . .

Not until I took three steps, and then it looked *exactly* like the bush maze in *The Shining*. Hope old *Heee-re's Johnny!* wasn't still around.

The initial fifty feet looked pretty easy. I skipped the first four openings, which probably dead-ended, but took the fifth, which was wider, because the path I'd been on appeared to terminate at a solid hedge.

A left and a right later, there was no place to go.

I turned to go back, and . . . all along the *empty* path I'd just come down were the headless bodies of fat ladies, about two dozen, propped up against the hedges. The heads were there, too, at the feet of each. *Big* heads, even more so in proportion to the bodies. Their expressions were, uniformly, one of total shock, which I guess made sense. None of the bodies were clothed, and the breasts—three per lady—were ponderous.

Do I have to tell you they were splattered with blood?

The perpetrator of this ghastly mess looked like Conan the Barbarian at the end of a really bad day. He was tall, slim-waisted, but bulging with muscles everywhere else, which gave him an illusory fat appearance. His *big* head was tufted with mounds of coarse black hair. He had wide, bloodshot eyes and a red slash of a mouth that was formed in a nasty scowl as he glared at me. And the worst of this picture was the bloody ax in his hand, which looked to be roughly the size of Oregon.

"I am Blogodox of Jaloba," he bellowed, "and during the Jaloban time notches 5328.7 to 5331.7 I slew twenty-six fat slovenly bitches, all of whom reminded me of my mother. Let me show you how I did it."

"Hey, no thanks, pal," I said, but he came at me anyway, swinging that mother of an ax. Fortunately he was slower than hell, and I sidestepped him easily. Probably the women of his world were just as slow, or these twenty-six wouldn't have wound up this way.

"I am Blogodox of Jaloba—" he began again, but I was outta there. I retraced my steps, chose a different passage, and this time made some good progress. But just like with any maze, I hit another dead end.

This person dressed like a clown and holding a knife stood waist-deep in dead bodies; all of them appeared to be males. The painted part of his face was grinning, but I couldn't tell what the guy was really doing.

"I am John Wayne Gacy of Chicago, Illinois, Earth," he said, "and in the years 1972 to 1978 I murdered thirty-three boys and young men, then buried them in the crawl space of my house and in the yard. Let me show you how I did it."

"Up yours!" I exclaimed, and ducked around the Killer Clown, as they'd dubbed him back then, before he could extract himself from his handiwork. Back out again, find the path, hope I don't get off it this time.

I did.

The bodies were too numerous to count. They were bats, for the most part, ranging from two to five feet tall, with humanlike fingers and toes, but heads that more closely resembled a hamster's. Standing before them, holding something that looked like one of those lawn spreaders for seed or fertilizer, was another of their kind, flapping her membranous wings (yes, I could tell it was a *her*). Her fingers were on the handle of the spreader.

"I am Vempis of Nasdakki," she said in a hissing voice, "and on the two hundred and fifth solar day of the Nasdakkian year 80971, I went absolutely bat-shit crazy and took out all these folks in a single afternoon. Let me show you how I did it."

Oh, yeah, bullshit (or maybe bat-shit)! I tried to get away, but somehow I knew this one would be harder than the others. Vempis lifted off and swooped down at me, the spreader throwing pellets of Christ-knows-what all around. I ducked under the stuff, squirmed between the bat corpses like a terrified snake, got on my feet, and tore ass.

This was one damn weird module.

Okay, back on the right path again. Not much farther to go now, I was sure of it. Probably could reach the end of the maze without another dead end.

Probably not.

They were human bodies this time, not many of them, but really messed up. Something vaguely familiar about them, too. I turned quickly.

The guy was short, with a scraggly head of long, black hair and an equally unkempt beard. A swastika was crudely drawn on his forehead. As he raised two fingers at me in an old sixties peace sign, other hippy types began to appear, literally coming out of the woodwork (or hedgework, or whatever).

"I am Charles Manson aka Jesus Christ of the San Fernando Valley, California, Earth," he said in a frenetic voice, "and during two August nights of the Earth year 1969 my children and me ran helter-skelter amid the elitist white pigs and brought them to their knees. Let us how you how we did it."

They surrounded me now, some of his Family: Susan Atkins, Tex Watson, Leslie Van Houten, Bobby Beausoleil, a couple of others whose names I couldn't remember. All looking as wild-eyed and disheveled as Manson himself, and worse: they were armed. Tex Watson waved a revolver, the others brandished knives as they moved around in a circle, like kids at play. They were chanting all kinds of weird shit, none of which made sense.

Hell no, I wasn't waiting around; ran right at Charlie, and through him. Sort of wished he was solid so I could've knocked him on his ass. On the other hand, I wouldn't have really wanted to touch the sonofabitch, even if it was only an organic simulation. He yelled for his Family to *get the pig*, but I turned the corner of a hedge, which probably deactivated that portion of the program, because their sounds were suddenly switched off.

I was on the final leg; not hard to figure with a door just ahead, and a sign that said, *Congratulations, You Made It*. Okay, I had coughed up my forty units, and I'd gotten exactly what I paid for, right? After all, I knew going in what this was about. Other users of *Mass Murder Maze* probably *tried* to go the wrong way, to have as many encounters as they could "survive."

But let me assure you, friends and fellow travelers, knowing what I knew didn't make running into the galaxy's craziest of the crazy any less unnerving!

CHAPTER 21

The Most Fantastic Attraction

I guess making it through was a big deal. Outside the door, an attendant—a beefstick on roller skates—tried to give me a badge that said, *I Survived Mass Murder Maze*, but I told him to keep it.

Okay, no more drug trips, no more violence. I'd promised myself one more module before rejoining the kids, and I definitely needed a change of pace. Something like *Pleasures of Pantrika* or *Brothels of Bordellus V*. I could pass on *Sheila Shows All!* and *Silk and Leather*; both of those, I think, were currently playing back home at the Pussycat Theater.

But you know, on *Star Trek*'s holodeck, when you touched a woman, you really *touched* her, and when you kissed a woman, you really *kissed* her, and when . . . you get the picture. If what they had here were only images . . . then big deal! Maybe they hadn't come that far yet, or maybe they never would.

Anyway, I was outside the module without yet having made a decision, when I saw that Vadera and Krill were back. Jillian and Robert were also there. The four of them waved frantically for me to come over.

"What's up, guys?" I asked.

"Jack, something awful is going to happen!" Robert exclaimed. He and Jillian were breathless. "You've got to listen to us!"

"Okay, I'm listening."

Jillian was more able to speak than her brother. "After finishing with our parents, we returned to the General Sector to look for you. Someone we knew thought he'd seen two Deltanians and an Earther going into *10,000 Fathoms Below*, so we went inside, but you weren't there."

Robert had caught his breath: "We exited early and wound up in a narrow alley, which turned a couple of times. Just before the last turn, which would have put us back on the midway, we heard an odd conversation. We hid there and listened."

"It was between a man and a woman," Jillian went on. "The man had a gruff voice. The woman asked, 'How much longer?'

and the man said, 'An hour or less.' Then he added, 'How simple. By cutting through one critical cable of the Lectronium power source, we shut down the whole system! Even when they discover the break, it will be days before everything is operative again. Imagine, Galaxyland *closed*!' "

"Jeez, that is bad," I said. "Did they say anything else?"

"They left, and their voices faded," Robert told me. "The woman said, 'Great plan,' and then, 'Tell me again where you put it.' All we could hear him say was, 'Right under the strangest, most fantastic attraction in Galaxyland . . .' Then they were gone. We looked out on the midway and saw them walking away; not their faces, of course, but we'd know them from behind."

"Did you tell the police?" I asked.

Jillian shook her head. "We were close by, so we came here first. Besides, there is almost no crime in Galaxyland, and the small security force stays invisible by being other things. We would have to go all the way to the central office, which is near the entrance, and there is so little time!"

"We must find where they put it!" Krill exclaimed.

"Put what?" I wanted to know.

"Whatever it is that will destroy the cable!"

"Oh, right," I said dryly. "What if it's a bomb or something? And another question: *You* tell *me* what the *strangest, most fantastic attraction in Galaxyland* is!"

"We . . . were hoping you could do that, Jack," Robert said. "The four of us have been discussing it, and we all have different opinions. Maybe after all the times we've seen them, *nothing* is special anymore."

I put a couple of fingers to my head in my best Peter Falk-Columbo impression. "Okay, let's do this by the numbers. Robert, you and me and the Deltanians will go and look for this Mt. Everest of modules. The cops have to be let in on this, so, Jillian, that'll be your job. Fair enough?"

"Oh, yes," Robert said. "Uh, Jack?"

"Yeah?"

"What is Mt. Everest?"

And this kid was from Earth. *Oy vey!* "Never mind," I said. "Jillian, get going."

Jillian ran off; the other kids looked at me like I'd looked at Ralph Ralph on his mountain. We started along the midway through the General Sector.

Okay, you've been with me through this, so how would *you* pick the most fantastic thing here? I mean, they were *all* pretty amazing. My first thought was that, whatever these saboteurs thought it was, they would choose something with broad appeal. In other words, forget *Bug-Eyed Monster Cave* in the Children's Sector and *Turkish Jail* in the Adult Sector. With less than an hour—according to Jillian—we had to concentrate on the General Sector.

So was it *Comet Adventure* or *Trouble on Toffarion*? The lines in front of *Earth Voyager* were really long, but not much different from *Ice Storm on Icora*. Jesus, I felt like an idiot doing this! I told Robert to keep an eye out for the man and woman, hoping they'd hang around the scene of the crime. But so far, nothing, and we were well into the General Sector, and time was ticking down.

Enough, Miller, do something. Now *I* happen to think that *Ice Storm on Icora* was nifty, and it was also Vadera's choice. Using his VIP pass, Robert walked right in (the life forms in line loved that). But when he exited a couple of minutes later, he was shaking his head.

"I found the junction box under a floor panel," he said, "but it was securely locked, and there was no sign of tampering."

Hey, this was getting hopeless. And by the way, where was Jillian with the police? Whatever was going to happen here couldn't be stopped; it was likely predestined. I could always hop ahead a decade or so and find out . . .

We were at the far end of the General Sector. The midway traffic was still heavy, but other intersecting paths were practically empty.

"What's down there?" I asked, indicating one.

"New modules are being built, and are scheduled to open soon," Robert said, then suddenly became excited. "Those people walking there . . . !"

Two life forms were approaching the midway. The humanoid male was short, and real fat. He wore a white suit and a Panama hat; sort of looked like Sidney Greenstreet with fifteen chins (I'm not exaggerating either, his face was a mass of lumps). The woman, a head taller, was probably an Earther and definitely a knockout, something I could tell even at a distance.

"Is it them?" I asked.

"I'm not sure," Robert said. "Perhaps when . . ." They

turned the corner and angled toward the traffic. Now he could see their backs. "Yes, it's them!" he exclaimed. "Come on!"

But we were too far past, and going in the opposite direction. By the time we had removed ourselves from the crowd, they had merged with it and were well along the midway.

"They were in an awful hurry to get somewhere," Vadera said.

I shook my head thoughtfully. "Maybe they were in a hurry to get *away* from somewhere. Let's see where that path goes."

Where it went was between two modules for about seventy feet, turned left, then right, and continued on. Remember before how empty I said these cross-paths were? Forget *that*. Life forms were feeding onto it from two narrow alleys, all of them headed in the same direction as us. No glitz on the module walls here, so I didn't have a clue what the attraction was.

The path widened, and just ahead we saw a throng. They were motionless, gathered around something; not a sound from their mouths, or whatever orifices they used. At first we couldn't tell what it was that held their interest. But as we reached the outer edge, the crowd did a perfect imitation of the Red Sea. My three little friends gasped in astonishment at what they saw.

"Oh, look at *that*!" Robert exclaimed.

"It's wonderful!" Vadera added.

We walked between the life forms. While everyone else's eyes were on the thing ahead, I was looking at their faces. Remember when you were a kid, the first time you went to Disneyland or Coney Island or whatever? Remember when you sat in your first movie house and watched a motion picture the size of a whole wall? Or when you saw the Grand Canyon? Mouth open, jaw hanging down, eyes as wide as an out-of-style tie? That's what these humans, humanoids, animals, vegetables, and minerals from all over the galaxy looked like, *especially* the kids.

These jaded little folks of the future, who ho-hummed *Boulder!* and *Comet Adventure* and *Trouble on Toffarion*, were turned on like you wouldn't believe! What was it that had this effect on them?

It was a carousel, an old Earth carousel, with carved wooden shields and tassels along the outer rim, and tons of mirrors everywhere else. The paint job done to each animal was excellent. In addition to the horses there were giraffes, dragons, unicorns, lions and tigers and bears (no, I'm not going to say it), even a couple of ostriches. There was one of those swing-out arms from where you grabbed the brass ring as you whizzed by. I found out later that the carousel had recently been restored and was going to become an official attraction of Galaxyland the next day. At the moment, it was being given a dry run. While a calliope piped Rosas's "Over the Waves," beings from all over the galaxy moved happily up and down, up and down, on this oldest of Earth wonders. A small celery stalk on a blue-and-gold unicorn was beside itself with glee.

"It's . . . *fantastic*!" Krill exclaimed.

The most fantastic attraction in Galaxyland, I thought, and I knew that Robert, on the verge of hyperventilating, was thinking the same thing. We knelt and peered under the platform, where the Earth boy pointed out a panel in the ground, near the base of the center pole. Vadera and Krill, squinting their little owl eyes, assured us that someone had tampered with it. Deltanians, I learned, had incredible vision.

"Jack, there's not much time!" Robert exclaimed. "We've got to do something!"

"Let's go!" I said, scrambling under the carousel and trying not to think about a mini nuclear device only a few feet away. The kids stayed with me.

Now you can imagine the uproar we caused among the onlookers. Well, tough luck, folks; this was for the good of Galaxyland. I removed the floor panel carefully, only now noticing the slash marks the sharp-eyed Deltanians had seen from back there. Inside was this chunky gray thing that looked like an old Earth fuse box. Its heavy lock had been cut through with something that must've generated incredible heat, because the metal had melted and then solidified. With the kids' noses practically in the hole, I lifted the door.

What in the name of Gary Larson was that?

Sitting atop intertwined strands of thick, multicolored cables was one weird little beastie! Picture a cross between a gerbil and an Ewok about a foot tall, with a long, razor-sharp tusk protruding down at a severe angle, and you got it. Cute little guy, actually. It was sitting on its haunches, and had already cut through nearly a third of the top cable.

"Why . . . it's a Deltanian Sawtooth!" Robert exclaimed. "I wouldn't touch it if I were you, Jack."

Hey, sound advice. At least it wasn't something nuclear . . .

"You under there!" a voice shouted. "Stop whatever it is you're doing!"

A dung beetle attendant with a baseball cap was crawling toward us; skillfully, I might add. He was flashing a badge. So this was one of Galaxyland's hidden storm troopers.

"Hold on to your carapace," I told him, "we're only trying to help out."

He could see down into the floor now. "Well, I'll be dipped in dung, it's a Deltanian Sawtooth!" he exclaimed.

"That's right," I said, "and you'd better zap it quick, or the lights are going out."

"No need to harm the creature," Robert said. "Vadera and Krill can take care of it."

The little girl butterball said, "Yes, all Deltanian life forms are in harmony with one another, which is why our planet is the most peaceful in this quadrant of the galaxy. Watch."

She held out a hand to the creature, and at the same time I felt, rather than heard, this soft hum. The animal pulled its tusk out of the cable, looked at the hand, sniffed it. Then the little guy's face lit up in a weird sort of smile, and it nuzzled Vadera's fingers with the top of its fuzzy head. The girl picked the thing up gently and sat it on her palm.

"A Deltanian Sawtooth is the most inoffensive of creatures," Krill said. "See that brown, sticky stuff on the cable? It's spice syrup, the one thing they have a weakness for. Those people must have saturated it."

"I still don't know what to make of this," the bemused dung beetle said, "but I want all of you out of here, right now."

Lots more stuff was going on when we crawled out from under the carousel. Jillian was there, and she waved vigorously when she saw us. Spinach leaf and dung beetle attendants were in abundance, four of the latter holding the fat, multichinned guy and his female accomplice in tow. Those two nearly dropped their gums when they saw the creature in Vadera's hand.

Jillian ran over to meet us and said, "On our way to look for you, I spotted those two and pointed them out. It didn't take the police long to *persuade* them to tell where they'd hidden whatever-it-was."

A human in a black jumpsuit and a wide-brimmed hat similar to Don Quixote's golden helmet of Mambrino had followed Jillian.

He was smiling broadly. Something familiar about this guy, I thought, but couldn't put a finger on it.

"I'm Melvin Butterwood, Administrator of Galaxyland," he said, shaking our hands. "Looks like all of you did a good piece of detective work. I'll send my technicians in, but I'm sure patching the cable will be a simple matter."

Indicating the fat guy and the woman, I asked, "What's going on here? Who are those two?"

"That's Otto Frump, and his secretary, Miss Diode."

"Otto *Frump*?" I exclaimed.

"Yes; he owns a theme park called Space World."

"I've heard of that," Robert said. "Everyone says it's an awful, run-down place."

Butterwood nodded. "It is; but it's only a few light-years from here. Frump thought that by shutting down Galaxyland and doing some heavy advertising, he could divert people there."

"It would've worked too," Frump said sourly, "if it weren't for that guy and these kids."

Butterwood motioned for his "men" to take the pair away. Otto Frump scowled at me; Miss Diode didn't.

Let me tell you about Miss Diode. About her long auburn hair and full red lips and legs that spanned the galaxy and eyes that flashed messages all healthy heterosexual males longed to hear. If only Miss Diode weren't on her way to being incarcerated . . .

As the pair was being loaded into something that looked like a helicopter without rotor blades, Butterwood said, "Well, Mr. . . ."

"Miller, Jack Miller," I told him.

"Yes, Mr. Miller. Needless to say, Galaxyland owes you and your young friends a cosmic debt of gratitude. The rest of your visit here is complimentary. Anything you want is . . ." He eyed me curiously, banging a knuckle on the golden helmet of Mambrino. "Did you say . . . *Jack Miller*?"

And that's when I knew why Melvin Butterwood was familiar. It was because he looked a hell of a lot like *me*!

"That's right," I said.

"I don't believe it!" he exclaimed. "We have pictures of you in an ancient family album. Jack, I'm your great-great—"

"Excuse me," I interrupted, "but I don't want to hear this!"

I really didn't want to know; I really *really* didn't. I mean, think about it: This guy was my great-great-grandson, or maybe my great-times-eight grandson. Whatever the case, he had *pictures* of me, maybe like I am now, or maybe as an old fart. He knew who I married, and what my kids' names were, and when I died, and how, and everything like that. He might even own a rare copy of a book I'd written in the early twenty-first century that won a National Book Award, or more importantly sold a few million copies by pandering to readers' baser instincts.

And what fun would life be if it were all laid out for me? Knowing *what* was going to happen, and *when*; hey, why bother? Or maybe I'd be like Marty McFly in all those *Back to the Futures* and try *too* hard to make sure things happened like they were supposed to. Uh-uh; leave me in my blissful ignorance, thank you.

"Oh, I understand," Butterwood said. "Sorry about that. Most time travelers feel the same way. I was just so excited meeting you."

Actually, I already knew too much. Since I obviously had a life that produced Melvin Butterwood and everyone else in between us, I must've survived all that happened to me in the gates along the Ultimate Bike Path. So I *never* had to worry about danger again; *right?* Somehow I didn't like that, either. Then again, if this was just one possible time line, and in some other time line I never made it past . . .

Okay, crazy stuff again. Best solution: Forget the whole damn thing!

"Yeah, well . . ." I nodded at my descendant. "You know, I wouldn't mind seeing more of Galaxyland, as long as I still have my guides." To this, the kids nodded vigorously. (At least, I *think* that's what Vadera and Krill were doing with their little owl heads.)

This pleased Butterwood; he tapped on the golden helmet again and said with a flourish, "The park is all yours. Uh, Jack . . . ?"

"Yeah?"

"I suppose coming home with me and meeting the family is out of the question?"

"Definitely; no offense, Melvin."

"None taken."

Anyway, I was issued this gold pass, and from then on I couldn't spend a unit there, not even to buy souvenirs for the kids. I gave all my skinny coins to Robert, who promised that they would be diverted to help life forms on some impoverished planet, a few of which remained in the galaxy.

No, I didn't go back to the Adult Sector. *Sheila Shows All!* and

Dismemberment Dreams would have to wait until another time. We did all the modules in the General Sector, and it was great. But the most fun was watching the kids bobbing up and down on the painted animals of the carousel, grabbing for the rings, enjoying the music. Even the serious Robert Kirby let out a squeal or two, much more befitting of a ten-year-old.

Then it was time to go.

Even though I was having a ball, the specter of finding out more than I wanted to know about this future—or about my past—was still hovering around. So, back to the *mhuva lun gallee*. No problem, except I was going to be leaving friends behind, and that was hard, and I told them so.

"I'll miss you a lot, Jack," Krill told me, echoing everyone else's words. "We sure shared a great adventure, didn't we?"

"That we did," I said. "Maybe I'll see you all another time, though."

"In *our* future?" Jillian asked.

"Hey, could be."

Now as it turned out, there *was* going to be a problem getting back. Galaxyland had been built at the "crossroads" of the galaxy, which happened to be on this lifeless, miserable little planet with a surface temperature that would cook a side of beef in three seconds, which meant no going outside. But inside the dome there wasn't anything remotely resembling a steep downhill slope that would enable me to get up over the required thirty-odd mph. Therefore . . .

Yeah, you guessed it: free-fall. The *easy* way, the Old Guy had always argued. Melvin Butterwood arranged for me to drop off the roof of the fifty-story Galaxyland Hilton. But after my experience in the module, free-falling shouldn't bother me all that much.

Right?

Scenario: Study Group observing Jack Miller pedaling furiously toward the edge of the Galaxyland Hilton's roof.

My Old Guy: "He's doing it! He's actually going to free-fall back to the *mhuva lun gallee*!"

Study Group Old Guy #2: "What is he saying?"

Study Group Old Guy #1: "It's in an old biblical tongue, and is called a prayer."

My Old Guy: "Now he is singing—I think—about free-falling

into nothing." (Sticks finger in ear.) "Ah, they are the words of an Earth philosopher called Tom Petty."

Study Group Old Guy #2 (holds out cupped hands full of ear plugs, which the others grab): "He has just gone off the edge. Hurry!"

Study Group Old Guy #1 (shoves them in ears): "Yes, without a doubt this will be his loudest scream yet!"

CHAPTER 22

The Fourth World

Well, guess what, I didn't disappoint the old boys. Don't suppose I impressed the folks at Galaxyland, either; definitely not those hanging out every window of the Hilton all the way down to the twenty-fifth floor, where I finally slipped into the Vurdabrok Gear. Might've done it sooner if I hadn't been scared shitless. Yeah, if you think I'm a chicken, *you* try jumping off a building of *any* height on a bicycle, and I don't care if there *is* a safety net below. You'll freak, guaranteed.

So, here I was back on the Ultimate Bike Path, and wouldn't you know, the first dominant stretch of gates had to be the creepy Bart Simpsons. Jeez, I didn't like those ones! I still felt that sooner or later I was going to give one of them a try.

How about later?

But after what seemed a long time there were less of them, and finally none. No dominant gates now, just the hodgepodge. I kept on riding, at the moment content to observe their kaleidoscopic passing. After the free-fall (which by the way provided a nice easy access to the Path) and the run of Bart Simpsons, I needed a while to get it all together.

My brain was running along two lines in regard to the next port of call. The first was to head home, spend the day with Holly Dragonette, find out if she was going to be the great-whatever-grandmother of Melvin Butterwood. And the second, in case you hadn't figured, was to keep looking for that elusive diamond of light and spend time talking (or more precisely listening) to Ralph Ralph. After all, I'd talked to spinach leaves and dung beetles and butterball turkeys and God-knows-what-else at Galaxyland, and the UT6 had performed quite well, hadn't it?

But of course, my choice turned out to be neither of the above. I still had the traveling itch, and Holly would still be there at ten A.M. on Sunday morning, even if I took a ringside seat to witness the whole evolution of man. And this time I didn't remain on the

Path long enough to find the glowing portal to the wise man who sat atop the incandescent mountain.

That's because another one of those black circles with the pulsating yellow lights sort of reached out and grabbed me, and when that happens on the *mhuva lun gallee*, you have to go with the flow. Making the necessary instant decision, I angled toward the gate. This time, although there were more of them, I didn't perceive the streaks as bread slicers when I passed through . . .

. . . and shifted out of the Vurdabrok Gear after feeling something hard under my tires.

The smooth surface was mottled black and white, looking sort of like fancy Italian marble. Above, the sky was even weirder, dominated by shades of blue and black, but not like what we would think of as day and night. I mean, the blue had no sun, not a single cloud, while the black was just that, no moon or stars. And there was no pattern to the colors. Here they were in squares, like a depraved checkerboard; there they ran in jagged, parallel stripes. There didn't seem to be any horizon, either; the same coloration filled the four distant "walls" or whatever of this place. It was almost like being inside a giant box.

"Looks *really* odd, doesn't it?" a raspy voice from behind me said. "Something will have to be done about separating the blue and the black and putting order into this chaos."

Preoccupied as I was, the voice nearly sent me jumping out of my bike shoes. I spun around and found myself face-to-face with a grinning coyote, who stood on his hind legs.

"Did *you* say that?" I asked.

The coyote looked around. "Well, who the heck else?" he replied. "You see anyone I don't?"

"Guess not. But—"

"Oh, bother!" the coyote suddenly exclaimed. "Locust stew and badger droppings! I can't believe what I forgot to do. It's always something, right?"

"What are you talking about?"

"You go ahead and have a look around. I'll catch up in a while."

"Wait a minute—!"

But he was gone, just like that. It happened so fast that I'm not sure if he winked out, faded away, dissolved, or what. It was weird, to say the least; but *weird* was commonplace by now, wasn't it?

Anyway, owing to the hard surface, I figured it was safe to get back on the bike. Pedaling slowly, I continued to look all around. There were low hills everywhere, and they appeared pretty normal, no marble or anything. Trees, too; white pine, black spruce, some others I couldn't recognize. (Gimme a break, my Peterson's guide was back home on a bookshelf.)

But probably the most obvious things about this *place* were four towering mountains, each standing prominently about dead-center before its respective "wall." They all seemed equally far away, which led me to believe—by heavy logic and deductive reasoning—that I rode in the middle of wherever-this-was.

Four peaks. What was it about four peaks . . .

These strange, clackety sort of voices rose from beyond some hills on my left. Leaving the bike, I scrambled up one and peered over. So, what do you think, something normal? Yeah, right.

A dozen or so man-sized insects were either walking or flying along a narrow stream of greenish water. In pairs, or groups of three, they discussed matters of the world animatedly, mandibles clattering, legs and feelers waving. There were at least three different kinds of beetles, some red ants, locusts, and a dragonfly hovering at the rear. Every so often the group would stop and dip their heads into the stream, which turned out to be a whole other weird sound.

The dragonfly was conversing with a sleek yellow beetle. They were a few yards in back of the others. Since they were passing below me, their words were audible.

"So, gorgeous, what do you say?" the dragonfly clacked (or maybe it was chittered). "You want to go into the reeds and see how much faster you can get my wings to beating?"

"Not today," the yellow beetle replied, "I have a headache."

Jesus, was it different *anywhere*?

The insect people continued up the stream. Insect people. There was something about them, and the four mountains, and the coyote, and this place, that should've lit a light bulb in my brain, even if it was only a ten-watt job. But so far I wasn't making any connection.

I should know this; I *should*. Walking back to the bike, I realized how much this was bugging me (no pun intended).

"There, that didn't take long—"

"Shit!"

The coyote again, popping up behind me and taking a few years off my life expectancy.

"Whoops, sorry," he said, but he was still grinning, so his sincerity was dubious. "Anyway, what do you think of the Fourth World so far?"

The Fourth World; that was it! Now I knew why this place was so familiar.

But the Fourth World wasn't real. It was a Navajo Indian legend, a myth.

I was inside a *myth*? Hey, Old Guy, is this part of the half I wouldn't understand?

Or was it real? Which was the same question I asked the coyote, or, rather, asked Coyote.

"*This* is real, isn't it?" he replied, stamping a foot on the hard ground. "And what about me? Aren't I real?"

He touched me with a paw, and I nearly jumped out of my skin, but decided it would be rude. Just remember, this was an *animal* staring me in the face, a big one at that, with *very* sharp teeth. Well spoken or not, he could still bite my head off. Yeah, he refrained . . . for now. From feeling his paw I had to admit, he *was* real.

Okay, why do I know about the Fourth World? See, I'm a big Tony Hillerman fan, and he writes these wonderful mysteries involving either of two cops (sometimes both together) who work for the Navajo Tribal Police. In addition to teasing your brain into solving a few juicy murders, disappearances, whatever, per book, Hillerman also offers remarkable insight of this unique tribe's fascinating, often enigmatic culture. Here is an Indian nation of about 130,000 who live—anonymously, to most other Americans—scattered across a reservation in the Southwest that encompasses more square miles than all of New England.

So, like most writers born to research, after reading the first couple of books I just *had* to learn more about the Navajo. (That's our name for them, by the way. They call themselves *Dineh*, which translates, simply, to The People.) That was how I knew a little about the Fourth World, which was part of their story of creation.

Right now, today, *as you read this*, the Navajo exist in the Fifth World. To get there, they had to rise up through four underworlds.

And in the process they didn't even become humans until their stay in the Fourth World.

Down in the red First World, the Insect People lived on an island surrounded by oceans. There were these four ocean gods, whom the Insect People called chiefs. Seems like the people angered the gods by committing adultery, so the gods decided to flood them out. They took to the sky and flew around the "ceiling" of the First World, until a swallow poked its head through a hole and invited them up.

Now they were in the blue Second World, which was inhabited by the Swallow People. Nice folks, these birds. They invited the Insect People to live with them, and for a few weeks everything was cool. But old habits die hard, and one of the Insect People got caught messing around with the chief's wife, which really pissed the chief off. Again they flew up, and this time were invited into the Third World by a grasshopper.

The yellow Third World (not, by the way, to be confused with any developing nation) was occupied by the Grasshopper People; don't ask me, apparently grasshoppers *were* different from locusts. The sexes became separated for a while, and the females gave birth to a host of fearsome monsters. Meanwhile, guess what, one of the males played patty-cake with the grasshopper honcho's wife, which stirred up the gods again, and there was another nasty flood. This time just about everyone, monsters included, was flushed up to the Fourth World, where a whole lot of proverbial shit was hurled into the proverbial fan.

"Anyway," Coyote said, "I give a pretty good tour. Let me show you around this place."

"Yeah, sure, that'd be . . ."

I looked at him suspiciously. This was *Coyote*, and in Navajo legend he didn't have the best reputation. Oh, he wasn't a monster or anything like that; he wasn't going to suck out your brains or do Nazi-style surgery on you or your children. He was more a troublemaker, a trickster, a real *mamser*. If there was a used-car lot in the Fourth World, Coyote would be out there wearing a smile and a plaid sport coat and writing the deals. In other words, to the Navajo he was a royal pain-in-the-ass. So you can understand my reluctance.

"Something wrong?" he asked.

"Just wondering what this was going to cost me."

His grin grew wider. Jeez, those were nasty teeth! "So, my

notoriety precedes me. Not to worry, friend. Being a trickster is fun, but it can get boring sometimes, too. We don't get many visitors here, and showing you around will be a nice change of pace. What do you say?"

Okay, why not? The guy didn't seem that bad, and I could always keep an eye on him.

"Lead on, MacDuff," I said, which made him scratch his fuzzy head.

CHAPTER 23

Birth of a Nation

The Nishiki came with me on the tour, which was good, because I didn't want to leave it behind. Even better, Coyote didn't mind if I rode it slowly, because he had this long, tireless stride and kept up easily. We were traveling toward the South (with a capital S), he assured me, in the direction of the sacred mountain called Tsoodzil, which on your Triple A map of Indian Country is called Mount Taylor and is located at J-16. From the beginning Coyote had been trying to explain something weird to me, but it took a while to catch his drift.

The best I could understand, we weren't just here at one particular moment of time in the Fourth World, but through its entire existence, so I could, in essence, see everything that ever happened here if I wanted. Coyote himself existed everywhere in time (that's Navajo time, I presume), from his creation in the Fourth World by the sky, all the way through the Fifth World. So at the moment he not only knew what had been, but also what was coming.

Are you grasping any of this?

Walking along streams and across valleys, we passed more groups of Insect People. They hardly even noticed us, and for a while I wondered if we were invisible to them, which wasn't so. Most of the conversation we overheard involved one hitting on another, all kinds of singles bar stuff. These were the horniest bugs, weren't they?

We were approaching a river when something whizzed across the sky. I'd hardly gotten a glimpse before it disappeared beyond some hills.

"What was that?" I asked.

Coyote grinned (which was redundant). "Look up there and you'll figure it out," he said.

Remember before when I said the blue *sky* was just that and nothing else? Wrong-o. There was a sun in it now, and it was sending down sunbeams that resembled long, twisting snakes. A

171

second one whooshed by like a runaway comet, then a bunch more. And racing alongside them were lightning bolts, which came out of clouds that now floated in the once-empty sky. I got the feeling this was the harbinger of something even bigger.

"What's going on?" I asked Coyote.

"The gods come," he said. "See?"

This *big* dude, I mean seven or eight feet, rode down on a sunbeam. He was naked and looked like a middle-aged Marlon Brando with the weight on, except his body was entirely blue.

"This is the god Blue Body," Coyote told me, unnecessarily. Real creative name.

The god, on his sunbeam mount, circled a few times and made a whole bunch of signs with his hands. Here was one language for which the UT6 wasn't going to do me a damn bit of good. Coyote answered, and Blue Body sped off.

"What was that all about?" I asked.

"Loosely translated, and with expletives deleted, he wanted to know who you were."

A second god came down on a lightning bolt, which was impressive. He was identical to the first, except for being entirely white (you can figure out his name for yourself). I don't mean Anglo-Saxon white; I'm talking French vanilla ice cream white. He did the same thing with his hands, then followed Blue Body.

So now sunbeams and lightning bolts were whizzing all over the place, and I got to see two more Brando clones, Yellow Body and Black Body, who also made with the hands and then followed the others.

"Where are they going?" I asked.

"You'll see," Coyote said. "But let me show you something first."

He reached up into the sky, stretching like Plastic Man, and grabbed one of the sunbeams, coiling it around his arm like a garden hose. There must've been fifty feet of it. He tied one end to a stone and tossed it into the river, paying out all but a few feet. Within seconds there was a tug on the line, and he pulled it out, which seemed to take a while.

When I saw what was on the other end, I wished it could've been even longer.

It was a little monster of some kind, about the size of a basketball, though hardly what you'd call round. Okay, try to picture this: A four-year-old of limited artistic ability tries to mold a model of Yoda's head out of strawberry jam, sawdust, green

Silly Putty, and Preparation H, but fails miserably. This nightmare had a small mouth, out of which Coyote popped the stone. It tried to bite Coyote's paw, but he pulled it back. So the thing rolled over and stared up at him with these wanna-be eyes that protruded like periscopes.

"What'd you pull me out for?" he said in a kid's whiny voice. "You're in deep shit now! Wait till my mama and papa find out!"

And as the river began churning I suddenly figured out what was going on. In the legend Coyote pulls the little monster from the water, and the kid's parents, who are gods, get really pissed off and flood the place, which sends all the Navajos up to their present existence in the Fifth World.

"Why, you asshole!" I exclaimed over the roar of the surging water.

Coyote kicked the sputtering horror back into the river. "Not to worry," he said as the water became still. "It isn't time yet. Come on."

We walked along the edge of the river, which twisted in all directions, but mostly south. Up ahead, something was going on. Lots of Insect People were splashing around in a shallow part of the river, not swimming, but washing themselves. They were doing this in a silent, ritualistic sort of way.

"The gods were angry at them for being so filthy," Coyote said. "If they wanted anything else to happen, they had to take a bath first."

"But what *is* going to happen?"

"You'll see."

The four technicolor Marlon Brandos were standing there with sunbeams and lightning bolts whizzing above them. They'd spread a buckskin on the ground, upon which they now placed two ears of corn, one white, one yellow. The Insect People, allegedly clean, came out of the river and gathered around to watch. The gods spread a second buckskin over the corn, then backed away.

"What you are watching, Jack," Coyote said, "is Creation itself!"

Yeah, I knew that! It suddenly occurred to me that this was the birth of the pair the Navajos called First Man and First Woman. Always right to the point with their nomenclature, huh? Aw-right, this was great!

A wind began blowing, and it puffed up the space between the buckskins. At about the same time these ghostly figures rose out of the ground and encircled the skins. Their shapes were vaguely human; reminded me of the apparitions that came down the stairs in *Poltergeist*. Anyway, the Mirage People, oblivious to the wind, went around slowly a few times, then sank back into the ground.

Blue Body peeled off the top buckskin. The white ear of corn had turned into a man, the yellow ear a woman. Was that *cool*! Their eyes snapped open, like they'd just awakened from the dead. The Insect People mumbled among themselves. Then the man and woman stood.

First Man was an ordinary guy, not big and macho, not wimpy. First Woman, on the other hand, was a piece of work. She was fat, and for one who had just been created at the hands of the gods, she looked like hell. Her hair was stringy and unkempt; her hands and arms up to the elbows were raw, like she'd had them in dishwater for hours. While First Man's expression was serene, she wore this scowl with a message written all over it: *You dick around with me, I'll shove a porcupine up where the sun don't shine*. She made the Insect People very nervous; me, too. But Coyote seemed to like her.

The gods had built a brushwood hut nearby and now pointed the pair in that direction. When First Woman looked at First Man for the First Time, she scowled even more. On their way to the hut she started right in haranguing him, using language that would have made the whole 30th Street Naval Station in San Diego blush. To his credit, First Man gave some of it back. But I'll tell you, I really felt sorry for the guy.

Inside the hut their fighting continued; it sounded like the Battling Bickersons on the old radio show. And *these* were the progenitors of the whole Navajo race?

But after a while the arguing dwindled, and the sounds that took its place were of some serious sex. The Insect People enjoyed this. I swear, the ground by the river was shaking, and the brushwood hut bounced up and down.

Then, silence . . . for a few seconds, anyway, until the bickering started anew. As it did, two tiny babies crawled out. Now this was *really* weird, because it was like watching time-lapse photography. In a matter of a minute they had crept through infancy, toddled through toddlerhood, walked through prepubescence, strutted through adolescence, stopped at young adulthood.

Seeing them up close I thought, What's wrong with this picture? They each had long hair and delicate features, well-formed breasts . . . a penis and balls. They were hermaphrodites!

The gods weren't too thrilled about this. Yellow Body pointed the chastened twins to another brushwood hut, and they disappeared inside. First Man and First Woman continued to scream at each other, but stopped long enough for a second roll in the buckskins. Again a set of twins emerged, and they matured as quickly as the first. The gods were pleased this time, and they told the new man and woman to stand by them.

Coyote said to me, "Things happen rather quickly in the Fourth World, don't they?"

"Are you doing something?" I asked. "I mean, are we skipping around, or whatever?"

"A little bit, but not like you think. These conceptions are usually carried out in four days."

Just think, four days from bedroom to baby. Hell of a timesaver! Obstetricians might not be too thrilled about it, though.

Anyway, three more sets of normal boy and girl twins were born, time-lapsed to adulthood, and united with the first pair. After the last birth, First Man and First Woman emerged from the hut. She still looked pretty awful, and he didn't look so great himself. I could imagine why. First Woman continued to harangue her mate, but with much less conviction.

Sunbeams suddenly swooped down, lifted the pair, and carried them off toward the east. The gods were right behind them.

"Where are they going?" I asked.

"The gods are taking First Man and First Woman to Mount Blanca, where they will be taught many things they need to know. It will be done in four days."

Four days again. "Now is that four days for real, or is it like I've been seeing . . . ?"

Never finished the question, because First Man and First Woman dropped from the sky, looking all sagacious and such. The four sets of normal twins were now carried off by sunbeams and lightning bolts, also toward the east, and were back just as quickly as their parents.

In the brief time they were gone these planted fields had appeared, spreading out from the river. The hermaphrodites were outside their hut, one building tools to tend the farm, the other molding this really fine-looking pottery.

But the eight who had returned from the east didn't start right in working, no sir. If everything else till now had been weird, then this next part was even weirder. First, the Insect People stood and began weaving in and out amid the twins in what seemed like a slow do-si-do. Then the Mirage People rose up and joined the square dance, which became rather ethereal, because—I swear—you could see through all of them. They were dancing more *inside* than around one another, and you could still make out the insect features of those who had risen up through the lower worlds, though they seemed less substantial.

Before long the square dance was over, and there were no more Insect People, no more Mirage People, only people, or more precisely People.

The *Dineh*.

"You just saw eight years of intermarriage and such," Coyote said, "and you know how long eight years can be in the Fourth World. Oh, by the way, this is about the time my brother Badger and I are born out of the sky. You want to see?"

I was still fascinated watching the *Dineh*, who were scattering to work on the farm. "I'll take your word for it."

"Anyway," Coyote went on, "lots more things happen in the Fourth World. The men and women are separated again for a while, which isn't the best way to develop a race of people. There are monsters, gods, heroes, all that great stuff on which legends are based. And of course there's *me* in the midst of everything, a real thorn in everyone's side. Ah, the fate of a trickster . . . But we can skip all that and get right to the grandest trick of all, when I pull the little monster from the river and—"

"Uh, I can pass on that, too," I interrupted. "Why don't—"

Coyote suddenly winked out or something, which didn't concern me as much as what else was no longer there.

My bike!

I heard this nasty little laugh from somewhere. The ultimate trickster had struck again.

"You sonofabitch!" I exclaimed, arms flailing. "Bring it back, you hear?"

My outburst hardly drew a glance from the *Dineh*, even though I looked toward them for guidance. They continued to go about their business, and again I had the same feeling as before, that I was invisible to them.

Well, no help here, and I had to start looking somewhere. The highest hill—not really *that* high—was a quarter mile away, across the fields. I walked between rows of corn, pumpkins, and such, all of it great-looking stuff that would've gotten top dollar at the Farmer's Market. Climbing to the summit was easy; but wherever I looked, there was no sign of either Coyote or my Nishiki.

The god Black Body was suddenly standing next to me, and my life expectancy again dropped a couple of notches. Nearly fell off the hill, I did. He made a bunch of hand signals, to which I stared dumbly and shook my head.

"Can you understand me this way?" he asked in a deep, rumbling voice.

"Yes, definitely," I said.

"So be it. Are you seeking something?"

"Yeah, my . . . the thing I was riding on. Coyote took it; thought he was pretty funny, too."

The ebony Marlon Brando sighed deeply. "Ah, that Coyote, he's such a penis-brain." (I swear, that's what the UT6 said he said, and not even a twitch!) "Always pulling stunts like that. Well, he was certainly rude to do it to a stranger."

"Can you help me get it back?" I asked.

"Yes, of course."

So what happens? This sunbeam snakes between my legs and then sort of snaps up, and I get a weird (but not unpleasant) tingling sensation in my crotch. Now I'm whizzing through the air, and for the first time in my life I know what it feels like to be a witch on a broomstick. *Nerve-wracking* is a mild description. The usual scream almost crossed the boundaries of my lips, but I managed to hold it in, especially when I noticed Black Body riding next to me on a lightning bolt, looking about as excited as Ozzy Osbourne at a Verdi opera. He'd obviously done this a couple of times before.

We cruised over the black-and-white surface of the Fourth World for what seemed a long time. I was hoping the god was flipping through time, same as Coyote had done. Who knows, maybe he was, and what we were doing would have taken ten months of real time.

In any case, we finally came across the furry bastard in a valley to the east. He was trying to ride the Nishiki, and would you believe, he was actually staying up on it, but no way could he figure out the toe clips and the pedals. So as soon as the bike's forward momentum stopped it was either hop off or fall over, and he appeared to have the former mastered pretty well.

"There's the little shitball (!!) now," Black Body said. "Your thing is as good as returned to you."

Coyote saw us and waved. "Hey, Jackie and Blackie!" he called, looking smug over his creative prowess. "Now you didn't think I was going to keep this, did you? Naah, I was just having a little fun . . ."

We had landed while he was talking; glad to get that sunbeam out of my crotch. Black Body did something with his hands, and the sunbeam re-formed into a big moccasined foot, which chased after Coyote, then caught him full in the rear end. He flew high and far, and on his downward arc he let out a scream that sounded like *aaah-hoo-hoo-hooey*, the same as Goofy does when you push him off a cliff or out a window. I didn't even see where he landed.

"Well, you have your thing back," Black Body said, "so it would be best if you returned to where you came from. Very soon now Coyote will fish the little monster from the river, and this time he will not throw it back." He pointed up at the sky, or ceiling, or whatever. "The *Dineh* will rise to the Fifth World."

I looked at him dubiously. "You know what's up there?"

"Of course. This has already been, remember?"

"Too bad they couldn't have remained in the Fourth World."

"Why?"

I was surprised. "Why? Because here the *Dineh* had already become humans, and the rivers flowed, and the land was fertile, and there were benevolent gods—"

"And monsters."

"Yeah, and monsters, too; but they weren't totally there in the smarts department, and the Hero twins whipped them all—"

"The Hero Twins whipped *most* of them, not all," Black Body said. "Hunger, Poverty, Old Age, and Dirt still survive."

"Isn't that the truth?" I said dryly. "Okay, but they survived in the *Fifth* World, right? Maybe down here they would've been slain, too. I mean, what'd they have waiting for them up there?" There was a distant rumbling sound, which meant Coyote was at work, so this discussion needed to wind down fast.

"They had the *Dinetah*, the Land of the People," Black Body said reverently, "which was their destiny."

"A rugged, arid land, not too great for a lot of things. And what about enemies up the walls? First, others similar to themselves, then the Spanish. And what about good old white America on its westward migration? Or are you forgetting the war against the Army, the Long Walk, virtual imprisonment at Fort Sumner and Bosque Redondo?"

"Am *I* forgetting . . . ?" The black giant shrugged like a father about at the end of his patience with a pain-in-the-ass child. "You seem to know a lot, and are quite passionate. But let me ask you this: In your present time and place, what have *you* done to help ease the lives of the *Dineh*, or for that matter any of the people known collectively as Native Americans?"

Right, he had me there. Jack Miller opens mouth, inserts foot deep down throat. I'm not sure what color I turned.

"Sorry," I said, quite subdued.

Black Body smiled and clapped me on the shoulder (touched by a *god*, wow!). "Your zeal, and its accompanying frustration, are noted and appreciated. Remember this: The People survived Fort Sumner and Bosque Redondo to return to their homeland, and in your time, though surrounded by an uncaring white nation, they still endure, mostly because they are as one with the *Dinetah*, what some call the Navajo Way. And in the future . . ."

He hesitated, looked away. It occurred to me that this minor Navajo god might know something more than he was saying.

"You've seen the *future* of the *Dineh* too?" I asked.

"Perhaps, or perhaps not. But if I did, is it knowledge you would wish to have?"

I think you know the answer to that. I could've learned everything about my world's future in a module or from a computer at Galaxyland. Anytime I wanted to, I could hop off the Ultimate Bike Path through the proper gate and check out the same thing. Uh-uh.

Not answering him, I said. "The rumbling's getting louder. Guess you have a lot to do. But can you *drop me off* first?" I tried to make that sound as literal as possible.

Black Body understood; somehow, he did. He called down a sunbeam, making it as wide as a carpet. This time we rose nearly as high as you could get in the Fourth World. Below, vast tidal waves threatened to converge at the center. I thought about the *Dineh* and wondered how they would reach the Fifth World, then remembered it was through a hollow reed or something.

The Navajo god who looked like Marlon Brando could've just pushed me off the edge, which was what I'd figured on, my dislike of free-fall notwithstanding. But instead—this was great—he slanted the wide sunbeam down, and I had a ramp that looked like it would never end. I nodded my thanks, and he waved somberly.

Less than a third of the way down the sunbeam hill, I left the Fourth World of the *Dineh*.

CHAPTER 24

The Afterward

Thoughts about this and that while riding along the Ultimate Bike Path:

Remember how hard it was for Marty McFly to resist picking up that sports almanac when he was in the twenty-first century? You know, the one with all the scores of games that from his perspective of time and place hadn't happened yet? All he could think about was getting rich from those sure bets, as bad guy Biff Tannen eventually did in one of the other time lines.

Okay, so maybe I didn't want to know the future—*my* future, Earth's future, whatever—but do you have a clue how damn hard it was controlling the urge to have a peek at knowledge that was there for the taking? Really, put yourself in my (bike) shoes and consider what you would do. If it doesn't make you crazy, then I sure as hell would like to know how you'd handle it.

Back in 1971, when I was a mere teen, there was a song out by Paul Revere and the Raiders called "Indian Reservation." While it was specifically about the Cherokee Nation, it represented the plight of all Native Americans collectively. Now realize, I was raised on these old shoot-'em-up westerns where Indians were always the savages in war paint ready to take your scalp, burn your house or wagon, rape your wife or daughter, whatever, all the while drinking firewater. At the end of the song they say that someday the Cherokee Nation *will* return, and tom-toms beat in the background. I used to get real nervous when I heard it, trying to *imagine* such an unthinkable thing happening. Fortunately, my enlightenment wasn't too long in coming, and subsequent hearings of "Indian Reservation" never failed to run a chill up my spine, thinking how fine that would be.

My experience in the Fourth World had got me thinking about that song again, especially after what Black Body had said just before I left. What happens in the future? Is the song prophetic? *Do* the Indian Nations return? And if so, in what way? Is it a normal, peaceful share-and-share-alike coexistence with white

America? Or do the ghosts of the ancestors rise up to destroy all those not of Indian blood, as another prophecy foretold?

Which leads right back to Thought Number One, to learn the future or to leave it alone. Maybe it hasn't happened yet at the time of Galaxyland. Maybe it doesn't take a hundred years, but a thousand or more; maybe . . .

Shit.

A thought about Holly Dragonette, whom I hardly knew yet, but was going to get to know a whole lot better in a few hours (more or less). Thinking about her, and all this other crazy business, reminded me of a wonderful movie, *Somewhere in Time,* which was based on an even more wonderful book called *Bid Time Return,* by Richard Matheson. In the film, Christopher Reeve (yeah, Superman) is a present-day playwright who falls in love with Jane Seymour, or her picture anyway, from over half a century back. (I used to flip out over Jane Seymour, but these days she has stiff competition from Michelle Pfeiffer and Jessica Rabbit.) He travels back in time to find her, and when they first lay eyes on each other, you know what she says? This is *cool;* she says, "Is it you?" And of course, that really freaks him out. One of the most romantic, shivers-up-your-back scenes from a movie ever.

No, that's not exactly what Holly said when she saw me last night. It was more like, "Hiya, I'm Holly, you must be Jack," and there was a handshake. I was only thinking that with all this time-and-whatever travel I was into, how neat it *would've* been . . . But of course, Matheson's story was just that, a story, right?

And a last thought about Henry Miller; that's right, the one who played some small part in my existence. He was thirty-eight when I was born, but an *old* thirty-eight, because he'd already had one *mild* heart attack and was on his way to bleeding ulcers and a couple of other less mild heart attacks into his forties. Add this to the fact that most of his adult life he worked six days a week, and I'm not sure I had much of a dad to fall back on. Oh, he did the best he could; occasional trips to the Bronx Zoo, Yankee games (now *also* known as the Bronx Zoo), the latest James Bond movie, stuff like that. But so much of the time he just wasn't there, or if he was there, he wasn't well enough to do anything. Like when I wanted to toss a baseball around, and he tried but had to stop after ten minutes because it hurt so much.

I'm glad I didn't have a date on the night I went to the movies to see *Field of Dreams*. It was just Phil Melkowitz and me. At the end, when Ray Kinsella's dad shows up, young and in baseball uniform, and they were talking and stuff, it was like seeing your life acted in front of you on the big screen. And when Ray asked his dad if he wanted to have a catch, and they started tossing the baseball around . . . It's hard to be cool with these tears running down your face like the Colorado River after a snowmelt. All these people were filing out, but I just sat there, because I couldn't get up, and the end credits rolled all the way to the copyright. Phil kind of knew, and he showed sensitivity by sitting there and saying nothing, until I got my shit together and was ready to leave.

There had to be something more than just physical about the Ultimate Bike Path, because it was unreal choosing the gate that I did, considering what was going through my brain.

It was a Bart Simpson; yeah, one of those creepy, chalk-on-the-blackboard, fork-on-the-plate, finger-down-your-backbone Bart Simpsons, which had been few and far between for a while. It came after a long run of Elmer Fudds, and it was ominous. But when it appeared, there was no doubt I had to go in . . .

So I did.

Jeez, was this place unreal! I shifted down from the Vurdabrok Gear as a natural action or something, because I sure don't remember doing it. First off, it didn't look like there was anything solid under my tires, which was enough to freak me out by itself. But I wasn't falling, and when I pedaled it felt like the Nishiki was going . . . forward, I guess, although I really couldn't be sure of *that*, either. It reminded me of an old *Star Trek* episode where the *Enterprise* is inside a black void, being pulled toward this huge amoeba-thing. When Kirk asks Scotty for reverse thrust, they go forward, and vice versa. Kind of made them crazy.

There was this gray haze all around me, like being in some factory town's record-breaking day on the air pollution index. Only this stuff didn't have any smell, or feel, and so far wasn't causing any adverse effects. I could make out nothing substantial through it, no buildings, no mountains. And because it wasn't solid—despite my tires grabbing hold of *something*—I couldn't even swear to you that I wasn't riding upside down, or sideways, or whatever.

And all the time, that creepy feeling from outside the gate

persisted. At least it wasn't any stronger, but it was still unnerving. The sooner I understood what was going on, the better . . .

Wait a minute, did I say it wasn't getting stronger? All of a sudden my angst was in overdrive. There was this devastating need to *escape*, as though I'd been tied in a chair for ten straight hours watching Mister Rogers changing his shoes and singing, "It's a beautiful day in the neighborhood." For a moment I was afraid of hyperventilating.

The gray haze seemed to pull back or something, and I was in a wider area; a "room," for want of a better description. It was lighter, almost white, though nothing like the place where I'd first met the Old Guy. Along most of its circular perimeter was—I swear—a bench. Something told me this was the place where I was supposed to be, and while it freaked me out no end, I got off the bike. No, I didn't plummet down into some infinite oblivion, but I'll tell you, the pumping action of my heart could've raised enough Alaskan crude to fuel all the cars in southern California for a week.

Remember I said *most* of the room's perimeter? There was one area, totally black, about four feet across and twice that in height. A "door," I suppose, though in reality (not a good word) it was more like the mouth of a cave. Staring at it, I thought my eyes were going to do a jack-in-the-box out of their sockets. Whatever anxiety I felt outside the Bart Simpson gate was enhanced a thousand times here. Still, something was drawing me. Laying the bike down on its side (I think), I started toward the maw.

Until now there had been absolute silence in wherever-this-was; I don't even think my derailleur made any noise. But I could hear something, and with each hesitant step toward the opening, it grew louder.

It was . . . music. An old rock-and-roll song: "Chantilly Lace," by the Big Bopper. I heard one line clearly, but then it became garbled as something else first mixed with it, then took its place: "Summertime Blues," the original one by Eddie Cochran. The same thing happened again, and this time I caught a piece of "Dream a Little Dream of Me" by Mama Cass, the same song they used to advertise the California state lottery.

What in hell was going on here?

Somehow I knew the "door" was open, but as yet I could see nothing on the other side. Mama Cass's smooth song became Ricky Nelson's "Hello Mary Lou," which became Frankie Lymon's "I Want You to be My Girl," which even more quickly became Buddy Holly's "Oh Boy." Now they were changing *really* fast; you know, like the snippets disk jockeys on the oldies stations play, and if you guess the song you win a dozen Winchell's donuts or something?

I was within an arm's length of the opening; my angst was crawling around in my throat.

A figure took shape in the blackness of the other side. Ethereal at first, then less so, but never what you could call solid. He turned and looked at me.

It was Elvis.

Not older and heavier and dressed in a Wayne Newton hand-me-down, but young and slim and boyish from the fifties and early sixties, looking like he just stepped off the set of *Love Me Tender*. He glanced at me, smiled the smile that millions of girls would have died for, threw me a two-fingered salute.

Then he sort of faded away.

No, I wasn't counting in my head all the money the *National Enquirer* would pay me when I got back. Seeing the King, hearing all the songs I'd heard, I was beginning to figure it out.

You've probably done that already, right? *All* those songs were by rockers who had died way before their time.

The blackness beyond this "door" was some kind of rock-and-roll *heaven*.

I took another step toward it.

"You got it almost exactly right, Jack."

The figure appeared suddenly in the doorway, growing like an out-of-control weed. I stumbled backward and would have jumped out of my skin, as the saying goes, were such a thing possible. The guy was tall, funereal-looking, sort of like one of the living dead in the Romero movies, except that he had a nice, reassuring smile.

"Who are you?" I asked, hoping my voice didn't sound like I was passing through puberty.

"You can call me the Doorkeeper. Sorry if I startled you, but you were about to step through here, and I don't think you really want to do that yet."

"Why, because this *is* rock-and-roll heaven? And by the way, did you read my mind or something?"

"Yes, something. And no, we never refer to this as *heaven*.

What you see behind me, Jack, is Rock-and-Roll Afterward. There are many different Afterwards, as you can imagine."

The music again. Janis Joplin's "Me and Bobby McGee" becoming Ritchie Valens's "Oh Donna" (I *loved* that song) becoming Otis Redding's "Sittin' on the Dock of the Bay."

"All of these Afterwards, they're located behind the Bart Simpson gates, right?"

The Doorkeeper pondered this for a moment. "Bart Simpson . . . oh, yes, precisely. You were uncomfortable passing them, weren't you?"

"Yeah, I suppose. But this one sort of . . ."

"Pulled you in, it did?"

"Uh-huh."

"There's someone here who wanted to meet you."

"Meet *me*?"

"Yes; it had to do with your thoughts as you rode the Ultimate Bike Path."

"Say what?" Now I was totally confused, and the Doorkeeper saw this.

"You'll understand, shortly. Please stay where you are; sit down on the bench, if you will. Our, ah, residents can enter the waiting area for a brief period of time."

"I got it; but I couldn't go in there unless I was dead, is that it?"

The Doorkeeper shook his head. "There is a way for you to travel in any of the Afterwards, but as yet you're unprepared. Perhaps in the future, Jack, but not now."

He retracted into the ground. To tell the truth, I wasn't sorry that he hadn't invited me in. The aura of the place was really getting to me, and it was a relief backing away even a few steps. But the anticipation of traveling inside an Afterward would sustain me for a long time, until—as Captain Picard of the *Enterprise* would say—I could finally "make it so."

I was sitting on the bench and trying to figure out what the Doorkeeper had meant, listening to Del Shannon's "Runaway" become Jim Croce's "Time in a Bottle." A figure appeared on the other side of the "door," hesitated a moment, then stepped into the waiting area. Seeing him, I understood.

"Hello, Jack," Harry Chapin said.

"Hi, Harry," I replied, wondering if my voice could be heard.

He pointed at the Nishiki. "Hey, nice bike."

"Thank you."

Harry Chapin sat down next to me. Maybe I should've stood, but my legs probably would have buckled. He looked the same as I always remembered him, either on television or the live concerts that I'd been to, a few in New York during the seventies, before I left, the last in California—shortly before his death in a traffic accident in the summer of 1981. A head of hair that had *not* been worked on by Vidal Sassoon; the benevolent face with the dreamer's smile that occasionally took the form of an impish grin. A flowered shirt, a pair of white slacks; no sequins, no glitz. An ordinary Joe who wouldn't warrant a second glance if he sat next to you on the subway.

But such a profound effect on my life, and the lives of so many people, not only through his music, but in other ways.

"So you heard what I was thinking," I said.

Harry grinned. "Well, heard, felt, something like that. And since you were in the neighborhood, I thought it'd be nice if you . . . dropped in. You being the first Earther to ride the Ultimate Bike Path and all."

This self-described "Third-rate folk/rock singer of long, wordy songs," who once did a nearly six-minute ditty about thirty thousand pounds of bananas, didn't have his den walls filled with platinum albums or gold singles. Ask the average person today to name two of Harry Chapin's songs and they probably could, but not much more. One choice would likely be "Taxi," his first biggie, which had nothing to do with Danny DeVito or Christopher Lloyd.

The other, without a doubt, would be "Cat's in the Cradle."

The song came out in 1974, and I fell in love with the simple lyrics. You know the story, how the father is so busy all the time that he's never around for his son, but the undaunted kid really thinks Dad is cool and vows to be *just like him* when he grows up. At the end of the song, Dad is old and retired, and he asks the son to come and visit, but now the son is too busy, and he's really sorry and all . . . And the old man, way too late, realizes his son *had* turned out *just like him*.

After my father died, "Cat's in the Cradle" took on a whole new meaning.

And after Harry Chapin died . . . I could never again hear that song without getting choked up.

Here are two "Cat's in the Cradle" incidents. The first happened in the early eighties, after Harry's death, when I was still married to Carol. Back then I was as interested in religion as

I am now, which is to say hardly at all. Carol, who had made a study of the world's religions, had a secular curiosity, even though her upbringing as a Catholic had been more intense. So in an attempt to share her interests, I would go along to services in everything from the Presbyterian Church to the synagogue to the Self-Realization Fellowship.

I'll never forget one Yom Kippur service, when this rabbi, a young and rather "hip" guy, read a "poem" to the worshipers. It was Harry Chapin's "Cat's in the Cradle." He didn't sing the words, didn't even recite the chorus once, just the meat of it. Looking around, I realized from their smiles and nods that about half the people knew what was going on. Even so, they were as riveted as the others by the words, and when he got to the end, there was *gasps*. I swear. The words affected the congregation, and me too, even though I'd heard them a thousand times. I vowed that when I had kids, I'd *never* be invisible to them.

A couple of years later, I was in what they call the black depths of despair (which sounds like prosaic bullshit). The marriage to Carol was ending; the job sucked. My body was going the way of Jabba the Hutt. And on this one morning, on the anniversary of my father's death, I was crawling along in early-morning traffic headed toward the aforementioned shitty job . . . when "Cat's in the Cradle" came on the radio. With everything else on my mind, I also thought about Harry Chapin.

I had to pull out of the traffic for a while until I could stop crying.

Now, lest you think I bawl like a baby at the drop of a sombrero, I can probably count on one hand all the times I've done so in the past twenty years. You just happen to know two of those times, that's all.

"Thanks for thinking about me that way, Jack," Harry said.

Oh, yeah, I forgot he could hear everything I had rattling around in my brain. "Thank *you*, Harry." He held out his hand. I looked at him. "Is it . . . all right?"

"Try it."

I shook Harry Chapin's hand. His grip was firm. I held it for a moment.

Then, what the hell, I hugged the guy. And he hugged me back.

"I have to go now, Jack," he said.

"You do? But . . . you just got here."

"We can only stay in the waiting area for a brief time."

I hadn't hardly said anything at all to this man, who had given half his concert earnings to combat world hunger and who had raised millions more by *noodging* other performers, politicians, and the like into doing something about it. I hadn't told him how much a lesser-known "story song" of his, "Shooting Star," meant to all the creative and weird people of the world, like me. I hadn't asked him *anything* about what it was like in the Afterward, a place that both terrified and beckoned me.

"There'll be another time for us to discuss all of it, Jack," Harry said, gesturing toward the opening. "It's not so terrifying in the Afterward, not when you know how to get around. I'll enjoy showing you through this one."

Harry Forster Chapin, 1942–1981, waved to me, stepped into the Rock-and-Roll Afterward, and was gone.

I had followed him across three quarters of the waiting area. The music was still playing. Roy Orbison's "In Dreams" became Jim Morrison's "Light My Fire," which became John Lennon's "Give Peace a Chance."

The Rock-and-Roll Afterward fell silent.

I knew that Harry was going to say good-bye to me with a song. I prepared myself for "Cat's in the Cradle," or "Shooting Star," or maybe "Remember When the Music."

The one he chose, bless him, was "30,000 Pounds of Bananas."

CHAPTER 25

The Sacred Pink Pools

So you're wondering, how did I get back here on the Ultimate Bike Path? I'll tell you: I don't know.

All the time I was in that weird place I was wondering about how I would find a hill or a mountain or a building to leap from in a single bound. Then I got back on the bike, and even though I was in twenty-first gear, my feet could barely keep up with the pedals. The slide into the Vurdabrok Gear had been simple; I wish they were all like this.

Under normal circumstances I would have been *more* than ready for reality time. Get back home, clean up, go and meet the potentially wonderful Holly Dragonette. But after the last one, I needed to finish with something a bit . . . *lighter,* shall we say? Hopefully, a gate that took me to a Three Stooges film festival, or put me inside George Carlin's brain. Okay, maybe not anything like those, but *something* to air out the head.

A snowman with the needles; no, not the one with the yellow ribbon. There were lots of others, most appearing shortly after I returned through the Bart Simpson head—which, by the way, didn't seem that creepy to me anymore. A random pick, here. Pop through a snowman and . . .

. . . come out in a place that looked pretty interesting, one with mountains and trees and grass and rivers and a sky with celestial bodies in it and all kinds of familiar-looking stuff.

But everything was the wrong color.

For example, the sky was amber with three fire engine–red suns, or maybe two suns and a moon, or . . . whatever. The bodies of water were either puce or pink. Most of the trees had black trunks with silver leaves, and there was also a ubiquitous bush with more colors in it than a Scotsman's kilts. The whole place looked like someone had screwed with the knobs of a Sony Trinitron.

The ground—which, by the way, was periwinkle-blue—wasn't

too hard to ride upon. It was tightly packed, a bit gritty on the surface. I got back on the bike and started pedaling, wary of holes or whatever, but there were none. The only things in my path were these foot-high, olive-drab tubers, each with a long, skinny protuberance; some sort of mutant potato, I guess. From the side, every one of them looked like a profile of Richard Nixon's head.

I had entered this place in the hills, but after about three miles of gradual descent I was on the floor of a broad valley. Those oversized Nixon potatoes were still around; more of them, in fact, though still not much of an obstacle. Yeah, this was the kind of place I had in mind to chill out (figuratively, of course, since it felt like about ninety humid degrees). Ride across the weird landscape, lay down by a puce river, maybe even take a swim . . . as long as I didn't risk pissing off something scaly and toothy.

A few minutes later the first sign of wildlife appeared: an orange duck. Now that's a *real* orange duck, not the French gourmet preparation of it. The little guy was gnawing (yeah, *gnawing*, with these sharp teeth) on one of the Nixon potatoes, which was a sort of Anusol-gray color inside. When I stopped to watch, the duck turned and looked at me with beady white eyes.

"Get the hell away, this one is mine," it said in a nasty voice that didn't sound like either Donald or Daffy.

"Hey, I don't want your potato," I told it, "I just—

It came snapping at my rear tire with those wicked teeth. Now I don't think a little orange duck could bite through Cycle Pro Mudslinger tires, but I wasn't about to prove myself right or wrong. I bolted forward, the fowl catching nothing but a mouthful of tread print.

"Hope to see you on a chafing dish someday," I called back. Sorry, but I didn't like the feathery little bastard.

Okay, rule number one here, beware the orange duck. I passed others gnawing on Nixon potatoes, and all of them took a run at the bike, except for one pair, who squawked and flapped and bit the shit out of each other. They raised a cloud of feathers, some of which got in my mouth, the derailleur, among other places.

The Nixon potatoes finally dwindled down to nothing, and with them went the orange ducks. Feeling safe now, I stopped and cleaned up the feathers. Got some grease on my hands from the derailleur, but that was okay, because twenty yards ahead was one of those puce tributaries I'd seen from the hills. Not hardly a river, more like a babbling brook. The water was real cold, and you barely noticed the weird color after you scooped it out. Yeah, but I still wasn't about to drink the stuff, only wash my hands in it. My water bottle was half-filled with warm Gatorade, and it was still drinkable in spite of all the places it had been.

So here I am, relaxing by this nifty little brook, tossing smooth green stones into it, when one of these seemingly solid "stones" crumbles between my fingers. Lifting the bits up to my face for a closer look, I caught a whiff of something familiar. Took me a few seconds, because it was so out of place: The pieces of stone smelled exactly like Cracker Jacks, which happened to be one of my favorite foods on the planet—*our* planet, anyway.

Sure, but the smell didn't mean anything; this could've been some deadly poison, for all I knew. So I made like the cops in the movies, when they want to see if the white powder they found on someone's table is cocaine or Coffeemate. I picked some up on my finger and put it on the tip of my tongue.

Hell, it tasted like Cracker Jacks, too. But again I made like the cops and spat it out.

This was interesting: Sitting by the brook, I had been idly picking up the green stones within easy reach. Most of them were about the size of your average marble. But on the other side the stones were larger, and many were clustered together. This weird rubble stretched for fifty yards toward some low hills, which in fact looked like even *larger* clusters of the same stones.

Cracker Jack hills? Naaah.

This warranted attention, especially after I heard a noise coming from that direction. No way could I roll the Nishiki through the rubble, so I hid it in a real dense clump of that plaid bush. Did a good job, too; you could be standing right over it and not know the bike was there.

Walking across the green rubble was easy, because the stuff practically disintegrated when you stepped on it. Forget climbing the hills, right? The smell of Cracker Jacks was stronger, and wonderful; it was like I'd fallen into a giant box and was sloshing around. I tried hard to concentrate on the sound, which was louder now. Definitely a human voice, chanting in some sort of a singsong. As yet I could not make out the words.

Now I was standing ankle-deep in crushed Cracker Jack stones. Peering between two of the hills, I saw something really weird. There was this guy, and he looked *sort of* human, except for his teal-blue skin. He wasn't wearing much, only what looked like a pair of yellow jockey shorts. I hoped that was their true color, and not some accident he'd had. Anyway, the guy's most noticeable feature was that he was fat; no, let me rephrase that: He was *fat*. You remember Lard Ass Hogan in *Stand By Me?* Nothing; a wisp of a boy. This fellow looked like a crew-cut, beardless Dom DeLuise after another one of his diets went awry.

Here's weird thing number two: The fat guy was standing at the edge of a pond, a *pink* pond, of course, with both chubby arms stretched toward the heavens. The pond was sort of round, about ten feet in diameter. He stood like that for a few seconds, then dropped to his knees, head bowed. He started to say something, and I knew this was the source of the chanting.

"O Sacred Pool, see me through the Season of Sustenance," he intoned. "Carry me along the Path of Provender. Guide me through the Valley of Victuals. I pray to you, Sacred Pool, in the Name of Nourishment."

The Season of Sustenance; a year-round season, if you asked me.

He got up, moved a couple of steps around the pond (the Sacred Pool, excuse *me*), and repeated the whole nine yards. This went on and on, and after a few minutes it got sort of boring. Still, I wondered what he was up to.

Finally he knelt by what looked like a canvas sack. He'd moved farther away from where I watched, and I couldn't make out exactly what it was he took out of the sack, but it was big and purple and mushy and I'm not sure I really wanted to know.

Standing again with the *whatever* held skyward, he said, "In gratitude for your guidance, O Sacred Pool, I offer you the Stomach of my Sister."

Jesus, the Stomach of his Sister? I hoped this was just symbolic or something. In any case, handling the Stomach of his Sister like a basketball, he arced it high toward the center of the pink pool. You would've expected a big splash, but it didn't happen. Instead, the—you know—sat on the surface for a moment, then was *blurped* under, like sinking into quicksand.

The ritual apparently over, this obese person walked away from the pool toward me. Five yards from the hills he sat down amid a really dense clump of green rubble; shook the earth for a hundred yards around, I swear. The stones beneath his butt were pulverized into microscopic particles.

You know what he did next? He began shoving the stones into

his mouth, swallowing without even chewing or tasting, shoving in some more.

Shove swallow, shove swallow. At least I knew now that the Cracker Jack stones were edible. But watching this guy, I really didn't have any appetite for them.

You think the rotund fellow was in ecstasy? To tell the truth, he looked more pissed off than anything. A scowl remained frozen on his face as *shove swallow* continued. The folds of his flesh flapped on the ground, pulverizing more stones; his stomach emitted a deep rumbling, like a Bay Area aftershock.

Shove swallow, shove swallow. Pretty soon all the rubble within reach was gone. I wondered how in *hell* he would get himself up on his feet, but he had the transportation problem well in hand. He leaned over on his side, rolled like a manic bowling ball to the nearest clump of stones, and began *shove swallow* anew.

Okay, enough of this. I was pretty much over the encounter beyond the last gate, so no great need to hang around. In three hours of real time I could be sitting across from Holly Dragonette, having brunch; or I could stay here and watch this guy stuff his face.

Tough choice.

So I pinpointed the nearest steep hill (hopefully not made of Cracker Jacks) as I walked back to the brook. It was only a couple of miles away in a different direction from where I'd come; hopefully I could avoid the maze of Richard Nixon potatoes and malcontent orange ducks.

Shit, the Nishiki was gone again! Not winked out of existence, like Coyote had done back in the Fourth World. The plaid bush was all torn up, and there were footprints around. Someone (more than one, I think) had carried it off. Probably saw me stashing it, because they would not have found it so easily.

Well, belay that brunch with Holly. Here goes the start of another chase. Now they couldn't have gotten that far. I'd only been gone a little while, and if they were anything like the guy pigging out on Cracker Jack–flavored rocks, their swiftness afoot would be dubious.

The tracks led along the brook, which soon wound through a sparse grove of those silver-leafed trees. Smaller versions of the Nixon potatoes began popping up, and I worried about running into more of the orange ducks. There was another ubiquitous growth here, a ruby-red mushroom with a long, twisty stem. It

gave off a strong smell of pepperoni. Hell of a cost-effective way
to top a pizza, I thought.

Damn, these guys were faster than I thought. The footprints
emerged from the trees and went on toward some hills about two
hundred yards away. I *had* to see them here, right?

Wrong.

Maybe I'd been following the wrong trail. Uh-uh, no way, it
was the only one. Now I was really getting pissed. I moved as
swiftly as I could through the hot, humid air, then up the easiest
slope I could find. You wouldn't believe the sounds I heard
coming from the other side.

You wouldn't believe what I *saw* on the other side.

First off, there were pink pools, plural. Not two or three or
eight, but . . . oh, *lots* of them, spreading out beyond my range
of vision. Seen from high above, they probably would have
looked like one vast lake. But they were definitely individual
pools, some smaller than the first one I'd seen, some larger, most
about the same. The space between them was often little more
than a couple of feet wide.

Near the pools stood a . . . village, you could call it, if you
were stretching the truth. A collection of broad, dilapidated huts
built of yellow and black wood and topped by roofs of plaid bush;
not your basic cover of *Better Homes and Gardens*. Fat blue adults
and fat blue children were everywhere, and yo! guess what they
were doing. Many chowed down on the Richard Nixon potatoes,
the Anusol-colored insides dribbling down their triple chins.
Others wolfed pepperoni mushrooms, while a few did the *shove
swallow* number on Cracker Jack stones. Most of whatever else
they were eating was unrecognizable. There was also a big fire
going, where ponderous-breasted women turned dozens of orange
ducks on spits. I was surprised these folks could wait long enough
for anything to be cooked.

And what a disgusting cacophony of belches, farts, and
stomach rumblings these sour-faced folk made. Jeez! That's right,
they looked about as happy with their lot as the first guy. Of those
who weren't eating, some were rolling around on the ground in
agony, hands clutching their stomachs. The rest were kneeling by
pink pools, going through that same stupid ritual.

All right, what about my bike? I didn't see it anywhere at first;
then I noticed one of the blue guys out amid the pink pools,
holding it over his head.

"In gratitude for your guidance, O Sacred Pool, I offer you the Stomach of my Sister," he called.

My bike was the Stomach of his Sister. Okay, then; what the first guy had thrown in wasn't really . . .

My bike was the Stomach of his Sister! Pardon my Klingonese, but fuck that, no way!

"*Hey, drop it!*" I shouted, running down the hill. But too late. He tossed it atop one of the pink pools, where it *blurped* under even more quickly than the other guy's Stomach of his Sister.

Well, that's great! For all I knew, this pool went down to the center of the planet. And even if it was only two feet deep, the stuff in it might dissolve the flesh off your bones. Shit!

Dodging past all the other fat blue people, I ran out into the maze of pools and confronted the guy who had just sank my Nishiki. "You asshole!" I exclaimed, gesturing toward the offending pool. "Do you know what—"

"Aaaargh," he grunted, and pushed me over on my ass like I was a twig. *Strong* sucker. Apparently he had a heavy date with an orange duck and some Nixon potatoes, and nothing was going to stand in his way. He waddled off.

I stood up and stared at the pink goop, hoping to see a handlebar or tire pop up. No luck. Maybe with a long stick or something I could poke around . . .

Wait a minute, these blue people had suddenly become real interested in me. Still belching, farting, and rumbling, they pointed fingers as they moved toward me amid the Sacred Pools. The expressions they wore did not foretell a dinner invitation.

"Who is that?" one of them asked.

"Not one of us, that's for sure," another replied.

"Maybe he's from the Far Tribe People."

"Or the Far Far Tribe People."

"Hey, listen," I called, "the only reason I came here is—"

"Who cares what Tribe he's from? We'll do what we want with him."

"Yes," the biggest and fattest said, "and as your Chief, I claim him to be the Stomach of my Sister!"

Oh, yeah, bullshit and a half! I retreated into the maze, figured I'd circle around, get back into the hills or trees, work out a strategy for retrieving the bike. But it seemed that no matter which way I turned, the damn pink pools were still there. And these blue bozos, slow afoot and all, were clogging up most of the arteries.

I even hopped a few of the smaller pools, but they kept right on a-comin'.

Pretty soon I was way the hell into the maze, and guess what, there was no place left to go.

Now this wasn't really what I'd had in mind for an end, becoming a sacrificial Stomach of a bunch of blue fat people's Sister. And my wonderful bike, either dissolved or deep down, *with the Vurdabrok Gear*. Might as well rub the Bukko and get the hell out of here. Can't worry about wasting a turn now, because without the Nishiki the Old Guy and his pals probably won't even send me back again.

Shit, I really liked that bike.

Okay, Miller, enough of this defeatist crap. You've gotten out of some pretty deep kaka before, and you can do it now. You'll get past these turkeys, and you'll pull the Nishiki out, and you'll say bye-bye to this off-color world.

I will?

They were on nearly every path. My only choice was leaping across one of the ten-foot pools.

In other words, no choice at all.

I squeezed the Bukko, then let it go.

"All right, wait just a frigging minute!" I bellowed, startling even myself. This brought them to a halt . . . for the moment.

The Chief took a step forward, hands crossed on his loudly gurgling stomach. His scowl could have cracked a mirror. He said, "What do you want?"

"I want to know what's going on here. Why did you throw my bike into that stuff? Why do you want to throw *me* in?"

"Because it is law, passed down to our people since the beginning of time from the Bird, who was the wisest and holiest, and we have never disobeyed."

"So, the Bird's the Word, huh?" I said, trying to keep a straight face.

"That is exactly right," the Chief said solemnly. "The Bird told the people, 'Put the Stomach of my Sister into the waters of the Scared Pool.' And so it has always been. You're next."

"Hold on!" I exclaimed as they started toward me again.

"What is it now?" he said real bitchily, after letting loose a fart that would have knocked birds off power lines.

Facing whatever I was here, I found myself getting bold. "Why do you people have to be so mean?" I asked.

His stomach gurgled. "You'd be mean too, if you felt like we did all the time."

"Well, maybe I could offer a suggestion."

"What's that?"

"Stop eating so much."

The blue folk all looked aghast; the Chief pondered this for a moment. "We never thought of that," he said. "Of course, it is the Word of the Bird. But maybe we'll give it some consideration . . . later. Take him!"

Okay, this called for *real* drastic measures. I whipped off my Padres hat and dipped it in one of the Sacred Pools. Once again the corpulent contingent stopped. Being careful not to drip any on my skin, I wielded it menacingly. They groaned, took a step backward.

Now, let me tell you about the hat I was sacrificing here. I'd bought it during the Padres' magical 1984 season, and it was on my head the night the Garv hit the home run in the fourth play-off game and broke the hearts of Cub fans for perhaps another half century. You think I was thrilled about the possibility of watching it disintegrate in front of my face?

But nothing happened, and I was able to hold off these turkeys . . . though not for long.

With my back turned for a moment, one of them managed to shove my arm.

The Padres hat went flying into one of the Sacred Pools.

When I turned to face the offending porker, the Chief grabbed me from behind.

I reached for the Bukko but couldn't get a grip on it.

The Chief lifted me high in the air. I didn't make it easy for him when he said, "In gratitude for . . . *oh* . . . your guidance, O Sacred Pool, I . . . *ah* . . . offer you the Stomach of my . . . *blaaah* . . . Sister!"

Jack Miller, son of Rose Miller Leventhal and the late Henry Miller, went flying into one of the Sacred Pools.

The blue people belched, farted, and rumbled in respect.

Being the heaviest Stomach of their Sister yet, I sank quickly.

The pool was four feet deep, and the stuff in it wasn't about to dissolve the flesh off my bones.

When I stood up and grinned, the people gasped.

The stuff in the pool had a familiar smell; the stuff in the pool had a familiar taste.

The stuff in the Sacred Pool was Pepto-Bismol, or a generic facsimile thereof.

"This . . . this is a *sacrilege*!" the Chief exclaimed.

"No, I don't think so," I told him. "Let me ask you some questions. This . . . uh, Bird of yours, he had a sister, right?"

"Of course."

"And back then, he and his people pigged, ah, consumed Victuals and Provender and what-not at the same leisurely pace as yourselves, so his sister could conceivably have had tummy troubles of her own."

"Yes, that's true."

"Now, are the words of the Bird written down anywhere?"

He shook his head. "They are passed along through the people."

"Well, there you are! Word of mouth often gets turned around. The Bird didn't say, 'Put the Stomach of my Sister into the waters of the Sacred Pool.' What he said was, 'Put the waters of the Sacred Pool into the Stomach of my Sister.' Here, watch."

They just about freaked out when I scooped up some Pepto-Bismol and drank it. Smacked my lips, which of course was bullshit. Reaching over into the next pool. I retrieved my hat and held it up to the Chief.

"You try this, and see what it will do for your stomach."

He took the hat hesitantly, sniffed the stuff, tasted it with his tongue, then downed it all. You know the little plastic cup that gives you an adult dose? I'd say he drank the equivalent of about fifteen of them.

The blue people watched and waited silently. After about a minute this wide grin broke out on the Chief's puffy face.

"It's working!" he cried. "My stomach feels better already!"

Well, the rest of it went like this: While the Chief pulled me out and put the Padres hat back on my head, his people began lapping up Pepto-Bismol like you wouldn't believe. Before long, the place was all smiles. They extracted the Nishiki and did a hell of a job cleaning it. Then, a feast was thrown in my honor. I gotta say, they took my words to heart and barely ate a thing. I skipped the Richard Nixon potatoes but sampled the Cracker Jack stones, the pepperoni mushrooms, and some of the orange duck (on general principles).

And they were still pretty happy when I pedaled off. Didn't want to overstay my welcome; I mean, with fifteen adult doses of Pepto-Bismol in every one of them, I'd say a dam was about to be raised across the river of their lives, wouldn't you?

CHAPTER 26

A Final Scenario

This kind of thing will sound familiar, I bet. You've been going to garage sales on weekends for years, and you've lost count of how many ceramic aardvarks with clocks in their bellies you've seen. Then, one day, you decide that a ceramic aardvark with a clock in its belly is the prize you've just *got* to have. So, now that you're looking for the thing, when will you find it? Probably at the same time Andrew Dice Clay is asked to do the benediction at Brigham Young University's graduation ceremonies.

The doorway back to Camp Pendleton was being conspicuous by its absence, and I was getting annoyed, because I really wanted back. I was more than ready for a big dose of reality time. And it wasn't just the gate to *my* place and time; *none* of the blue gates with pyramids leading into Earth's past or future or whatever had popped up for the longest time now.

What was going on here?

Just to show you how much I wanted back, somewhere along the Ultimate Bike Path I even passed up the diamond of light that would have led me to Ralph Ralph, and you *know* how hard I'd looked for that one. Okay, I was committed; but the run of Floridas with Stetson hats and Elmer Fudds and triangles with fireworks and so on was without end. And get this, a new gate suddenly shows up, a lemon-colored one shaped like Gorbachev's birthmark. Not only a *new* gate, but one that *really* wanted me to come in, I mean *badly*.

But resolve and perseverance always wins out, right? My gate showed up rather suddenly between a black circle and a Bart Simpson head. Bingo! I raced through happily . . .

. . . and was hurtling down the Stuart Mesa hill at thirty-two mph, only a few yards behind my old friends Muriel and Walt, who even on a steep declivity somehow managed to ride slowly.

"Ohhh . . . *shit!*" I exclaimed and swerved to the left to avoid them. Into the road, of course, where a marine humvee truck nearly put me into the ravine. The driver laid on his horn; the troops in back of it grinned at me.

I don't understand. Stuart Mesa Road had been deserted when I left, and it should've been the same now. I'd have to ask the Old Guy . . .

Who, by the way, was waiting at the other end of the Santa Margarita River bridge. In fact, three of *him* were. They all looked the same, and each was straddling an identical Schwinn World, and they were dressed about the same, which is to say, inappropriately. I knew my Old Guy because *his* Dockers were still tan, while the others wore blue and gray respectively.

"Well, Jack," my Old Guy said, "you're probably curious about how you came to lose"—he looked at his watch—"over eight minutes."

Eight minutes. Well, at least it wasn't three hours. "Yeah, I am," I told him.

"You came through your gate just to the left of center. It happens, sometimes. But do be careful in the future."

"Or the past," I said jokingly, but none of them got it.

Muriel and Walt finally got across the bridge, nodded at the Old Guys and me, and went on their merry way. Study Group Old Guy #1 (I think) said, "We've been so looking forward to meeting you, Jack."

"Oh, I was going to tell him that!" Study Group Old Guy #2 exclaimed.

"Thanks," I told them. "Then you're the whole study group?"

"Yes, but that might well change," my Old Guy said.

"Indeed," Study Group Old Guy #1 said. "You are one of the most interesting subjects we've ever followed along the *mhuva lun gallee*. We have spoken to others about you, and I know many of them will sit in with us during at least part of your travels yet to come."

"Yeah, well, that's nice," I told him, "but I can tell you, it's not going to be for a while."

"Some more *reality time*, Jack?" my Old Guy asked.

"You got it."

"What will you be doing?" Study Group Old Guy #1 asked.

I shrugged. "Let's see, start a relationship, go to the beach, catch a couple of Padres games, call my mother—or maybe that's next week—keep writing down what's happened to me."

"We know you started doing that, Jack," Study Group Old Guy

#2 said. "Uh, you're not planning to try and have it published, are you?"

"It crossed my mind. Why, are you worried I'll be giving something away? No one's going to believe this, trust me. *Especially* coming from a guy who wrote *Wasp Women of Naheedi* and *Blood Roaches of Ibasklar*."

"He has a point there," my Old Guy said. "But please, Jack, will you discuss it with us first?"

"Okay, sure. Now I have a question for you."

"Yes?"

"How much of the Ultimate Bike Path did I *really* see?"

The three of them grinned; my Old Guy's was better. He stuck a finger in his ear and said, "You've barely seen the tip of the iceberg, you haven't even scratched the surface . . ." He pulled the finger out. "Soon, Jack?"

I thought of Hazel the Healer and Ralph Ralph and the kids at Galaxyland and Hormona the Vulvan and Black Body . . . and Harry Chapin. "Yeah, soon."

They each shook my hand in their electric way, then started off on their Schwinns toward the Stuart Mesa hill. My Old Guy was going to show them how to ride. I didn't want to watch.

Okay, so now I'm pedaling toward my car, and the *only* thing on my mind is Holly Dragonette. Hey, thanks for hanging with me, and don't worry . . .

You remember what Arnold Schwarzenegger said as he left the police station in *The Terminator?*

No, it wasn't *"Fokk you, asshull!"*

He said, *"I'll be back."*